What readers say about Penny Pinter Smith's
The Last Legwoman:
A Novel of Hollywood, Murder...and Gossip!

"I enjoyed *Last Legwoman!* I really liked your book's loving depiction of our beloved journalistic endeavors back in the day, as well as the Hollywood syndicated columnist intrigues. Good job-hunting advice in there, too...really good story...writing was beautiful...."

> —Don Wallace, author of *The French House* and four other books, the documentary *Those Who Came Before: The Musical Journey of Eddie Kamae*, Contributing Editor of *Honolulu Magazine* and Editor of *The Hawaii Review of Books*.

"What a fun read! Interesting characters in a vivid setting should appeal to those who love the glamour of Hollywood and the stylish old-school gossip columns...."

"Anyone who has ever followed the goings and comings in Hollywood will enjoy this tale. Such an adventure and well written, too...."

"The most striking feature of this book is the beauty of the language... a joy to read.... The clues are all there, but the killer is difficult to identify...."

"Can't wait for the sequel...."

"This book is too good not to have a sequel...."

SUNSET WEST
GUNS, GRIT AND GOSSIP!

A Meredith Ogden Hollywood Legwoman Mystery

PENNY PENCE SMITH

ISBN: 9798526341103

Cover image: BDFC/Shutterstock
Cover design: Cynthia Gunn
Author photograph: Malia Leinau Myers
Interior design: Elizabeth Beeton

150 Hamakua Dr. #357
Kailua, HI 96734

For Frank Baron, Ed and Cheryl Crane, Betty Lam, John James, Stan Brossette and Regina Gruss, Stan Rosenfield, David Brokaw, Booker and Maria McClay—and all those behind the headlines who shined up Hollywood's stars and made gossip go 'round. Hooray for Hollywood!

CHAPTER 1
AUGUST 1986
LOS ANGELES, CALIFORNIA
THURSDAY MORNING

"Where the hell is Meredith?" Cassie O'Connell glanced at the empty desk sitting in the glare of the studio lights. The backdrop was emblazoned with the logo "Hollywood Newsroom." She ran a hand through her short, curly dark hair, turned and rushed to the phone on the wall nearby.

"Where's Meredith?" she barked into the receiver, "It's eight-thirty and we only have a half hour to get this segment shot. Is she still in the office?"

"No—didn't she reach you?" puzzled Sonia, the assistant in the small Los Angeles editorial offices headed by Cassie and her news partner Meredith Ogden. "She called me at five-thirty this morning from the Santa Monica Airport's private terminal! Told me something dire had happened on the set of the movie *Sunset West* and she was catching a private plane the studio already had parked at the private terminal. Some execs had flown in a day or so earlier. Told me to prepare to put a breaking story on the wire this morning, and to cancel other appointments for the day. She was going to call you right after she hung up!"

"Damn," snapped Cassie. "I turned the phone off because Bob had to get up early and I didn't want to wake him last night. I forgot to check the messages this morning. Damn,

damn!" What's going on? What's the breaking news? Where's she going?

"Flecha Dorada, New Mexico—apparently private or tiny airfield. Dusty sent the studio plane."

"New Mexico? Dusty? Wow—That's a surprise. I thought that was over long ago. But what's the crisis?"

"I don't know—she couldn't really say because she only knew it was 'dire,' and had to do with some kid dying on location—as she put it."

"Where's Raymond?" asked Cassie, suddenly reminded of a long-ago tug of war between Meredith's two relationships. Dusty Reed was a newly minted high-ticket movie director on his first big project, and T.K. Raymond was the Beverly Hills "Special Cases" detective who had helped solve the murder of famed Hollywood columnist, Bettina Grant, Meredith and Cassie's former boss.

"Not sure, but I know he's out of town at a law enforcement seminar. I think Washington D.C."

"Not good," sighed Cassie, "for a lot of reasons, but I need someone in the anchor chair right now. It's Meredith's day, but I guess it'll be me. No alternative." Cassie hung up the phone and mentally checked off preparations: script on teleprompter, background tape and material ready. She walked quickly to a side table where a production assistant had hung his blue blazer over a chair back. She looked at the jacket, at the man himself, slight, not too tall. She stepped in front of a mirror on a small portable dressing table and took a hard look at her own yellow T-shirt with jeans. She grabbed the blazer, shrugged into it, rolled up the sleeves to look trendy, and went in search of a scarf. A female staffer came running out of the adjacent hallway with a brush in hand.

Five minutes later, Cassie had instructed the technician in the control booth about the order of the stories and graphics to display behind her, then settled at the desk in front of the logo, nodded to the cameraman focusing on her and called, "Roll it."

☆☆☆

Above the southwestern desert, headed to the easternmost corner of New Mexico, Meredith Ogden sat by herself, the only passenger in the twin-engine aircraft. She gnawed on a thumbnail cuticle and wondered about the wisdom of the emergency trip. She was a widely syndicated Hollywood news columnist, privy to some of the most dynamic stories about movies, TV and music. Her old friend and former lover Dusty Reed had phoned openly frantic at three that morning, begging for her help. "I really need your media expertise and wisdom right now," he said in a voice she recognized in total stress mode.

He was directing a highly touted contemporary western movie in a remote desert location, his first high-budget, intensely publicized project. His leading lady, Sonora Hutchinson, one of the highest paid actresses in the industry, had returned home after dinner the night before and found her 15-year old son on the bedroom floor, dead from a drug overdose. Dusty instinctively knew that the situation would quickly become high global drama and cause chaotic controversy for the film as well as the star. Before the morning light, the determined director had called Meredith, imploring her to come to New Mexico, write an honest and factual story, before the predatory frenzy of paparazzi and press heard the rumors and descended upon the movie site.

Meredith pondered the situation and wondered how a mother could agree to be interviewed by national press less than six hours after the tragic death of her only son. However, she reminded herself, this is Hollywood, a state of mind with rules of its own. And a celebrity's brand is all about public image. "I'm not on the studio's publicity team, Dusty. I'm not managing your press exposure." Meredith had admonished.

"The studio will take care of that, believe me, and that's one reason why I'm so worried about an honest and straightforward accounting to start off," Dusty's tense voice responded. "The pros will arrive in a few hours and they're masters of creating a circus and then ring-leading it. It'll be a disaster. But I know you'll write it honestly and without prejudice or hysterics. I don't want this to get away from us before we even know what happened."

"Sonora's okay with this? Her son literally just died," Meredith persisted. The director assured her she would have immediate access to interview time with the actress and himself, no one would dictate what she could and could not write. It was a big story, "an old-fashioned scoop!" And she'd be home for dinner.

"Was the boy a druggie?" Meredith asked as carefully as possible.

Dusty hesitated to respond. Then, "I don't think so. Never saw it, never heard about it. I admit I'm suspicious."

"Why? How do you think he died? Suicide?" She heard what she considered an audible shrug.

"I think we should let the authorities figure that out. I'd advise you to be sensitive—and careful—with your questions. We may not want to know the answer."

"Um…," Meredith started a question, but faltered. "Dangerous? Am I stepping into a viper pit?"

"I hope it's too early for that to develop just yet," sighed Dusty. "Once the law and the execs and the press arrive later today…anyone's guess. But in and out this morning and don't pack your gun."

She was still hesitant, realizing that soon she would have to explain this surprise journey to Raymond with whom she mostly lived these days. And who knew of her past with the now-troubled director. Expecting only a few hours in and out of the high desert for a good story, she dumped extra food in her cat Paco's bowl and left for the airport. She had no idea what Flecha Dorada had in store.

CHAPTER 2
FLECHA DORADA, NEW MEXICO
THURSDAY MORNING

Hot dry winds sifted through the small town of Flecha Dorada, lightly tumbling grit from the surrounding desert through the half dozen streets of the downtown. Meredith looked through the windows of the sand-whipped van that bumped along from the airstrip location on a private ranch a few miles away.

"Where do you all stay? Motels?" she asked.

"Only two around," chuckled the compact, solidly built, ruggedly appealing driver, Dusty Reed. "Some of the crew stays there. Most are in rented ranch houses or cottages, some as far away as 15 miles. Not much available near here for large groups."

"And Sonora Hutchinson? Where will we meet her?"

"At the main house on a large estate where a few of us are staying. It's like a mini-resort, and the headquarters for the production company. Its real name is El Rancho Descanso. But we all just refer to it as 'the Villa.' It looks like one. We've moved Sonora to the main house for the time being. Her usual spot was a guest cottage, really the pool house, on the recreational section of the property. More private, had its own gated entrance. But she can't stay where the kid died. And it's already cordoned off by the sheriff. This estate is big and sprawling—absentee owner who uses it for family and business holidays, retreats and parties. Several guest wings, close to town—small as it is. Hardly a 'town,' more like a small crossroads shopping area."

Meredith looked at her watch, smiling at the bold numbers on the stylish timepiece that had been a Christmas gift last year from T.K. Raymond. "It's only 8:15 in LA," she said, noting a two-hour time difference. "I have to call the office as soon as I can."

"Use my car phone." He lifted up the cover to the black instrument in the van's center console and handed the receiver to Meredith. "I remember the number," he joked as he punched it in. Sonia answered in an efficient voice.

"Hi," Meredith spoke. "I don't have much time to talk right now. Just got in. But within the hour I'll be faxing in a hard news story for the wires, and then rewriting the column for a more in-depth follow-up this afternoon. Time is short and staying on top is critical."

"What do you need from us now?" Sonia shot back.

"Nothing now. I never got through to Cassie. Is she okay with doing the TV shot herself?"

"Maybe a little miffed, but she's on it," Sonia chuckled.

"Good. Talk later." Meredith hung up.

"We'll be at the Villa in a couple of minutes. We'll put your stuff in one of the empty suites," Dusty explained. Meredith silently sighed, remembering the familiar years she and Dusty had spent together, sometimes under the same roof, mostly not, because of conflicting schedules and intentions. But when they were, they were rarely in different bedrooms.

"How are you doing with this crisis—on your first big movie?" she asked, changing the subject.

A perturbed sigh came from the driver's seat. "I knew a big budget, big-star power project would be complex, a test and learning experience. I've enjoyed the challenge, and working with top-line pros. But this—this crisis—is a whole new level of stress. Huge pucker factor. Sonora, rumors to the contrary, had been just fine. Sweet, in fact. Until now. Her co-star, Beau Hastings, comes when he's called. Does good work. We've gone along well so far, I guess a problem bigger than life was inevitable."

"Why inevitable?" quizzed Meredith.

Dusty shrugged. "Not sure—intuition when I signed on to the project. Maybe I'm just a little pessimistic, or maybe just tired."

"I wasn't surprised you were awake and functioning at three this morning, but I figured you'd be on location in the desert by now."

"We're just shooting background stuff at night right now. Regular cast and most of the crew had a long weekend off. Most went home to LA. Only us chickens left this morning and that means I'm juggling a lot of balls until they get here. Everyone who knows about this is on comment lock-down."

"So, we have to work quickly," surmised Meredith. "Who knows I'm here?"

"Me, Sonora, the two Villa managers. Even the full investigation team isn't here yet. You beat them all."

Meredith softly whistled in disbelief. "You took a huge risk bringing me here. Won't the studio be pissed?"

"Maybe. But when we arranged a set visit, no one knew this would happen just hours before your arrival."

Meredith groaned. "So that's the story. You've made me an accessory to this ruse. Given me a leg up on the story but without studio sanction…for what, Dusty? You could lose your movie over this."

"Won't happen. And Sonora deserves this. Her story, her way. Once the law enforcement guys get here, the studio marketing and publicity people, it'll be a carnival. You know that. And I know you'll tell an honest straight forward story before the dark innuendo begins—you know it will. "

"A silly question, Dusty: is there any danger for me—us—on this escapade. A death you think is mysterious. A major movie star involved, a possible black-eye on a big-ticket movie. And the death scene? Still raw. You told me not to pack my gun?"

Dusty snickered. "Even if you had, would you know how to shoot it?"

Meredith took a deep breath and gazed out the window. "So, what's the cast of characters here, Dusty? Besides you, Sonora Hutchinson and her deceased son Carlton?"

"You probably know the landscape, Meredith, and I'll bet you've already read the *Sunset West* info sheets I faxed this morning. Since we're on a production break—and have a big crisis on our hands—schedule's a little fluid now, but normally, the day-to-day line producer is Steve Bankleman. He works for MEGAWATT Productions, the company making this movie for CenturySonic Studios. He's the guy who keeps our 'local trains running on time.' He's on his way back from break in LA. During your short visit, you'll, of course, meet Sonora, maybe her co-star Beau Hastings. A lovely woman named Fastida is the Villa's guest manager. Caleb Wurtzman runs the facilities around here. Otherwise—well, me. And the regular ant village of technicians who make a movie happen."

"No higher-ups from the production company or studio? Even with this crisis?"

"Well, the executive producers are typically scattered from Europe to Asia—most making money deals. One of them, Marv Snelling, will be here this afternoon from New York but we won't see the rest here on the set. Lou Marquand, CenturySonic's VP of marketing and publicity, is also on his way in, a rare visit, but he'll be husbanding the hordes of press that will be arriving to delve into this mess. Lou's underling, Laurie Shoup, the publicist in charge of this movie, can't get here until Monday."

"I thought your close friend Renn Burton was a producer of this film?" Meredith probed, referring to a popular action screen star.

"He is—but in name, and money, only. His buddy— entourage pal—Hank Torbin, has been nosing around. I guess reporting back to Renn." Meredith raised an eyebrow.

"I know are uncomfortable with Hank but he's not here now. You probably noticed that Bert Solver, one of the owners of MEGAWATT, is also a producer. We don't see him much, but his teenage kid, Frankie, is nearby for the summer with a bunch of friends from their Philly home territory."

Meredith nodded then asked, "Any problems seem obvious between Sonora and her son before last night? Know anything about him?"

"No. He's been kind of a ghost around here, but she seemed worried about him all the time."

"She ever say why?"

"Uh-uh. He's apparently never liked to be on location with his mother. His dad, Sonora's ex, lives in Europe which is where the boy usually lives as well."

"When did Sonora find his body?"

"Early this morning. About two a.m. Which is why I called you as early as I did. We both wanted to get ahead of this before it snowballed out of control."

"Where was he—or she—until two? That's only about seven hours ago."

Dusty shook his head. "Not their baby-sitter."

"You're sure Sonora is up for this interview, now?" Meredith puzzled over the facts as she tried to piece together the scenario and how to approach the grieving mother whose dead son was just barely discovered.

"She knows she only has a couple of options, managing it from the get-go, or being at the mercy of the rags and rumor. She's been in the movie business for a long time. Thanks for giving her a choice." Meredith scowled at the thought and looked out the window as the van made a bumpy turn into a well-paved road between two long rows of scraggly mesquite trees. "Ignore the condition of the trees. Not a lot grows tall and leafy here."

"So it seems."

A few minutes up the long and curved road, a large white-washed compound loomed against the horizon. Tall walls topped with red tiles, a wide arched entrance with wooden gates and copper lantern-style lamps on either side. "Welcome to the Villa," murmured Dusty. The gates opened when he pushed an electronic control. Inside, a circular drive was surrounded by emerald green grass up to a massive carved metal door. Dusty beeped the horn and a slender, angular gray-haired man emerged, moving purposefully from the house, followed by a solidly-built woman, about 60, iron curls framing her face and an apron over jeans and a denim shirt.

As Meredith hesitantly opened the car door, Dusty stepped quickly from the driver's side. "Meet Caleb and Fastida," he announced. Meredith stepped out, closed the door and walked around the front of the van to shake hands.

"How's Ms. Sonora?" asked Dusty.

"Shaky," answered Fastida. "But she is fixing her hair and face for the visitor—reporter," she nodded toward Meredith. Caleb's wiry body was busily unloading packages from the rear of the van. He reached for Meredith's bag, regarding her with dark, flinty eyes.

"Take Ms. Ogden to the guest suite we prepared," Dusty directed. Fastida nodded, took the duffle from Caleb and guided Meredith into the cavernous foyer of the house.

"Have the police been here with Sonora this morning?" asked Meredith, trying to learn where the situation stood at this early hour.

"The sheriff. He's our only law here, but he has called in more experienced people," answered Fastida, her light Mexican accent noticeable. "He says because there are so many famous stars involved, someone higher than him needs to be involved. They are coming from Albuquerque so it will be a while before they arrive."

Meredith flinched. "Is the…deceased…body still at Sonora's cottage?"

Fastida shrugged and shook her head. "I don't know. It's on the other side of the creek where the pool is and has its own driveway and entrance. I stay away. Too spooky."

There was no time for Meredith to settle down, gather her thoughts or be more prepared than she already was. She needed to beat the next round of law enforcement officers who would soon descend on Sonora and Dusty. She dropped her purse on the colorful, fashionably-appointed bed, realizing she had not taken time to eat or even drink anything more than a cup of acrid coffee in the waiting room of the Santa Monica Airport. Fastida seemed to have read her thoughts.

"You will be meeting with Miss Sonora on the back veranda with breakfast and coffee," she said with a hint of maternal concern. "We've closed off the area to everyone else."

A quick stop in the suite's airy, pristine bathroom to run a hand through her hair and wipe the travel grit from her face, Meredith idly wondered if she would ever not be in a hurry, pressed for time or on deadline. Tiredness was part of the landscape in her world. She grabbed her small recorder, two pens and a notebook from her bag and followed Fastida down the long hallway through cool, tiled and southwestern decorated corridors and out to an expansive veranda. Dusty wasn't exaggerating—the place was like a small luxury hotel.

Stepping through broad, etched sliding glass doors to an expansive flagstone veranda, Meredith found herself almost gasping. The view was uninterrupted, a vast desert scape with two small rounded mountains covered in clots of golden undergrowth—as far as the eye could see. In the morning light, the land seemed to have a personality all its own.

She walked under a bougainvillea covered pergola to a stone-walled edge of the patio where Dusty stood. He turned to her and swept an arm across the sight. "I always told you there was magic to the desert," he smiled. Meredith just stared silently. "Sonora is on her way," he quickly added. Meredith noticed a freshly laid breakfast table, covered in seductive foods and made her way there. From a bright ceramic pitcher, she poured pulpy fresh orange juice into a blue glass. She eyed the food as she tasted the sweet liquid.

Then Sonora Hutchinson entered the area. "Hello, Meredith. Thank you for coming and I believe we met a couple of years ago on the set of *NOT ME!*" She extended her hand. Meredith took it. "Let's have something to eat while we talk." Sonora wore a soft blue gauzy caftan, her raven black hair pulled into a bun at her neck. Her makeup was artfully applied around her striking blue eyes, but the orbs themselves were as tortured as any Meredith had ever even imagined, her face a pastiche of misery. Still, the movie star was gracious, at a glance, seeming like a hostess at a glamorous patio party. Meredith expressed her deep condolences, but in reality, was confused by the seeming lack of emotion, at least here in public. Her own words replayed, "…but this is Hollywood and anything is possible."

"Before we start, there are some rules, as I'm sure Dusty has explained," Meredith began as the trio took seats at the table. "Honesty and truth. Don't tell me part of a story you change later for a different listener. This is an exclusive interview for now. Dusty tells me that later today the studio will have a press conference based on whatever the authorities find. The publicity department will have taken over by then. My story already will have broken. Finally, no one edits my work, I tell the story I find. I'm so sorry to be so crass, especially now, and I can only imagine your sadness and shock— but I came a long way at a difficult time to help out a good friend. And, I'm sure you'd rather be elsewhere right now. So, my rules." She shrugged, a little embarrassed.

Dusty smiled quietly. Sonora toyed with a warm tortilla and murmured. "Of course."

CHAPTER 3
WEST LOS ANGELES
THURSDAY MORNING

When Cassie arrived at the vintage West Los Angeles cottage that housed the editorial offices, Meredith's news story from Flecha Dorada was clacking in over the fax machine. Munching on a piece of toast, Cassie perched on the edge of Sonia's desk and read the text, shaking her head.

"Quite a break," shrugged Sonia, the dark-haired assistant to Cassie and Meredith. They were now established, respected journalists who covered entertainment and mostly Hollywood "news"—once called "gossip." Inherited from the late famed gossip maven Bettina Grant, their positions with a global news distribution syndicate had cemented their own journalistic partnership as stellar in the burgeoning world of show business. Newspaper columns, short television "Hollywood updates" to local stations across the county, and a daily short radio spot on a major radio network's national programming had made them known names in a very short period of time.

"Production has been halted on the big budget film, *Sunset West*, in New Mexico after its star, Sonora Hutchinson, early this morning discovered the body of her 15-year old son Carlton, dead from what local authorities are calling 'a drug overdose,'" Cassie read aloud. "The Academy Award winner spoke from the

New Mexico ranch where she is staying during filming. 'I've never known my son to do drugs. He's an introspective boy and pretty much a loner, so I don't understand where he got the drugs or why he took them.'

"…Local law enforcement officials were just arriving at the scene as Hutchinson gazed out to the desert from the veranda of the ranch house and wept. Friday, Saturday and Sunday are days off for most of the *Sunset West* cast and crew. Producers and studio administration had returned to Los Angeles for the break, according to Director Dusty Reed, who remained at the location to oversee night filming. County Sheriff William Bardo, first official on the scene, said, 'Until the Medical Examiner and other investigators from Albuquerque complete their work, we have no answers—including the official cause of death.'

"The deceased boy's father, financier Merit Sturgiss, Hutchinson's ex-husband, is expected to arrive in New Mexico this evening from his home in Geneva, Switzerland."

Sonia hurriedly began to mark up the story to send to the New York syndicate headquarters for immediate release over the wire to newspapers across the country and several foreign countries. Cassie scowled and chewed on her pencil. The fax machine began its rat-a-tat clack again, and she pulled another page from it. "Meredith's working today from Dusty's office in the ranch complex where he's staying, there's the phone number. A column lead to follow shortly, hopes she can come home tonight."

Cassie hoped so as well. Besides needing the help with office and news duties, she also knew that Meredith's partner of the past two years, police investigator T.K. Raymond, probably didn't know she was in New Mexico working with her former lover Dusty Reed. A problem? Maybe. Maybe not. But Raymond had been good for Meredith, grounding, and Cassie hated to imagine a wrinkle in that scene.

In a moment of total serendipity, Ito, the office manager, thrust his head into Sonia's small office with the announcement, "Raymond's on the line from D.C., asking for Meredith. What shall I tell him?" Sonia looked at Cassie who rubbed her eyes then waved to Ito that she'd take the call. She picked up the extension.

"Raymond."

"Cass—Where's Meredith? She out of the office?"

"Yeah—for sure. Quick change of plans. She's in New Mexico."

Cassie felt the surprise from Raymond even over the phone lines. "When did that come up? I talked with her last night and she was headed to bed for a good beauty sleep since she was doing the TV shot this morning."

"I don't know the whole story yet—but apparently there was a crisis—maybe more like a tragedy—with the leading lady, Sonora Hutchinson, very early this morning and Meredith had an inside glimpse—and access—and took advantage of it. On a plane, wheels up just at sunrise. That's all I really know because I've been the one in front of the camera this morning. I just got back to the office and Meredith's first news story came in a few minutes ago and is already on the fax to New York."

"Huh," said Raymond. "Any idea how long she'll be there or when she'll be home?"

"She said in a quick call to Sonia that she plans to be home tonight. I have a phone number where you might reach her. Want it?"

"Yeah, sure. But I'll try her at home later tonight. We'll catch up then. I wanted to let her know that I'll probably be here for another couple of days. Not happy about it, but things came up here and I need to stay around."

Cassie read him the number Meredith sent, then asked, "Can she call you at your hotel there in DC?"

"No," he responded thoughtfully. "I'll be out most of the day—I'll have to catch up with her." They said hurried goodbyes and were off to their own endeavors.

Raymond absently dropped the receiver into its cradle and stood quietly for a minute as the situation pinged around in his brain. He got the connection between *Sunset West,* New Mexico and Dusty Reed. Meredith had mentioned the project to him when it was announced. And he wasn't really worried about it. Meredith retained friendships close to her soul, but he knew she easily let go of the intimacy part of "relationship," if they had existed. She was basically monogamous and had been with him since the first night of their own intimacy, the night of her friend Gloria's elegant Christmas party two years before.

He was more concerned with his own current deceptions. It bothered him deeply. It was totally uncharacteristic of the life he shared with Meredith. Yet, in many ways, her unplanned trip into the field left him more room for his own needs. He hurriedly collected his back-up gun from his well-concealed safe under the floor of the bathroom vanity in his Malibu house, seaside west of Los Angeles. He thrust the weapon deep into the suitcase with his already travel-weary clothes. He doubted he would need it, but he was stepping into new legal territory without a map. He retrieved an empty duffle from his bedroom closet and filled it with a pair of casual jeans and polo shirts, then headed back to his car. He glanced around with some trepidation, making sure no one saw him entering or exiting the place, empty because his son Will, and girlfriend Sophie, were away for summer break, not staying at the house as usual. He turned the car north to head to the Ventura Freeway and to the inconspicuous house in the hills near Agoura. On the way, he thought about how to deal with the deceit he was perpetrating on Meredith. He felt guilty beyond words, but helpless. It's not a perfect world. We aren't perfect people, he told himself. He was on a complicated and serious case, loaned out from his own local police unit to the FBI because of his familiarity with and ease of movement in the music and entertainment industry.

Raymond met Meredith Ogden when he was assigned as the "High Profile Cases" detective, handling only sensitive cases with star quality, on the murder of world famed gossip columnist Bettina Grant, murdered in her home. The same home housed the offices where Meredith, the assistant/ "legwoman" worked as center point of Grant's editorial staff. As the investigation had unfolded, Meredith, also Grant's closest friend and associate, had twice been assaulted, her home broken into and ransacked. Raymond came to know her well, a forthright journalist with copper blond hair and large brown eyes, and a steel determination to find answers and a truthful story. First, he protected her and then fell in love with her.

From their first encounter, there were information ground rules vital to each of their professions, but candor and honesty about those rules had been the heart of it. As Raymond drove up the narrow, rustic road through the underbrush and unkempt trees along the ridge of the mountain south of the Ventura Freeway, he shifted his focus to what he was about to undertake. And the fact that he could not tell Meredith the encounter which awaited him.

The car chugged up the gritty hill, surrounded by original Southern California houses, some now expanded giving clues to modern interiors. But none majestic or the McMansions so prevalent in nearby neighborhoods now. Around a curving corner he pulled into a cracked concrete driveway that led to the back of a modest single-story house. A caramel-colored hillside rose behind a tall, well-aged wooden fence surrounding the place. He parked, extracted his briefcase, travel case and duffle from the passenger seat and made his way up the steps to a service porch. The screen door was opened by a tall, striking redhead in jeans and a t-shirt with "Morning Glory" emblazoned across her ample front. "I was worried you wouldn't get here," she said in welcome.

CHAPTER 4
WEST LOS ANGELES
THURSDAY MID-DAY

"Hey. Lunch today? I'm three blocks from you and I'm buying. Copper Lantern?" The voice of Vanessa Collier, Cassie's friend who worked in the literary agency representing Cassie's Hollywood fiction book was a welcome break in the morning's confusion. Cassie fingered her desk calendar to see what the day was to bring. "Sure. But it'll have to be early and fast. It's already been a nutso day."

"Works for me," said Vanessa.

The two women subsequently curled over salads, glasses of white wine at their elbows, and exchanged idle conversation in the small, trendy hole-in-the-wall restaurant. "Things are quiet on the show biz front," sighed Cassie. "Slow time. Meredith's covering the *Sunset West* movie location today. And Sonia is chasing details of some of the news releases we got in. We could all just call in our work from home."

Vanessa snickered, reaching for a crisp cracker in a basket midtable. "I don't even have any good personal gossip for you. Other than who's on vacation with whom. But nothing very titillating." Both women chuckled and picked up their wine glasses. "And we know that good juicy stuff is the meat in your sandwich, Cassie."

The journalist sighed and nodded. "I am the sponge that absorbs the juicy stuff. Meredith really likes the business side. But both are important these days."

"Talk about how the Hollywood news content has expanded. Even the studio financial stories are part of the 'gossip' scene now." The table was silent as both women dug into their salads, chewed thoughtfully and considered the statement. Vanessa broke the silence. "There's a rumor—nothing more and not verified or even detailed—that Sterling Music is under some kind of investigation by the feds. And the financial director seems to be 'away' on vacation." She glanced around surreptitiously hoping no one overheard her conversation.

Cassie winced. "Boy, investigating that story is a one-way road to trouble."

"Yeah, well, keep your ears on alert. As I said, nothing real yet, just some murmurs around the office. Not our client, but a lot of the musicians they publish and distribute are ours. And there's a lot of angst in the air."

As they walked to their cars, Cassie turned to Vanessa seriously. "It's a little above my pay grade, but would you keep me in the loop on what you hear about Sterling Music?"

Vanessa agreed, they hugged the perfunctory industry hug, and went their own ways.

At her office, Cassie toyed with her pen and drew squiggles on her desk blotter. The idea of a major controversy against Sterling was heavy. Many of the hottest music artists were on the Sterling label.

"Hey, Sonia? Can you spend some time in the next couple of days and get us a list of the artists who are on the Sterling Music label?"

"I'll see what I can find."

Cassie turned her attention to other matters until the diminutive form of Ito quietly entered her office. "What do you want to know about Sterling Music?"

She looked up at him, surprised as always about the depth of his involvement with the stories and article content. By his own insistence, he loved Hollywood, movies and movie stars. But he was a whiz at accounting, financial matters—and cooking. "I'm just following a very vague lead down an equally vague path about some of the Sterling music people."

"What do you want to know? I have some friends in a couple of the clubs where Sterling groups play and some of the management guys hang out."

"Oh, well," Cassie held back a response, avoiding any mention of the actual allegation or even any possibility of it. "Just wondering what the relationship is like between the performers or artists and the label itself, the management. I'm always curious about who wields the power—how stringent are the contracts? Do the artists make what they should even when they're successful...all the usual stuff."

"I can pry and probe a little," said Ito.

"Don't get yourself into any trouble," Cassie quickly replied. "This isn't a big deal, just trying to fill out some information on a segment of the industry we don't see much. Don't do anything if it makes you uncomfortable and puts you in a difficult spot with your friends...oh, and maybe you can find out who now owns Sterling? It was founded by musicians, but I seem to recall it was acquired by someone, hedge fund or something."

"Okay," said Ito, turning and leaving. He was reliving a night a few weeks ago when Brent, one of his club friends who enjoyed the music and night life of West Los Angeles, elaborated on his own job at Sterling Music. He had also mentioned another friend who enjoyed the club scene and was also employed at one of the companies owned by the same conglomerate as Sterling. Ito went to his desk and thumbed through his Rolodex.

Cassie mused that this sometimes humorous, always focused, mostly insightful man was a more valuable colleague than anyone had ever predicted. He had been the houseman of their murdered boss, Bettina Grant. But unbeknownst to most, he not only cleaned her house, offices and yard, he managed her bookkeeping, taxes, all manner of financial matters, and cooked most of Bettina's meals. Originally an MBA student from Japan at one of the local universities, he finished his degree, then signed on through an agency as Bettina's domestic support person in order to "taste the spice of Hollywood," as he put it. When she died, and before the details of the house and office were sorted out, he became a vital and permanent member of the news team when the media syndicate for whom they worked solidified the organization and assignments. In the two-and-a-half years since the traumatic bombshell of Bettina's death, he had also become a key financial operative for the media syndicate on other West Coast dealings. But Hollywood, and popular music, were his passions.

As Cassie turned her head to her computer screen and wondered how Meredith was faring in the summer desert of New Mexico, her mind returned to the call from T.K. Raymond. Something seemed amiss. Something about his voice and about the sound of his call. It was so clear it could have come from next door. And there was a familiar sound in the background— only vaguely familiar but not what she would have expected from an office or hotel room on the other side of the continent. Feeling foolish and even a little guilty, she picked up the phone and dialed the now-well known number of Raymond's Malibu house. An answer machine picked up the call offering a brief but well-spoken request from T.K. to leave a message for him, Will or Sophie. Softly in the background she could hear the surf. It was clear and refreshing. She frowned and shook her head.

Her ruminations were surgically sliced through by Sonia's shrill voice cutting the quiet. "It's Meredith—quick, pick up. She sounds frantic!"

Cassie snatched the receiver to her ear and demanded, "What's going on? Are you on your way back? What's the matter?" Sonia clung to the phone, listening intently, in her own office.

On the other end of the line, Meredith took a deep breath and blurted out, "I can't leave! They won't let me come home."

"Who? What do you mean?" persisted Cassie.

"The whole shebang got here about two hours ago—studio big wigs, producers, lawyer, publicist, and all the law enforcement people from Albuquerque. The Sheriff insists I'm a material witness since I was here before anyone else and actually talked with Sonora, saw the crime scene, and so on and on." She gasped with almost a hiccup. Cassie could tell she was close to tears.

"Can't Dusty clear this up?"

"No. Because he brought me here so quickly and before anyone else was around, now we're both up for questioning. Damn!" She exploded. "I knew this was a bad idea and I warned Dusty about it."

"What's the schedule? The process?"

"I'm not sure. But since my story broke so early this morning, we've already got a half dozen foreign press here—out of LA, two local TV channels from Albuquerque and one from El Paso and you know many others to come. I don't even know where they'll stay. There are no rooms left here. At least I have that!"

"So, you don't know when they'll release you or how you'll get home?"

"Uh-uh," sniffed Meredith.

"Is there wine close by?" Cassie heard a slight chuckle. "I knew we could ground you. So, you have proof you were nowhere near the place when the overdose went down. It's just a formality...."

"Dusty will be the one under scrutiny," said Meredith, forthright again.

"You need to keep some distance from the whole investigation so no one tries to accuse you of some kind of advance knowledge or planning. Sooner or later someone's going to realize the relationship you and Dusty had—even if it was a long time ago."

"They don't even know if the overdose was accidental, suicidal, or some kind of crime— more to this than I thought," murmured Meredith. "I realized that Dusty said Sonora discovered her son dead in their cottage when she returned from dinner—on the patio of the main house. But he called me around three in the morning and said she'd just found the body. Dinner until three? Something doesn't make sense."

"You go girl," Cassie sighed. "But be careful. Watch your own back. It's an unlikely and unexplained death. Someone's bound to know something they don't want anyone else to know. And, they won't want anyone, much less a gossip reporter, looking for it. Keep us updated and let us know what you need from us."

CHAPTER 5
SAN FERNANDO VALLEY, CALIFORNIA
THURSDAY MID-DAY

"Margo."

"T.K. Raymond. Glad you could make it." She smiled a flirty smile the detective suspected was simply play acting.

"We'll see how it goes," he shrugged and entered the nondescript 60s-style Southern California ranch house in the San Fernando Valley foothills of the Santa Monica Mountains.

"Come in and meet our numbers king," she invited as he tossed his cases and jacket onto a plain beige couch. She led him into a dining room off the living room. Bright fluorescent lights had been installed and a large conference table was strewn with stacks and flying pages of paper. At one side of the table, eyes focused on the ledger in front of himself, a massively-built man sat, scratching his shaved head. He stood up, unfolding six-foot-four or more frame, the light deepening his naturally dark skin into a walnut wood patina.

"Jerrold," he smiled, waving across the messy table.

"T.K.," responded the detective as he walked around to extend his hand. Jerrold was as large and solid as any linebacker from the LA Rams. Raymond was taken aback by the incongruity of his appearance and his exact, precise profession.

"Jerrold is our forensic accountant," Margo explained. "That means he dissects and parses the books of our suspect companies."

"I understand forensic accounting," said Raymond almost as an aside. "Found anything worth noting yet?"

"Little streams, tiny tributaries," said Jerrold, returning to his seat. "But there's a main channel somewhere and I hope these will take me to it." He scratched his head again.

"Where's our whistleblower?" asked Raymond.

"Napping in the back room," Margo answered. "He had a long day of questioning yesterday and then watched movies most of the night. And worked all day today with Jerrold. He got tired."

"Do we have enough to start the boots on the ground investigation?"

"Probably, but maybe wait to meet him in person and let us brief you on what we know. Tallyure will be in first thing in the morning," she continued referring to the regional FBI head.

"Then why am I here now?" asked Raymond. "I literally came here from the airport, and I could have gone home, changed clothes and at least caught up with my family."

"Not a good idea," muttered Jerrold.

"Our whistleblower, Melvin, found out about the irregularities in the books from his boss, a tough as nails woman," Margo continued the explanation. "She had the balls to ask about the irregularities from upper management at Marlborough—Marlborough, Newlin, Solver mostly known as MNS...."

"She was hit by a car two weeks ago, hit and run," Jerrold interjected. "Still looking for the driver and the car."

"She had a chance to mention to Melvin about the oddities and management's reluctant reaction to her questions. Your role is to slither around the Hollywood elite—your turf—and interface with any conduits in that population who can help. The next few hours are to strategize who and where they are. You'll be the one following the person-to-person connections on the shadowy edge, so plan to keep your head down, T.K."

"It's not like I'm an unknown entity in the entertainment or music industry," he said with a scowl. "It's perfectly normal for me to be asking questions about companies, artists, profitability, etc."

"But when you do, you—and we—don't want your interest to be thought of as unusual or to leak back to what's going on here. You know where to look for streams of information, who needs to be consulted and how to get to them."

"And for that you're keeping me captive here? "

"Yup." answered Jerrold.

"Especially with your red-carpet visibility with a popular gossip queen," added Margo.

Raymond shook his head. Ignoring her, he asked, "Where do I set up shop and where do I sleep?"

"You'd think we were holding you for ransom, T.K.," Margo spoke up. "You're only here for two days so we can brief you well enough on this case to keep you from stumbling into trouble. You are out there in the community a lot. We want you to be aware enough to avoid stupid mistakes. You and Jerrold have the first bedroom down the hall on the right. Melvin is next door," she continued, "And I have the master suite." There was slight embarrassment in her voice. "You can work here or set up a desk in the living room. Or even the side patio. Up to you."

He nodded, returned to the living room and picked up his bag and jacket, heading toward the hall.

"T.K.?" He turned to see Margo, hands on her hips, a serious look in her eyes. "Apologies. It's been tense around here. I'm just messin' with you."

He grinned. "Yeah. I know."

"But I'm not joking about the investigation. It's serious. Bottomline is that we have intelligence that someone at MNS is funneling money from large scale drug imports into the country. Not quite like a rock music entrepreneur stealing profits from his artists. That's bad enough—and that's your back yard. Drugs? Big time? That's mine." T.K. Raymond nodded.

CHAPTER 6
FLECHA DORADA, NEW MEXICO
THURSDAY EVENING

A fiery sunset settled on the brown mountains surrounding Rancho El Descanso, the Villa, and a slight breeze stirred up the sand and brush. A hawk dove toward the ground long in the distance, likely chasing dinner for the night. Meredith looked out from the wide window in her suite, her mind still trying to piece together the discordant puzzle surrounding her.

A 15-year old boy had overdosed on drugs. His mother was a hugely famous, high-trend movie star, father a world traveling financier. The movie was the film version of an epic novel, high budget, emerging director. Costs: unspeakable loss for the parents, numerous delays and high overages and less profit to the movie production, a child's life cut short. More or less in that order, as far as Meredith assessed the film industry's perspective.

Benefits: More than usual international attention to the film, and not focused on the quality or the production itself, lots of sympathy for the movie star for her loss which translated into generosity at awards time. But there were the collateral damaging effects, as well, Meredith assessed. Dusty's first major directorial project would be lost in the drama surrounding it. A lot of production personnel and actors would be out of work or stuck in a holding pattern, possibly delaying other work, until the situation was deemed under control. Meredith would have some exclusive material that would solidly ground her role as the Hollywood insider's insider, but she would be tethered to New Mexico longer than she wanted. And, the collateral gossip might unearth more than she or Dusty wanted to make public. And who knew what else might emerge that was not intended to be public knowledge. Just gossip.

Two investigators had kept Meredith sitting in an uncomfortable metal folding chair at a make-shift worktable set up in the ranch house dining room. For two hours she politely answered questions, often the same ones over and over. She showed her receipts from the coffee vendor at the private terminal in Los Angeles, given them every possible lead to her whereabouts—at home in Brentwood—until sunup that morning.

"Why did you come in today, when production was closed and most everyone gone, and why so early?" was the gist of repeat questions.

"Dusty is an old friend and he had asked me to cover the set—unofficially—scheduled set visits are the studio's job—just as a courtesy. He anticipated a quiet day today and a good opportunity to spend quality time with him and Sonora. I thought I'd be home by tonight."

"When did you find out about the boy's death?"

"I knew by the time I got to the Santa Monica airport—but I'm a news reporter and it only made the visit more vital…No, I didn't know it was a day off…No, we never went to the pool house…No, I didn't slant my story to make Ms. Hutchinson look innocent. I only quoted the sheriff…No, Mr. Reed didn't tell me anything about where the boy got his drugs or who else might have been involved with his death…I didn't know if the studio knew I was coming…."

Finally, she had asked, "Do I need a lawyer because I can call him right now, but it will make good copy." They allowed her to leave the table. It was six o'clock in the evening. She made her way to the suite she'd been assigned and plopped down on the bed. Had it only been this morning that this whole thing had started? She was tired again. Her news story had broken, her column written and filed before the Albuquerque investigators talked to her. Tomorrow's column would be a doozie. Hopefully, no one would stop her from writing—or sending—it. The material also would be a good short on-screen story. If only Cassie had her cameras here.... Meredith picked up the phone in the suite, hoping no one would prohibit calls, and dialed Cassie at home.

"I can see if one of the Albuquerque stations has a camera person with a hand-held, I guess. I doubt the Syndicate would approve a trip for me or Sonia, but hiring someone freelance wouldn't be any cheaper if there was travel involved," reasoned Cassie.

"Dusty, if I can get to him, might have a solution. Someone here who wanted to make a few bucks...just thinking that we have another TV spot on Tuesday...good material...," Meredith was thinking out loud.

"Put it on the next private flight to Santa Monica and we could pick it up...," Cassie continued the drift. "How are you doing now?" she persisted.

Meredith sighed loudly. "Not the best situation but I should be able to get home tomorrow...unless...."

"What?" asked Cassie?

"Someone mentioned the local coroner, a pediatrician here in Flecha Dorada, has suggested a coroner's inquiry since no one seems to have any definitive or even real subjective clues about the cause of death."

"Crap!" spat Cassie. "You'll all be stuck for days. Why would he do that?"

"Let me get back to you on that," snarfed Meredith. "Has Raymond tried to reach me again? I haven't had a minute to myself, but I'll try to call him tonight."

"Good idea. He has your number in New Mexico and it didn't sound like he was very accessible there in D.C. I hope they let him through," said Cassie unwilling to mention her own reservations about the source of the detective's last call to the office.

"This place is set up like a hotel. I have a line into my suite...I hope all else is going well with you, with Raymond...I can't focus on anything but what's happening here," said Meredith. "I'm signing off and going to try to find Dusty about this film idea."

"Be careful," Cassie reminded one more time.

"Sure," muttered Meredith as she hung up and swung her legs off the bed, grabbed her shoulder bag and headed out the door to find Dusty. The white-washed, red-tiled hallways were surprisingly empty and quiet but she reasoned the action would be an acre away at the pool house. She found her way to the room Dusty used as an office and even more amazingly found him sitting at his desk, staring into space. "Are you still employed?" she asked.

He snorted, "Yeah. But what a cluster fuck. I've been running all day to try to organize the changes, prod the people. We've put principal photography on hold, just second unit stuff until we can get Sonora refocused. Fortunately, most people weren't here and won't be back until Monday. God, I hope this is straightened out by then."

"Murphy's law, Dusty," said Meredith. "Those pesky producers in yet?"

"Yep. And thank God. I just want to direct the damn movie, which is enough. Good to have the bosses around and their decision-making authority. By tomorrow morning this place will be like a beehive."

Meredith sat down in a leather side chair, dropped her bag on the floor and leaned back. Dusty turned his office chair toward her and slumped in resignation. "Sorry about the intense interrogation today. I'm sorry I got you involved in this...yes, you did warn me."

"We got what we got, Dusty," sighed Meredith.

"There's no way anyone suspects you of anything except letting me coerce you into coming out here...I thought it was a good idea. Stupid."

"You know me too well. I could've said 'no', but I didn't. A good story is a good story and I have a hard time passing one up. Try to explain that to a couple of hard-nosed investigators." Her mind quickly segued to thoughts of Detective T.K. Raymond, waiting for her at home in California, and she almost blushed with guilt and recrimination.

"What did they ask?" Dusty broke into her reverie.

"What you might expect. When did I know about the death? Why did I come out when I did? Had I visited Sonora's room? Did the studio sanction my visit? What did Sonora tell me? Where were you when the kid died? Lots of stuff that I didn't know." She rubbed a hand over her eyes. "Haven't they interviewed you yet?"

"Oh yeah." He visibly shuddered. "And more to come, I'm sure. The meeting with the production execs tomorrow won't be any better, I'm sure."

"Will I be the center of their angst around you? Non-sanctioned, so to speak?"

"No, I don't think so. I think the focus will be on Sonora...her son, and me."

"That has an interesting ring to it. You were an innocent bystander who happened to be near-by at the same time?"

"Well…there's a little more to it than that…."

Meredith snapped to full attention. "Three in the morning, after dinner. Give Sonora a fighting chance, she's so sweet. There's a whole lot more, isn't there?"

"Look, Meredith, I had—have—something good going with Sonora…didn't want to say anything because…well, you and I have a history and I didn't want…."

"Didn't want to what?" Meredith cut him short, "make me feel bad? Kidding? I'm very happy with my current life and partner and I wouldn't want anything but a happy one for you. Did you really think I wouldn't want that for you? So, you kept me in the dark and now I'm the one making up false scenarios because the one person here who promised me an honest story didn't deliver!" She looked out the window, face hard set in disappointment.

"Sorry. Very few people know about us. I mean 'us' as in me with Sonora."

"Sure, and someone will have leaked it by now if not to the studio, to the law, and so it'll be public knowledge in about ten minutes. I don't care about the relationship, Dusty. Hope it's a good and happy—and long—one. But the trust between you and me. Boy, those investigators must have thought I was one stupid broad." She shook her head.

"I'm sorry."

No one spoke again for several minutes. Then Meredith pulled herself out of her slump.

"You have a camera person on deck who might like to make a little extra money?" she asked.

He gazed at her guardedly.

"What do you have I mind? Don't get yourself or me in more trouble."

"Ha!" Meredith snorted. "It's a little late for that. I'd like the story on video—maybe some good background shots," she said, looking away. "Me on camera, you and...well, anyone else we can arrange. Cassie and I have a TV shot due on Tuesday. I figure between now and then we could get the stuff to her."

"We got a guy who might be interested. He's here, but you contact him yourself. I don't want to get involved any more than I am right now." He scribbled out a name and phone number on a scratch pad, tore off the page and handed it to Meredith. "You need anything else now that you're our overnight guest?"

She shook her head, "There'll be more, for sure, but not now. I have a change of undies and a blouse for tomorrow. After that, if I'm still here, I'll be looking for the closest Walmart."

"Go with God," mused Dusty. "I'm sorry about this. You warned me...."

"It's the woman's role...warning adrenalin-addicted, testosterone-addled men," snorted Meredith as she turned to leave the office.

"Dinner is served each night on the terrace—in about an hour," called Dusty. "At least eat well and keep up your energy. And so far, you haven't needed a single gun!"

Meredith returned to her room quickly and dialed the number Dusty had given her. To her amazement, the photographer answered. He agreed to meet her at two o'clock the next afternoon and together they'd film something worth showing on national TV a few days later. She had a plan.

CHAPTER 7
WEST LOS ANGELES
THURSDAY EVENING

Ito moved through the crowd that flocked noisily in the popular restaurant/disco in West Los Angeles. He curled furtively against the bar. Across the crowded room, a popular band and front singer belted out Huey Lewis and the News' "Power of Love"—not quite so well as the originals—but plenty loud. Ito was hardly noticeable tucked in amongst the throbbing mass. He beckoned to the bartender and ordered a tequila, straight up. He glanced around the room looking for the familiar face of his friend, Brent.

An accountant, like Ito, Brent had talked idly about his job at a popular local recording studio. Ito knew from just being around the women of Hollywood Newsroom that any casual conversation could lead to a good story, or at least a line into one. He scanned the throbbing room and then his eyes fell on the familiar face of Brent. He quickly made his way through the crowd to the corner where the tall man stood surrounded by several other people.

Brent nodded and waved him over. "I've got someone holding a table over this way," nodding to his left. "A little quieter. We ordered some calamari. Hope you eat squid." Ito laughed. "A favorite." At the table, Brent introduced his friend

Mel, a pudgy balding man with a scruffy moustache and horn-rimmed glasses. He, too, worked in finance for a company. Ito billed himself as an accountant underling at a small media syndicate. Ultimately the conversation among the threesome meandered around the music, focused for a few minutes on a few hot girls gyrating on the dance floor, and eventually centered around their work.

After a couple of drinks, Mel commented with an audible groan, "There's audit fever in our company. And that's no fun forecast. I work with the local office of a subsidiary of the music company where Brent works. We're just one arm of a many-legged holding group. And, apparently some funds are missing from the corporate books. The headquarters financial officer died—I've heard stories she was funneling money into her own pocket, maybe contributing to someone else's well-being. Now, her assistant is on the lam...."

"Real intrigue—not what we usually worry about," mused Brent, chugging the last of a beer. "Both our companies are part of a larger holding entity. I'm glad I'm just an accountant, not our Financial Director at Sterling Music. He'll have the higher ups all over him, probably the law as well. That's why he gets the big bucks. Probably why he decided to take an impromptu vacation today. I think the auditors wore him down."

"Now's not the time for you to know too much," smiled Ito.

"Both our employers are part of a big global organization and I'm only a small potato in one small division," mused Mel.

"What company?" probed Ito. "American?"

"MNS, Inc. is the big guy—in Switzerland—into a whole bunch of entertainment and recreational stuff—toy company in Europe, music division, a TV production company in England, a popular electronic game company, a soccer team...stuff like that."

"Games? I love computer games. They're pretty raw but can't you imagine what they'll be one day? I play them a lot," continued Ito.

"I actually work for Quality Fun, the local game developers," said Mel, leaning on the high-top table.

"So, how much do you have to interact with the corporate group? This...audit...does it involve you guys?"

"Not so far," said Mel. "Could change, though. We've been warned the investigations could dig really deep and into even the most obscure holding. Numbers being numbers—they can hold mystery even people like us don't realize."

"What artists are on Sterling's label?" Ito persisted, looking at Brent and pushing into a new conversational direction. Brent listed some well-known names, musical groups and individuals, and added, "plus a whole bunch of musicians from back a couple of decades." Ito nodded.

"Quality Fun Is the computer games company where I work," Mel spoke up. "New technology, exciting new industry, actually. But complicated relationship to Sterling Music. They're a subsidiary of MNS and we're a subsidiary of Sterling."

"Sounds like a domino game," laughed Ito. "One company owns another that owns two more...and on and on."

"Life in the economic world of the 1980s," chuckled Mel.

"Still, nice gig—and to be there in the earliest phases," said Ito as the conversation progressed. A plate of calamari and other bar snacks arrived and were quickly consumed.

"Hey, maybe you'd like to come on down to Culver City one day soon and take a look at our game manufacturing facility. We take parts and pieces from lots of different vendors—but the final coding and assembly gets done here," offered Mel. Ito nodded enthusiastically. Mel handed him a business card. "Let me know when you'd like to visit."

Soon Ito made a discreet exit, claiming a large project with an early start the next day. "I'll call you," he said to Mel. He was anxious to get home and make notes about the information he'd gleaned. Sitting in his sweatshirt and skivvies later, he jotted down the details of the evening, pleased that he could be a part of the investigative group even for a few minutes.

CHAPTER 8
FLECHA DORADA, NEW MEXICO
THURSDAY NIGHT

The sun gently morphed into a crimson-purple ribbon across the horizon as Meredith entered the Villa's veranda dining area. Not sure who might be at the long tables—studio personnel, law enforcement officers, complete strangers—she made her way timidly, looking for a familiar face.

"Meredith Ogden, over here," commanded a gravelly voice. She looked across the patio and saw the gnarled face of the studio's VP and Senior Publicity Chief, Lou Marquand. Relieved that the individual dispatched to the scene had been a friendly contact, and glad he happened to be on the terrace at that moment, Meredith hastened her step to his table. A vacant chair was opposite Lou's and she sat down cordially. "Join us," he said, and proceeded to introduce his companions, the producer and one of the executive producers of *Sunset West*, visiting only to show the executive "flag" during the crisis at the film's location.

"Hear you had a busy day today," Lou said in a characteristic chortle.

"Yeah, you could say that," Meredith answered, looking around for evidence of food. She noticed a long cafeteria style table bearing a variety of options: salads, local entrée dishes and side selections, way more than the assembled group would ever finish.

"Go get something to eat. You look like you could use it," urged Lou. She excused herself without further comment and headed to the spread.

"So, you want to talk about this," he said when she had returned with a full plate and seated herself. He was smiling but she knew his concern was deep. Still, there was a bravado added for the sake of the producers who were listening intently.

"Not a lot to talk about, Lou," said Meredith, arranging her food plate and utensils as she sat down. "Everything I know is in the stories we released. After two hours with the local gendarmes, I can honestly say that there's nothing more I can tell you." The old publicist reached across the table and patted her hand. His rough-hewn face with its bushy grey mustache smiled, resembling a well-used leather hide.

"No one's taking you to task, my dear," he said, a slight theatrical lilt in his voice.

"We all appreciate your being here and not sensationalizing the situation," spoke up one of the other diners. "Steve Bankleman," he introduced himself, extending his hand. "I'm the Line Producer here on the movie." Meredith shook his hand. A forty-something muscular man, sun-tanned face, solid like a boxer or wrestler, Meredith thought. "Thank you for coming. I'm sorry for everyone's loss here," he added with rapt and sincere solemnity. "Let us know what we can do to make your visit more...comfortable," he said, searching for the most accommodating word. He introduced her to the other diner, Executive Producer Marv Snelling, the administrative visitor.

"I'd sure like to head home in the morning," laughed Meredith. "Any chance of that?"

Again, with a deep sense of condolence, Bankleman answered, "I hope we can help you there, but we're still waiting for the instructions from the local coroner."

"There seems to be quite a heightened sense of mystery about this death," Meredith commented quietly, loading a warm tortilla with a spoonful of refried beans.

Blank looks met her from around the table. "Who knows?" said Bankleman. "None of us are real sure why the need for an inquest. There's a whole contingent of law people here from the state out of Albuquerque who can investigate with plenty of rigor, but the coroner...well, he's the local coroner and has the authority. He wants a 'thorough investigation.'" Everyone groaned.

"He's a retired pediatrician, for God's sake," muttered the Executive Producer.

"Well," smiled Meredith with a forced sincerity, "Then I hope you won't mind if I use the extra time to grab some background and color film for my TV shot next week." The three other guests looked at one another cautiously, then the publicity chief nodded. "Might as well make good use of your time since you're here. Just be careful—and don't get into anyone's way." Meredith shot him a look that made him openly cringe. "Sorry, that was condescending, wasn't it?"

"If I have to stay," Meredith continued. "I'll need to borrow a car or driver because I didn't come prepared for an extended visit and need a couple of clothing items. Walmart around here anywhere? IF I have to stay, of course." She looked around.

Bankleman finally answered, "Sure. But the closest Walmart is in Albuquerque—couple of hours away but there's a small, pretty complete mall much closer. We'll have someone for you as soon as we know the score tomorrow morning."

"Thanks," said Meredith, biting into her thickly filled tortilla. Twenty minutes later, the studio executives finished their meal and were about the leave the table. Meredith wished them a good evening, about to leave as well. She noticed Dusty had just arrived and was moving down the food layout. She waved him over.

"That was a bevy of royalty," he chuckled as he set his plate down and arranged himself in one of the vacant chairs.

"I've known Lou Marquand, the Publicity Chief, for years. He was also a very close friend of Cassie's in the early days," smirked Meredith. "Lucky the studio sent him here instead of some ingenue. I got permission for filming and a driver—IF I have to stay. I'll want you on film, you know."

"Don't miss a beat, do you?" Dusty shook his head and smiled at Meredith. "You aren't going to embarrass me, are you?"

"You've pretty much said what you're going to say to the public already."

"Get Bankleman on camera. As the line producer he 'makes the trains run on time.' And he loves publicity. And, he's really the go-to guy now that he's back on site."

"What about Marv?" Meredith asked, referring to the Executive Producer.

"No. He hates the limelight. His only concern is about money—making as much as possible and spending as little as he can—not people. That's why we never usually see him here."

Meredith nodded, then spoke up quietly and almost intimately. "Dusty, how did you and Sonora's boy get along? Were you friendly? Close? What do you think went on last night?"

"I'm always friendly. Carlton? No, we weren't close, not his style. I have no idea what went on last night, but I believe it's more than anyone wants to admit or find…but hold on. Please don't make this into a fan magazine ditty. It doesn't merit or deserve that."

"Hey, you brought me here because you trusted me.…" The two were quiet for a few minutes while Dusty ate his dinner and

Meredith stared out at the desert, sipping on a glass of red wine from the food table. Finally, she smiled softly and spoke up quietly, "So, is it good with her, Dusty? I hope so. You deserve it."

"I wonder if a relationship with a super-public person is ever 'good,' Merri. But it was pretty nice until...this...this death happened. Who knows at this point?"

"Well, you're now a public persona, too Mr. Big Time Director...." She dodged a piece of bread he tossed at her, and giggled. Suddenly, a hearty, "Hi there Meredith! Good to see you. And Dusty!" interrupted their conversation. A tall, attractive sun-bleached blonde man with a wide affable grin approached the table, pulled out an empty chair and sat down.

"Hank Torbin," smiled Meredith. "Wow, the gang's all here!" Torbin was a member of super-star and *Sunset West* producer Renn Burton's moviemaking team, the team from which Dusty had graduated from stunt person into directing.

"I'm in the movie," said Torbin. "But you're a busy reporter, I'll bet. You sure chose the right time to visit *Sunset West*, didn't she Dusty?" The director smiled accommodatingly and said, "You bet. I didn't know you were back, though, Hank. Just get in?"

"More or less. Crisis time," he said. Meredith struggled to stay in her seat and not to leave. She knew Hank Torbin from an earlier encounter. Several years before, still fairly new to the gossip game, she traveled to a southeastern college, location of a football movie starring Renn Burton. The studio had taken over a stadium during summer to film. Meredith had spent one day covering the filming, interviewing various actors and the director. In the afternoon she talked with Renn himself. Dinner followed with the star and several of his entourage, including Hank Torbin, at the rural area's only hotel restaurant. As the meal progressed and Meredith chatted with dinner companions, Torbin became more and more attentive to her. She moved around the table several times to distance herself from him. She knew the dance from encounters with other would-be partners, part of being young, attractive and in a super-charged culture.

"Let's have a drink and I'd love to hear about your work," he said to her as guests were leaving the gathering. She declined, explaining she had work left to do. He followed along to the lobby, once again encouraging her to join him at the bar.

"Not tonight, I'm afraid. Long day, early flight out tomorrow and writing to do. But so nice meeting you." She saw more than disappointment on his face—determination. "I'm going to have to excuse—or embarrass—myself after all the coffee I drank," she smiled and rushed into the open elevator, gasping in relief when the door closed before he could follow. Later, packed, wake-up call set, she climbed into bed and turned off the lamp. Falling to sleep, she heard a fluttering sound around the door to her room, carefully locked when she arrived from dinner. She crept out of bed and to the door which opened into a small vestibule leading into the actual bedroom. She looked through the small magnified peep hole and was stunned to see Torbin standing outside her door, staring at it.

She pondered what to do—call security, yell "go away." He hadn't done anything wrong—yet. He was a known, visible member of a respected actor community. And well-liked. She was just a gossip reporter. And it would be a "he said, she said." After a few minutes, he walked on down the hall. Maybe his room was on the same floor.

She considered dragging the chair from the wall desk and placing its back under the door handle, then wondered if she wasn't overreacting. She crept back into bed, her hand on the nightstand telephone just in case. She still had concerns about the incident as she left for her flight the next morning. Over the months and eventually years after, she only caught glimpses of

Hank Torbin at various events. There never was a follow-up discussion or even mention of his attempted visit to her room that night. Once in a while she revisited the dilemma—did she overreact? He was handsome, gentlemanly, always pleasant.

Sitting opposite her in the remote movie location in New Mexico, he asked, "What have you learned? Talking to lots of the employees? Would love to talk with you more."

Meredith cringed at the intrusion. "Just the usual stuff, Hank. There's a local paper with today's column in it over on the shelf. You can check it out." Instead, Torbin made his way to the food table and Meredith sighed deeply.

She quickly bid good night and made her way to her room. A bath in the opulent tub, and a vigorous toweling off, she melted into the crisp, welcoming sheets. Then Raymond called. Relieved to hear his voice, and anxious to calm any concerns he might have about her being here, in crisis, with her former lover, she recounted the day's events in quick succession. She noticed a hesitancy in his voice but didn't attribute it to jealousy or worry about her. More as though someone else were listening and he was being guarded.

"Stay safe. Be careful around those execs," he cautioned her. "I'm still out of town, but I'll probably be home before you get there! I'm hard to catch right now. Lots of meetings and updates in the offices. But I'll try to reach you tomorrow around dinner time." And they both signed off relieved to talk with one another but neither satisfied with the conversation.

"The old guy actually called an inquest?" Cassie listened to Meredith's woeful announcement at eight-thirty the next morning. "What's going on with that slick investigative team from Albuquerque? Can't they handle it?"

"It's a travesty, Cassie. Everyone here is puzzled by it. How about calling Russ in New York and seeing if his legal team can't spring me loose. I'm fine with one more day. I want to get some of this on film and the video guy is ready to work tomorrow afternoon. But, damn, that's enough! I've done my favor for Dusty, got a good story and now it's time to go home."

"I'll see what I can do. Everything else okay, Meredith?"

"Sure. I guess. Business as usual. The studio has given me a car and driver. Apparently, there's a small mall about a half hour away and I'm starting my day buying a quick change of clothes for another day or two. What's going on there? Anything I should know about?"

"Nah. Ito's chasing down some early information on a rumored federal investigation of one of the record companies—actually of its parent company in Switzerland. Doesn't sound like anything local is very involved...but interesting."

"Good for him! How about you? You sound a little subdued."

"Not really. Just distracted. Working on a new book. Nothing exciting. Have you talked with Raymond?" Cassie asked the question with a forced nonchalance.

"Last night. He sounds distracted, too. Maybe August is the month for distraction. Once I get out of here, it will all normalize."

"Probably. I better get off and try to reach Russ about getting you out of there."

"Thanks, and I'm gonna see if Fred Barton has heard anything from the grapevine about this delay. Bye." Meredith hung up. Cassie pondered her partner's words about Raymond and distraction and hoped she hadn't made a miscalculation about the phone call from Washington D.C. that had the sounds of surf in the background.

From New Mexico Meredith placed a call to Fred Barton, her former colleague and long-time friend, at his editor post now at the prestigious show business chronicle, *Daily Channels*. He answered in his usual serious yet buoyant voice, "Ya. Barton here."

"So, Fred, I'm in Flecha Dorada, New Mexico, covering *Sunset West*. The star's kid OD'd, and half the investigative power of the state is in from Albuquerque digging under rocks to find out how and why. Any idea why the coroner of this small one-horse town used as a movie location would call for a formal inquest?"

"Lucky you!" Fred chortled. "No place like the desert in August! Hope there's a swimming pool and a margarita!"

"Probably. But I'm stuck here until some retired pediatrician functioning as the local coroner decides to release us. Could be months."

"If he's really old, let's hope he doesn't die before it's over. You'll never get home."

"There's a pleasant thought!"

"Can I call you back? Or call me in a couple of hours. I'll ask around and see what I can find out. It is a mysterious death, though. So, someone's got to investigate—and knowing you, stay in your room and lock the door. You okay otherwise?"

"Yeah—you?"

"Yep. Talk to you in a while." The line went dead.

Meredith reflected on Fred's wise directive to stay in the room and lock the door. They'd had some dangerous adventures together in pursuit of a good story. Yet, she made her way down to the Villa entrance. Waiting there was her ride. Leaning against a dark SUV was a tall, sinewy Latino man, dark hair stylishly cut and almost shining in the bright sunshine, and wearing a dark brown shirt, sleeves rolled to the elbows, jeans, and hot-shit sunglasses.

"Ms. Ogden?" He offered his hand. "I'm Reuben."

She shook his hand. "Please call me Meredith."

"I understand we're going shopping at the Montana Mall. It's about twenty miles south, twenty or thirty minutes." He opened the car door and she slid into the back seat.

CHAPTER 10
SAN FERNANDO VALLEY
FRIDAY

"You're sure you got all this?" Margo gazed intently at Raymond. She was wearing a "Hot Stuff" tee shirt with a pair of cut off shorts that even Jerrold had commented on. "Lady, for someone with the chutzpa you have and the brains, that's not what's showing!"

The three of them were sipping coffee from take-out cups from the closest Starbucks and sitting on the sparse patio in the back of the house. Bags, duffels and file boxes were stacked at the front door, ready for departure. Their ward, the whistleblower, had been picked up by another set of agents for delivery to a distant safe house.

"My head is full, and I've converted everything to what looks like the drabble from the notes I took in DC. Now I'm ready to go home," said the detective, a sense of finality in his voice.

"We hit the pavement tomorrow," said Margo. "Melvin will be under lock and key in Ojai in a couple of hours. Jerrold, you've already situated yourself in Brentwood, not far from Raymond's usual digs?" The big accountant nodded.

"And you, Raymond. Maybe stay off the red carpet until this is over. Probably not a great idea to have your face everywhere in the glitter news while this case is going on."

"Do my best," he said. "Staying away from some of the limelight actually might be more noticeable to some, but I'll try to keep out of camera range."

"And what about your friend George Masner? Are you sure you can handle that one?" Margo referred to one of Raymond's oldest friends from college, and the husband of Meredith's best friend Gloria. George was also a high-powered theatrical agent, well connected and had lines into the music industry, including artists at Sterling.

"I have to strategize 'that one' carefully," Raymond admitted. "I can handle it, but with subtlety."

"Strategize quickly. We need to move on this, "concluded Margo.

"And folks, this isn't a benign look into a set of books," cautioned Jerrold. "Watch your backs. So far as we can tell, with a hit and run and the 'vacation' of Sterling's financial officer, this is wider and deeper than we realize." With that warning, they all rose from the canvas chairs, gathered their belongings and materials and headed to their cars.

☆☆☆

The day was already evolving into a hot, smoggy sponge. Leaving the Valley, Raymond was glad to be heading toward the beach. He realized he didn't spend nearly as much time there as he would like during these sooty summer months. He took unnecessary detours along the way, to add assurance that his trip was not being shadowed by anyone else. Once in Malibu, he circled the block twice until he saw no other sign of life on the street and could quickly open the garage and pull in.

The detective used his house on the beach like a part-time guest cottage most of the time. Son Will and college girlfriend

Sophie lived there, occupying the guest room. Both were engineering students at nearby Pepperdine University. Raymond stayed mostly with Meredith at her Brentwood townhouse because of its proximity to both workplaces, and they often used the Malibu house on weekends.

He tossed his bag on the couch, opened up the windows and took a deep breath of the cool breezy ocean air. It felt like a tonic to his anxiety-clinched brain. He longed to take a run down the beach, drop into the Seashack Diner down the road and settle into the wooden patio chairs with a margarita and plate of clam strips, watching the evening creep in over the water. But he also wanted no one to realize he was back in town, and in Malibu. He was actually expected home—but to the Brentwood condo— later this evening. But there was work to be done before that. And he felt a strong pull to the calming ocean air and solace of his beach house.

He ran a laundry load of his "beach casual" clothing items taken to the San Fernando Valley, repacked the duffle, hoping no one would realize he'd ever been there. The kids wouldn't, he realized looking around the place at the student-lifestyle clutter. Sitting on the deck with the cool, light breeze calming his concern, he thought about the assignment he was undertaking and wondering about the wisdom of it. His special profile unit was shared among several of the Southern California law enforcement agencies and dealt with the glamor industries: celebrity assaults, glitzy white-collar crimes, show business break-ins, royal visits. He'd seen his share of suspicious deaths, the most notable of them gossip columnist Bettina Grant, the case where he met Meredith.

He remembered interviewing her the evening after the murder. Bettina Grant worked in a luxury office in her Bel Air home and her small staff, primarily Meredith, shared those offices. The younger journalist was in shock as she talked with the detective that first meeting, overwhelmed not only by the unexpected death of her long-time boss and mentor but awed by the task ahead—keeping the news material flowing and the office functioning. Over a very short time, Meredith herself, known to be the person closest to Bettina Grant, became the object of assaults—on the office, her home and her person. Regardless, she moved forward in spite of her own fears, sadness, weariness and confused professional future. Resolution evolved on all fronts, work, past personal history…well, the rest.

At first, he managed her in order to ferret out clues to the murder. Then he protected her as a valuable witness and then as a personal concern, and ultimately as someone he valued. Over the holidays that year, it became clear she welcomed his company as much as he hers. Christmas came and both went their own planned ways for the short break. When he returned to LA, he didn't know how to approach her, without the investigation as an excuse. Her parting words as she left their pre-holiday dinner date was "Get your tux cleaned, Raymond." After Christmas, he drove by the office from which the news team would be moving very shortly. He walked in, greeted Ito, the houseman turned editorial secretary, a former "person of interest" with whom Raymond had become friendly.

"She here?" he asked. Ito smiled broadly and pointed into the furthest office back. Meredith was perched on her toes struggling to reach a box on the top shelf of her office closet. Raymond stepped up next to her and easily extracted the box. She smiled and said, 'Happy holidays, Raymond. You found your way back here." She was blushing. He realized he probably was as well.

"Thought I'd see how the move is going. And where it's going."

"It's going. That's about all the news right now. Probably sign a lease in the next couple of days. Cassie flies in from New York in two weeks—for good—husband Bob follows in a month. And the news moves along as always. Want some coffee?"

"If its Ito's—you bet." Hearing his name, Ito was already heading to the kitchen.

"Sit down," Meredith said with a laugh, indicating two patio chairs now used as office furniture. They both settled into them. "How was Laguna?"

"Good. Always pleasant. My mom lives in a nice apartment building converted to condominiums for the elderly, complete with caretaker companions. Will and I go down every Christmas, rent one of the vacation rental apartments about a block away and it's a nice Christmas.

"You look rested," he said regarding her with a smile. Ito cordially interrupted and handed them both a mug of coffee, leaving as quietly as he arrived.

"For now. But oh my God! So much to do—moving this office, getting everyone's new job organized, and," she sighed, "getting Cassie set up with the local TV studio so we can start taping our TV segments in March." She shook her head.

"Business as usual?" Meredith nodded. Both were quiet for a moment, then Raymond said, "I thought we might have dinner or get together soon."

Meredith gave him a subtle smile. "I'd like that."

Suddenly at a loss for words, Raymond said, "My tux is clean."

"Good. You can wear it in a couple of weeks to the Golden Globe Awards—that is, if you want."

He cocked his head and looked at her, puzzled.

"Oh crap—I'm sorry. I forgot that life is all different now— me as the ward of law enforcement is over," she grinned almost wickedly." I just thought maybe you'd like to go with me. I have to go and it's always the funnest award party in Hollywood. I mean, well, you know, as my date?"

"Date. Sounds interesting. Lots of big events going on in tinsel town, I imagine," he said, standing up.

"Some," she said. "Big season coming up—Oscars, Emmys, and on and on. I'll actually be glad when Cassie gets to town and can take some of the events. As it is, I give a lot of screening tickets and concert stuff to Sonia. She loves it and I need quiet time."

"Well, the Big Ball drops on New Years' Eve, lest we all forget!"

Meredith snorted. "Sure, of course. The most over-rated night of the year. Everyone seems to need to have a party or an event of some kind. Way too much stuff going on that night and little of it very worthwhile." She dramatically shuddered.

He reached over, squeezed her arm, said, "Call me with Golden Globe details. We're on." And left the offices, realizing he hadn't thought of an evening out with an attractive woman as a "date" in years. But it was two weeks away, leaving him slightly disappointed.

New Year's Eve rolled in, as it always does. Meredith closed the office early and sent everyone home. All seemed to have plans for celebrating. Including Meredith. Hers were to close her house door, crawl into a bubble bath, a rare treat, and pour a glass of wine. But as five o'clock loomed, she felt restless, and had other thoughts on her mind. Taking a large drink of Prosecco, she picked up the phone and dialed Raymond. Trepidation shook her hand. What if…? He answered sounding half-asleep.

"Happy New Year, Raymond!"

"Well, thanks. This is a nice surprise. What's on your agenda for tonight?"

"Prosecco. After that, I haven't really settled on anything yet. What are you doing?"

"Listening to an old Dave Brubeck album, having some 12-year old scotch and planning to put a steak on the grill. Would you like to join me? The steak is huge."

"I like steak. I could bring Prosecco. And brownies. I picked them up on my way home this afternoon—a chocolate craving."

"Can you drive," he chuckled.

"I can now. But maybe not later."

"Then bring your pajamas."

Meredith poured a huge volume of dry cat kibble into Paco's bowl and scooped out a sloppy cup of wet food for him. "Be a good boy," she directed him. "Don't be a glutton and eat this all at once. You have a whole day ahead." The big feline looked at her with disdain. She locked up and left for Malibu.

She didn't come home for two days, calling the office on Monday morning, rationalizing that the column for Monday was complete and ready to send. "I'm taking a vacation day." With crime quiet during the holidays, Raymond did the same, his partner, Marty, chuckling slyly at the phone message he received at his desk that morning.

And so the schedule went for months. Usually one night during the week for dinner out or in together with the Brentwood condo as the landing pad afterward. Then one work event, sometimes with Raymond, sometimes not, but with Raymond's Malibu place on the weekend. He learned that in spite of her social energy, she protected her time alone and only allowed herself two evenings a week away from her personal cocoon. Malibu had become part of that. Time moved along, birthdays, holidays, red carpet events, movies, even an occasional long weekend in Cabo San Lucas or Laguna. Raymond's son Will had come home for graduate school, with a car full of clothes, books, two pairs of skis—and a diminutive young Asian woman named Sophie. Raymond offered them the guest room and bath at the Malibu house. They eagerly accepted. He mused at the picture of himself— evolving from a single, alone cop who focused almost exclusively on work, to a guy with a very active, albeit irregular set of family—the veritable full house.

One day in the fall of 1985, he called Meredith at her office after he had just flown in from a work trip to Sacramento. "Hasn't she called you or talked to you today?" Ito probed. "No," he said.

Cassie quickly came on the line. "Raymond, Meredith's in the hospital. She has pneumonia, really sick. I'm surprised you didn't notice that she's been feeling terrible—bronchitis, coughing. Fever spiked last night at 104."

"I've been away for the past four days," he stammered. "She said she had a cold. I talked to her yesterday afternoon. She said she was going to bed early and we'd catch up today."

"Well, Sonia's there now, and is trying to get her mom to take her 12-year-old son so she can drive Meredith home and stay with her. Otherwise, she has to stay in the hospital. They want someone with her, and you know Merri—she wants no part of a hospital."

"I've got it, Cass. Call Sonia off. I'm on my way there now." He was spurred on, and worried, by memories of the months spent caregiving for his late wife Lilli as she slipped through the grasp of breast cancer and then left them. He took Meredith home, too depleted by her illness for her usual insistence on self-reliance, but nonetheless determined not to spend time in the hospital. For three weeks Raymond settled into the condo full time, working mostly from there except when Sonia or Cassie would spend a few hours and he'd go to his own office and caseload. He was relieved that his partner, Marty Escobar, had matured into the job well enough to work independently and well. A former street cop whose instincts had made his superiors notice him, he applied for the "special cases" (read celebrity or public person) position with Raymond and won it without competition.

By week three of Meredith's illness, Raymond was going into work again as Meredith's strength had returned and she was writing from home, resting often and finally eating regular meals. Her gaunt face was gaining definition again, her lustrous copper blond hair shiny and full, and her athletic, lithe form once again straight and almost ready for aerobics.

Packing up to move back to Malibu, he caught Meredith watching pensively. "What's up?" he asked. She shrugged. "Seriously," he probed, "are you okay? What can I do to make you feel better?"

"Stay," she said.

"Just stay?"

She nodded slowly.

So, a deal was struck with little negotiation. Weekdays in Brentwood because it was close to both offices and she felt attached to her cocoon. Weekends at Malibu. Some nights Raymond would escort Meredith through the maze of Hollywood's cacophonous glamor. Red carpets, screenings, concerts, always navigating her, firmly by the elbow, through the throngs of photographers, other press and hangers-on.

After two and a half years, he sat on his ocean front lanai, taking in the breezes and listening to the gulls' cry, and felt a sense of peace with the family that now surrounded him. And they allowed him to function well, even notably, in his role investigating the glamor world's murders, assaults, felony burglaries, and other miscellaneous bad stuff.

But the new FBI assignment, handed down from a longways away from Southern California and from much higher up than the hills of Beverly, was both an acknowledgment of his skill, but also many times more deadly than his previous ones. He rose from his patio chair, rechecked to find his handgun in the bottom of his bag, and closed up the house. With a cautious eye for onlookers, he drove to the Brentwood town house, not totally certain what would await him there.

CHAPTER 11
FLECHA DORADA, NEW MEXICO
FRIDAY MORNING

Meredith spent the morning adding to her scant travel wardrobe: underwear, T-shirts, socks and jeans. The studio-assigned driver, Rueben Alonso, drove her to a small mall that included a local department store. "Take your time," he told her as she left the car. "I'll be down the road having coffee at the diner." Forty-five minutes later they were back on the road.

"Took you less time to fill your wardrobe than it took to get here," the affable young man commented.

"I hope I'm not here that much longer. I'm really frustrated that I can't get home."

"Awful lot of unusual happenstances," commented the driver. Meredith sat quietly thinking about the phone conversation she'd just had with Fred Barton from the pay phone in the mall. "So, there doesn't seem to be a hardline reason for the inquest—other than the overdose and death," chuckled Fred. "No one at the studio understands it any better than you do, but it stands because it's legal. One of the attorneys I talked to said he 'got the impression' that the tourist business arriving because of the celebrity death was too good to ignore. Every motel within miles of Flecha Dorada is full, restaurants, car rentals and what not are slammed. My contact said his contact told him the area hadn't seen that good a tourist influx in years."

"You think the town is using this as a PR draw?" Meredith asked Reuben.

"Why not?" he responded. "This area doesn't get much play any other way. Not much to bring people here unless they come to the Villa as guests of the owner. Or want to live far away from anything else." The car was silent for a while. Reuben broke the spell soon with, "You live in the LA area?"

"Westside. Brentwood," Meredith murmured.

"Nice part of town. I grew up in Glendale, went to UCLA and loved that area—especially the beaches."

"What are you doing here? In this isolated desert?"

"I'm a studio driver. I go where the work is. I often work with the same crew who is working this movie."

"You like driving people around?"

"Sure, I get to know a lot of different people—that's really interesting. Movie people are kind of their own tribe. And I've made some pretty good friends." He named a half dozen other movies he'd work with, mostly in the southwestern region.

"You must like it here."

"As you said, it's quiet, I can do my job and still have time to myself. I like to read, study language," Reuben glanced into the rearview mirror and scowled.

"What's happening?"

"Nothing. Truck coming up on us faster than it should. Just keeping an eye on it." He continued to stare at the mirror. "Got your seat belt on?"

"Why?" she asked, looking down to make sure her belt was strong into its holder. As she did, she noticed Reuben's hand idly reaching under his seat and sliding a metal object forward. She was pretty sure it was the handle of a gun.

"Just a good idea," he said, both hands back on the wheel, watching as the large red truck drew up on their tail to pass, yells and hoots coming from its inhabitants. "Maybe stay down as low as you can." She hunched forward and held her breath.

Besides the driver and passenger, the truck boasted three animated young men shouting and laughing in the vehicle's bed, one with a rifle waving in the wind. Meredith saw Reuben grimace and subtly slow his own vehicle. As he did so, the speeding red image streaked by, the rifle aimed well above the car, but in its direction. A series of loud "pops" punctuated the air and faded down the road with the truck.

"Kids!" snorted Reuben. "There's some troublemakers around here. Nothing to worry about." Meredith's heart was already beating in her throat. A few minutes later, Reuben pulled into a timeworn gas station fronting a tired convenience store. "I need to fill up the tank. Be just a minute. Stay put, unless you need to use the bathroom."

She opened the door shakily and made her way into the store. The plump, wiry-haired clerk noticed her and pointed toward the restroom signs. Meredith splashed cold water on her face and smoothed her hair.

"Heard those idiots going by," said the weathered clerk, standing solid in her work apron, hands on her hips. She shook her iron-grey curls. Meredith scowled in question at her comment. "Couple of sure-ass stupid kids that come here from time to time. They like to go out and just shoot guns. No reason, just to make havoc, I guess Daddy owns both the air strip and ranch and part of the fancy place the movie people are staying at....How about a cold drink?" Meredith accepted, still shaken by the sudden mayhem, happy to stay behind closed doors and out of the open.

Soon, they were on the road to the Villa. Meredith was even more shaken noticing him absently pushing the gun butt far back under his seat as they had climbed back into the car.

"You seem pretty shaken—will you be okay?" Reuben asked.

"Yeah—a little PTSD from a couple of incidents a few years ago. I can handle it. Are you doing okay?"

"Fine," he grinned in the mirror so she could see. "I'm Teflon coated!"

CHAPTER 12
WEST LOS ANGELES
FRIDAY

"So...let me get this straight. You need our lawyers to get CenturySonic Studios to free Meredith from the confines of a coroner's inquest in New Mexico?" United American Media's Managing Director Russ Talbot sighed, and Cassie could almost hear him slapping a hand to his forehead. "What's she gotten into there?"

"Nothing all that much, Russ. Not her. It's the situation." Cassie explained about the movie set visit that coincided with the overdose death of the star's son, how Meredith had managed to spend some time with Sonora Hutchinson quite serendipitously within hours and how Meredith was now part of the subpoena to contain all parties at the location until the inquest was completed."

"Any idea when that might be?"

"No. The heavy hitter investigators are all there from Albuquerque, but the local coroner seems to want to be in charge. He won't close the case even for now. Word on the street is that business in and around Flecha Dorada is just too good these days to let go of it this soon."

"You're kidding, right?"

"No."

"Shit."

Ito walked quietly into Cassie's office. "Is Meredith in trouble? She need help?"

"Yes, indeed. Stuck in the outlands of New Mexico. But I hope we have it under control right now." She commented confidently, but deep inside she felt like the situation in Flecha Dorada was volatile, and worried for her friend.

Ito shook his head, then quickly changed the subject. "I have information on Sterling Music. Artists, current lawsuits, problems and so on. What is it you are looking for?"

"We heard there's a federal investigation about embezzlement around it. We want to know what, where, why, how and who. All the usual suspects." She looked at him expectantly.

"I think it's higher up the corporate ladder than Sterling. Maybe not, but that's what I was told. The headquarters Chief Financial Officer was killed in a hit and run accident. Her assistant disappeared—just vanished into thin air. I understand there's lots of a behind-closed-door-meetings locally, strangers moving around the offices, and anxiety. The local people have been told it's about a federal audit at headquarters—in London—with no real impact on California operations. But...."

"Don't you wonder who's involved here?" probed Cassie.

"I'm not sure my contacts are that deep or forthcoming, but I'll do some careful snooping."

"Ito, please be careful. These kinds of stories aren't always worth the dangerous ground we have to cover to get them. I heard that there may be drug stuff involved. Back off if it's going to cost you anything—friends, credibility, safety...anything." He nodded, quietly stood up and left the room. Cassie picked up the phone and called her literary agency friend Vanessa Collier who had tipped her off about the audit initially.

"Hey, Cassie. What's up in gossip land?"

"Not much. But I have a question about the issue you mentioned at lunch. The audit? Have you heard anything new on that? I have some distant rumbling?"

"Mine's not so distant, but I do know that our main contact there, the talent coordinator, has suddenly been sent to London to work on a 'special' project for a while. And there were a couple of new client folks working the account that were here for a couple of weeks and then gone. They were a little strange."

"How so?"

"They just sat in the meetings, asking off-the-wall questions, sometimes completely off topic or out of context. Like they're from another planet."

Cassie chuckled. "Now there's a descriptive sentence I want to use."

"Uh-uh," replied Vanessa. "I'm not kidding. We all walk around looking straight ahead when the client is in the office. I don't think this is a story to fool around about." They ended the call and Cassie sat chewing on a cherry lollipop, substituting for her usual fingernail, and gazing out the window. Who did she know she could call on to learn more about this company? Then it came to her and she was instantly sorry Meredith was caught up in the New Mexico turmoil. This was her kind of story—and she had the exact right contacts. But she wasn't there and the story, like all good stories, needed to be farmed now before the results got stale. Cassie went to Meredith's office and flipped through her Rolodex.

☆☆☆

Cassie decided to park in a public lot near Little Santa Monica Boulevard and Rodeo Drive, several blocks from the law offices of Gloria Masner. In spite of the gritty August heat, she enjoyed the walk down the high fashion pathway through the center of Beverly Hills. The display windows with their flirty and colorful mannequins were seductive even in the low-hanging smog of summer. They lifted her spirits, helping to remind her that she was part of show business's pastiche of imagined glamor.

A small low-rise brick building housed the trendy offices where the Honorable Gloria Masner, Esq. practiced. A respected attorney mostly specializing in trust cases, Gloria was also the best friend of Cassie's editorial partner. And the wife of one of the entertainment industry's most respected and powerful artist agents, George Masner. And Cassie hoped she was in her office, and in a receptive mood.

Cassie's visit took the attorney by surprise as she welcomed the journalist to her small but well-appointed office. "Cass, what brings you over here? Wished you'd called earlier. We could have had lunch—I could have used the break. I've been buried in a project all day and didn't notice the time. Glad you showed up."

Lowering herself into a buttery leather side chair, Cassie dropped her purse and sat back. "You probably know Meredith's kind of stuck in New Mexico, and I need some perspective on a brewing story. You might have it for me, so I took the liberty of stopping by."

Gloria tucked a strand of raven black hair behind her ear, reached back to secure the clip on the knot at her neck, and looked closely at Cassie. "What's Meredith doing in New Mexico? I didn't know she was going."

"Short story made long—went to cover Dusty Reed's new movie and ended up snagged into the middle of a set drama— overdose of the star's son—and is currently bound to stay put by the local coroner's inquest."

Gloria slapped a hand over her mouth and chuckled.

"Wow—she does find the intrigue, doesn't she? But Dusty?"

Cassie shrugged. "Started out as a favor. Turned into a nightmare. She's beside herself."

"I can imagine," said Gloria, narrowing her glance at Cassie. "Can't wait to hear the rest of that story." Her husband George was one of the few close personal friends of T.K. Raymond. The two couples often shared social time. "So, what can I help you with? What's this perplexing story?"

"It has to do with a seemingly serious audit, or financial investigation of some kind by the Feds of—maybe more appropriately—its parent company. I seem to remember that you or your company had some connection to Sterling Music, thought you might have some insight on the situation."

Gloria brought her well-manicured hands together in a prayer-like pose and rubbed them together idly. She suddenly rose from her chair and gestured to Cassie. "I need to get out for a break. Take a walk with me." Puzzled, Cassie rose and followed her out of the office, through the reception area and into the street.

They walked a block before Gloria spoke again. "We're going down the street to the coffee shop on the corner and there, we're going to talk about how your joint enterprise is going. Until then, all I can tell you is that this is George's realm, not mine. He's mentioned what you're talking about. I've heard him say the implications are so wide-spread and deep he's doing independent audits of his own company's connection, just to be certain there's no spill-over from client to agency. But I don't know any details. We have an agreement not to discuss our client specifics and honestly, they don't usually intersect. But I couldn't help but overhear some of the conversations. There seems to be very high-level financial irregularities, wide-spread impact on a lot of people, and…," she took a breath, was silent for a moment, then added, "maybe drugs involved, but I don't know any more than that. Oh, here we are. Let's go in and get a cup of coffee."

They did and talked for another half hour about the Hollywood Dateline offices, the nature of Hollywood gossip and how Cassie's husband was faring in his photographic editor job at a long-standing magazine. As they left the coffee shop, they bid one another a happy afternoon, Gloria striding down Rodeo Drive with her crisp, confident gait, her green and blue scarf trailing behind her perfectly tailored blue suit. Walking back to her car, Cassie was more intrigued about the Sterling Music story than ever. Maybe it was time to let Ito get his hands truly dirty in the business of investigative journalism.

CHAPTER 13
FLECHA DORADA, NEW MEXICO
FRIDAY AFTERNOON

The Villa, production headquarters for *Sunset West*, pulsated with activity as the death of the star's son brought executives and crew back early from what was to have been a four-day break. Lunch was being served on the terrace with a conversational buzz filling the air. Reuben dropped off Meredith at the front entrance and she carefully avoided notice as she went to her room but could not miss the voice of an upset guest. His accented voice haranguing and challenging a group standing near the Villa main office.

Splashing cold water on her face, brushing her hair and taking deep breaths to calm her frayed nerves, she reached into her bag for her sneakers—a must when covering movie locations. Usually habitually organized with her travel belongings, she was puzzled by the rumpled condition of the contents in the duffle.

I was really rattled by Torbin, she told herself. Then she noticed her notes and studio handouts scattered on the desk, a page on the floor. She knew those materials had been well organized inside a file folder when she left the room that morning. Housekeeping? She wondered. Not likely, especially considering the state of the overnight bag. Her quandary was interrupted by a discreet knock on her door. She opened it to

Fastida, the house's manager. The woman seemed frazzled and distracted. She handed Meredith a folded slip of paper.

"Mr. Bankleman asked me to give you this. He says he will meet you on the saloon set at one-thirty with your photographer." Meredith grimaced at the name of the producer, realizing his presence meant he would be orchestrating the filming she had planned for the afternoon. Already control of the story was evolving into the hands of the studio.

"Thank you Fastida. What's going on in the lobby? Someone's sure not happy."

"That's Mr. Sturgiss, Miss Sonora's ex-husband who just arrived. He's unhappy about the investigation, says it's unprofessional. He's going to take his son home to Europe for burial as quickly as the inquest is over. He thinks the local coroner is a 'jerk,' he says. Miss Sonora will accompany him for a few days while their son is…put to rest. Then she'll be back. Mr. Sturgiss wants them to suspend filming so she can stay in Europe, but…well…they aren't going to do that."

"Oh, Fastida. Have you noticed anyone entering or leaving my room today—besides me?"

"No, only the housekeeper early this morning, but I don't see the hallways from the office." Meredith shook her head, then dismissed the concern.

"You are a real rock here, Fastida," said Meredith. "Do a lot of movie companies use the Villa? Other than the *Sunset West* company?"

"Oh yes," replied the short, squarely-built Latina woman, "but the producers here with *Sunset West* have used it a lot. Many years. They like it here, but we never see the big guys. Just the workers."

"I know how difficult Carlton's death and the drama around it has made your work," Meredith smiled. "I'm sorry—I wish I could do something to help." The older woman ran a hand through her greying curls and shook her head. "That boy should never have been here. His mother just couldn't take care of him and work too."

Meredith carefully looked at her and asked, "Was he running wild? You know, disappearing, drinking, taking drugs— how was he acting?"

Fastida shrugged shyly, "He just hung around with a gang of stupid ranch boys. Most of the time Carlton was buried in a book. Miss Sonora never knew where he was—but didn't seem to worry much. She had—other things—on her mind."

"Like Mr. Reed, the director?" Meredith asked with a complicit grin. Fastida laughed heartily, wagged her finger and left. The note directed Meredith to the appointment location and let her know that the photographer would meet her there. Her driver would deliver her—twenty minutes away. She shrugged off the disarray of her belongings and headed to the afternoon's activities.

☆☆☆

As nonchalant and forgotten as the morning's drama had become, both she and Reuben seemed to be looking into the rearview mirror or over shoulders to see who might be following them en route to the movie set constructed in the desert. At the temporarily built western town, Reuben pulled up to the saloon building. "I'm on set until you're finished," he told her. "There's a bathroom in the wardrobe mobile trailer across the road and Bitsy, the costumer, is there today, so feel free to knock."

Meredith realized she was a few minutes early and the only part of the video team on site so far. She walked to the extended trailer and rapped on the door. A 50-something blond swung it

open and said, "Ah, you must be the reporter." They exchanged
pleasantries and Bitsy pointed to the back of the mobile's
hallway. As she emerged from the tiny bathroom, Meredith
looked at herself in the wardrobe mirror mounted on the wall.
She dug a comb from her bag and slicked back her copper-blond
hair, pulling it into a sleek ponytail. The wardrober suddenly
appeared with a western straw hat in hand.

"Here, you should be wearing this—too hot out there to stay
more than a few minutes in the sun without it." Meredith smiled
as she adjusted the hat to her hair. "You did the first story about
Sonora's kid, didn't you?" asked Bitsy, perching on the edge of a
built-in sofa.

"I did," Meredith answered. "Did you ever meet him?" Her
question brought a burst of chuckles from the wardrobe mistress.

"He was around here a lot. I got to know him—no one else
seemed to talk to him, or maybe it was the other way around."
"Was he as distant and quiet as most people say?"

"He was miserable. He lived most of the year with his dad in
Europe and I guess, by the divorce agreement, spent summers
with Sonora. He hated it when she worked and he hated being
here, in this isolated place. He really wanted to go home."

"I'm surprised she didn't let him do so. Did he make any
friends around the area?"

"For a while, Trent Hastings—son of the co-star Beau
Hastings—was here. Nice boy, about Carlton's age. But he left
quickly. Told his dad that he was leaving one afternoon whether
Beau arranged it or not. Just up and kind of ran, like he didn't
want to have anything to do with this movie.

"The rest of the kid gang was mostly stupid teen dudes from
the fancy ranch down the highway—probably where you flew in.
They have a private airfield. Anyhow, it's summer and the
owner's kid, Frankie, is home from boarding school along with a

couple of other of his pals. Their families sent them out here to keep them occupied. They're arrogant and pushy, take advantage, entitled like they own the place. Had no respect for the rules around a movie set, yet no one threw them out. And they took Carlton under their wing but teased him mercilessly about his famous mother. But he took it—had nothing else to do, I guess."

"Besides their arrogance and bullying, what made them so bad?" Meredith straightened her clothes a little, pulling at her shirt to get rid of wrinkles from the warm day.

"Oh—they smoked a lot of weed, boasted of how they could get anything anybody wanted. They'd openly offer drugs, booze. Sat on the back stoop of my trailer—kind of out-of-sight—and watched the movie stuff—smoked and bantered about. Maybe it was just who they are that turned me off," shrugged Bitsy. "People gossip about the kid's dad who owns the ranch and air strip, say he's heavy into the drug business. Mexican border isn't far, you know. El Paso and Juarez are a couple of hours. I never heard about any investigations or arrests, but, well…it seems to be a local belief, anyhow. The kid seems to take advantage of it—tosses his weight around, plays off the privileged gangster image."

"Interesting. Poor Carlton. Did you tell anyone about this?"

"Bitsy shook her head. "When it all went down, we were on break. I got called back— just got here, and I'm sure I'm not the only one who's seen and heard this stuff." Meredith noticed the photographer walking toward the saloon set with his gear, and she thanked Bitsy for the use of the facilities and hurried over. Shortly, the producer arrived and they began shooting. Bankleman on camera, Meredith on camera, then co-star Beau Hastings on camera. As they wrapped the co-star's interview, Dusty arrived. "You're next," Meredith announced. Dusty looked at Bankleman who nodded. The interview was short and focused totally on the movie.

As they finished, the producer turned suddenly and said, "I better use Bitsy's loo before heading out. Back in a minute."

Meredith grabbed the sleeve of the photographer and pushed Dusty in front of the camera. "No argument," she cautioned. "Just do the interview. Tell me about Sonora Hutchinson. Will she recover from this terrible blow? You know her well—what's she like?"

Nonplused but compliant, Dusty struggled to sound prepared, "Sonora will recover. She's a tough and grounded person, but she is complex. She's compassionate and lighthearted on one side, but tough as nails and demanding on the other. So people sometimes do take her the wrong way. But her son meant a great deal to her and she is devastated by his death. Still, she plans to resume work next week after taking her son home to Europe for interment."

"How did you find working with her?"

"Working with her was great! She's very professional. We got along very well…." Dusty stammered for the first time. "We found a good bond between us."

"How good a bond was that?" she winked at the camera, feeling guilty and frivolous at the same time.

"Very good," answered Dusty. "Sonora and I have no secrets about that."

"Did you know Carlton well?"

"Not really. He was a nice boy, smart and courteous, but Sonora had a policy of keeping work and personal life separate."

Meredith saw Bankleman emerging from the wardrobe and closed off the interview. "Thanks all. I really appreciate it," she said to the group, reached to a nearby bench and plunked the straw hat from Bitsy on her head to shield herself from the sun.

Reuben watched from under the overhang of a false-front building and she waved at him. He walked quickly over. "I have a message for you from the office," he said. "You're supposed to call Russ Talbot in New York as soon as you can. He left this number. You can use my car phone."

Before anyone had a chance to talk further or inquire why Meredith's boss, the head of United American Media, would phone her in New Mexico, she turned and gathered her belongings. She thanked the photographer who told her he'd deliver his material by eight the next morning, then she sprinted to Reuben's Jeep.

"You can go home tomorrow, Meredith," came the calm, if weary, voice from New York. "But there's a catch. You have to stay the night and cover the press conference the studio is holding this evening at seven. That's the deal. They'll fly you commercially from Albuquerque tomorrow afternoon." He could hear her sigh—whether in relief or resignation. He couldn't tell.

"Thanks Russ. Sorry you had to get involved in this. I just want to get out of here. It's hot, gritty and August. But I hope I made the most of it."

"I heard something about shots fired?"

"Really? Sonia? She tends to overdramatize things. The local guy driving me said kids were joy riding with a shot gun—pretty wide open around here! Even the clerk at the gas station we had stopped at said kids firing off guns wasn't uncommon."

"You do get into these kerfuffles, don't you?" he chuckled. "Try to stay out of trouble—at least until you get back to LA."

CHAPTER 14
WEST LOS ANGELES, FLECHA DORADA, NEW MEXICO
FRIDAY NIGHT

Raymond unlocked the front door of the Brentwood townhouse and snapped on the lights. Dropping his bags on the sofa, he looked around at the well-appointed home that Meredith had purchased a decade earlier for herself. Soft pastels and beiges in the living room, a comforting brick fireplace, bookcases, a hanging staircase to the upper floor bedrooms and bath. He smiled at the concessions to a masculine presence in the house for the past two years: a large comfortable leather recliner and large TV off to one side of the living room. She'd chosen well.

But this night he longed for the Malibu beach house they now hung out only on weekends, its breezy solace and cleaner fresh air. The open ocean into which he could toss out concerns, questions and dilemmas—like the massive one on his mind. He looked around and mechanically went back out the entrance to the neighbor's door, ringing the bell with a sigh. A portly, ruddy-faced, white haired man opened the door only a sliver and looked out.

"Hi Norman..." Raymond began, but before he could finish, the neighbor thrust his arms forward, handing him a large silver and grey cat. "Paco's been a good boy," said the neighbor, and as Raymond took the cat in his arms, the door shut. "Good boy, huh?" he mocked. Paco looked at him with detached disdain.

The tall detective immediately fed Paco, understanding well the cat's role in the household. Then took his own belongings up to the bedroom and den, catching his own image in the hall mirror and stopped for a moment. His thick dark hair had developed a scant, but fine lattice of silver. He thought it made him distinguished. He was after all, fifty. But he scowled at the recent bags under his wide dark eyes, a few brush-stroked lines around them. "Just tired," he rationalized, wondering if Meredith, twelve years his junior, would ever age. She never seemed to.

He spent the rest of the evening drinking good Scotch and listening to John Coltrane.

☆☆☆

Flecha Dorada, New Mexico, was a thousand miles from Brentwood, "as the crow flies." Meredith curled into a chair she had pulled to the tiny, wrought-iron-bound "patio" outside her room at the Villa and wondered if a crow every really flew from LA to Flecha Dorada. Why? She puzzled. And she wondered about—well, everything. Raymond and his distant conversations since she'd been ensconced in the drama here in Flecha Dorada, how to handle the film and material she'd assembled that day on the *Sunset West* set, what to say about its star Sonora Hutchinson and her elusive overdosed and now dead son. She pondered her own future in the kluged–together entertainment news business she and Cassie and a handful of advisers had constructed out of the debris left behind by Bettina Grant's murder. But the entertainment industry news landscape was quickly and continuously changing. So the combined business package of the daily columns, the twice-weekly five-minute TV spots syndicated by their base, United American Media, plus Cassie's books and Meredith's weekly radio news spots had become cumbersome. It seemed the whole package wasn't all that economical for UAM, not in light of what the networks were doing on their own.

Meredith sipped a water glass of white wine and let the night sky gently blanket her tumbling thoughts. The sunset's watercolor oranges and reds had morphed into a night of uninterrupted star scape—one into which she found she could escape. Until the biggest problem emerged, like a rock under the sole of her conscience. What to do about Dusty Reed. The affair with Sonora was the kind of gossip treacle she really preferred not to pursue, particularly within the context of a boy's death and everything else going on with the movie. She was again surprised at how much she rued the celebrity gossip style of earlier decades. She'd certainly participated in the fomenting of them: affairs, out-of-wedlock children, bad girl or boy behavior in public. But show business stories were wider and deeper these days and she relished covering and writing the good ones.

As strong as the developing *Sunset West* "story" was, the past two days had been an emotional tumbleweed. Let's see, she thought—being used by Sonora, lied to by Dusty, missed her TV spot, and side-stepped a teenage shoot fest—kept hostage by an aging pediatrician so the local motels could reap better profits.

She pondered the stories about the local kids and their impact on Carlton but was frustrated by not enough information to put it in context. But the same large question resurfaced to bedevil her: to capitalize or not on the affair between Dusty and Sonora? If she didn't write about it, someone else eventually would, making her look foolish. If she did write about it, the story might diminish his stock as an effective and reputable director. Not that many movie directors didn't share the beds of their stars and coworkers. This production, though, was now world-wide news fodder.

She also didn't want anyone to believe she still held a candle for her old lover. That ship, she laughed at the cliché, had long ago sailed the minute T.K. Raymond walked into the bedroom.

She took a long drink of wine, and idly wondered if her parents, now gone, would be proud of her. She let the night pour over her psyche and remembered her mother's old adage, "Tomorrow's another day…."

CHAPTER 15
ALBUQUERQUE, NEW MEXICO
SATURDAY MORNING

Dusty stood in the archway entrance of the Villa early the next morning, as Reuben, the studio's driver, loaded her bag into the Jeep, along with the video materials the photographer had dropped off. Meredith climbed into the car. Dusty waved. She waved. There was a look of turmoil and sadness in his eyes. She splayed her hands out, and shrugged, then blew him a kiss. A suggestion of a smile crossed his face.

"It's a little over two hours," Reuben reported as they pulled away from El Rancho Descanso—the Villa. Meredith sat back into the seat and replayed the memory of her phone conversation from the night before with Raymond. Better than earlier ones, but still…she also worried over the disarray in her room the day before. Finally shrugging it off, she decided it was her imagination and that the housekeeping staff had unwittingly disturbed things.

"What do you know about the guy who owns the big ranch with the air strip," she finally spoke up. Reuben looked at her, puzzled, in the rearview mirror. "Not much," he answered. "Why."

"I heard his son was hanging around with Sonora's kid—kind of a local posse thing and they weren't too kind to Carlton."

"Don't know a thing about it," he said. "Local kids around for sure and some kind of gang-ish. But I didn't know Bert Solver's kid, Frankie, was even living here," he said, referring to the ranch owner by name.

"I guess he comes in during the summer. One of the other movie kids left in a hurry after spending time with the summer gang—including Carlton. And I also heard the dad—Bert, I guess—is rumored to be like a terminal station for drug trade between here and Mexico."

Reuben chuckled loudly. "A popular rumor. Where'd you hear it?"

Meredith shook her head lazily. "Here and there. Couple of people from the set. Don't even know their names. I was just asking about Carlton." As she repeated the comments Bitsy had told her, she also instinctively glanced over her shoulder for anyone tailing them. And she wondered about the gun under the seat she'd seen the day before.

"What else did you hear?" Reuben asked.

"Not anything that's worth repeating. Real sleaze-type gossip." The admission made her cringe with its truth. The rest of the journey was punctuated by personal stories and backgrounds—schools, studies, travels. They each had movie stories to share. Arriving at the airport, Reuben asked her, "Want some of the best nachos around? There's a really fine little restaurant in the airport. My treat. You have a couple of hours before your flight leaves."

Realizing she'd decided against the breakfast crowd at the Villa, avoiding possible delays and errant discussions and gossip, she quickly agreed to lunch. Checked in and ready to go, she followed Reuben to a small cavern-like diner not far from her gate.

"I was watching for anyone following us," she stammered.

He laughed. 'No need to do that."

"What's with the gun under your seat?"

His eyes narrowed and he scowled darkly. "Movie set security can be a little dangerous at times."

She focused on her meal and made small talk for a while. As they finished up, Reuben asked, "Are you finished with this story now that you're going home?"

She shook her head. "I'm never finished with a story until whatever ending comes along—or the resolution. I won't consider it finished until the final questions are answered: how and why did Carlton die?"

"How will you determine that if you're a thousand miles away?"

"I'll have to find a way to get a copy of the final inquest report. Or, any other decision about the situation."

Reuben smiled warily. "You always this determined?"

"Yes," Meredith answered bluntly. "I'm a detail wonk. And my colleagues call me relentless. I like to be accurate and thorough. Integrity is important to me." She snorted. "I sound like a politician."

As he paid the check and they rose to leave, he walked her outside to a quiet place in the terminal corridor. He handed her a card with no details, just a phone number. Then slipped from his pocket a leather-bound case, flipped it open and flashed a credential with his image and DEA logo. Just as quickly, it was back in his pocket.

Meredith shook her head. "Why tell me?"

"As you say, you're detail-oriented, accurate and honor integrity. Maybe we can help each other."

"Like how?" she asked, suddenly looking around. "Like the coroner's pathology report as quick as it's available. It could tell us what killed him."

"And what do you want from me?"

"Any bit of info can lead to another. One of these days you might know something that will help me. Just understand that no one can know about this alliance."

"Alliance?" sniffed Meredith. "Discretion. Secrecy. Informants." She shook her head and blinked her eyes. "What's going on in Flecha Dorada that demands you folks? And is that why that red truck made you so nervous?"

"Not really," he smiled. "There's something going on that we're interested in just about anywhere, anytime." Dazed by the exchange, she handed him her own business card, took his.

"Stay safe. I'll be in touch. And shh." He shook her hand and pointed her to her departure gate. She went, still stunned, not sure what had just happened. Looking over her shoulder, there was no sign of Reuben.

CHAPTER 16
PLAYA DEL REY, CALIFORNIA
SUNDAY MORNING

Cassie poured a cup of coffee into her favorite vintage Arrowsmith mug, added a splash of milk and took it along with the file folder on Sterling Music out to the stucco terrace of the three-bedroom apartment she and Bob had rented when they moved from New York to California. The complex sat on a bluff where the wide Marina Del Rey boat channel met the open ocean. On weekends, like this one, the parade of sail and motor boats was a perennial Fourth of July celebration. Even at eight a.m., activity was underway. Cassie shook her head and felt the cool breeze in her dark, curly short hair. Her burly husband, Bob, had already taken the stairs two floors down to the building's small exercise room.

Cassie missed the Sundays in New York, teeming with energy and activity. Always somewhere to go, something to do. Walk out the door and you're in the midst of it. Neighbors moving about, a street musician playing soulfully on his saxophone. Los Angeles was about cars and driving, part and parcel of Cassie's earlier professional life. She pondered her current work—two satisfying elements that were hers alone: her independent novel writing and its progression, and producing the short television Hollywood news spots syndicated by the

Media company to small stations across the US. Her work with the column gave her little satisfaction in the wake of Meredith's acclaim and the TV spots were short and ran only on local TV stations here and there. Cassie could see that an increasing number of broadcast entertainment shows and daily celebrity talk fests would soon overshadow the need for the short, generic gossip offering her team currently produced.

She stood up and looked over the railing into the bright, marine landscape and let herself settle into the internal rant. Work, she thought, was not very satisfying, and the home front needed to be more than an apartment that didn't even enjoy the trappings of New York. She picked up the phone set with its extendable cord, and called Cynthia, her best friend in Manhattan, an IRS agent who seemed to know all the scuttlebutt on corporations in legal trouble. Eight-thirty a.m. in California, it was eleven-thirty a.m. in New York, Cassie figured.

☆☆☆

In the Brentwood townhouse, sunlight crept into the bedroom, splashing the Sunday morning in cheerful promise. Meredith stretched her strong athletic form long as she awakened to the light, nestling her body deep into the bedsheets and the luxury of being at home. She glanced at the clock, eight-thirty, sunshine, and a recollection of Raymond's quiet voice sometime during the night. "Miss me?" She chuckled softly as she sat up and heard him downstairs rustling around in the kitchen. She pushed out of bed, shrugged into one of his old soccer jerseys and padded down the stairs.

In the kitchen, watching her descending the stairs, Raymond nodded to the cat, sprawled on the top of the refrigerator. "Told you she'd be down as soon as she smelled the java." Paco yawned. Raymond handed Meredith a cup of coffee. She took it enthusiastically.

"Whew, that's a welcome gift." She reached up and tickled Paco's paw, opened the fridge door, grabbed the milk and poured it into her mug. She sat down with a thunk into a chair at the table. Raymond pulled another out and joined her.

"Thoughts about how you'd like to spend today?" he asked.

"Since we've both been away," she answered, blowing on her coffee, "maybe there's something you'd like to do?"

"We could spend the day at Malibu. The kids won't be back for a couple more days. Lunch at the Seashack. Or, George Masner has suggested we join him and Gloria at the Club—we'll probably play some racquetball. You and Gloria can swim and catch up. Lunch. What sounds good?"

Meredith stared idly into her coffee cup, both hands wrapped around it. Then she stood up and moved over to him, sat down on his lap and put an arm around him. "Quiet day at home? Laundry, crossword puzzles—fried clams at sunset at the Seashack?"

"Done."

Detective T.K. Raymond pulled up to the impressive portico entrance to the Westside Country Club between Beverly Hills and Bel Air. At the last minute he drove past the drop-off curb and found the self-park, reminding himself that he had long ago chosen to back away from the façade of Southern California's fashionable best. Then he chuckled, reminding himself of his current lifestyle with Meredith, the gossip girl. He made his way through the opulent lobby of the clubhouse, finding his former college roommate and now good friend George Masner peering out a massive window overlooking the golf course's 18th green. Shorter than Raymond by several inches, the prominent theatrical agent had thinning hair to the point of balding in front, a soft but affable face and blue, laser-like eyes. His tight body was wrapped in a well-tailored grey suit, white shirt and paisley tie.

"Wishing you were out there today?" asked Raymond. George Masner turned to him. "Nope. Lovely at eight in the morning, but by ten it'll be too hot and smoggy to breathe. You playing any golf now?" The two made their way to the club's dining room.

"No time. Too busy making red carpet appearances," snickered Raymond.

"Yeah, that," mused George, heading to a remote location on the patio and settling into the table. "I hear that Meredith was stuck somewhere in the wilds of New Mexico."

"Yeah—covering *Sunset West*. The star's kid died of an overdose and the local coroner decided to hold an inquest. Even with half of the state's investigative team on site, the word on the street was that the motels and diners were full, and they wanted to extend the interest. Took the legal department of Meredith's news syndicate to spring her." A waitress took their breakfast order.

"Meredith sure likes to excavate her stories, doesn't she?"

"Like an adorable, aggressive Pekinese—gets her teeth into something and shakes the truth out of it until there's nothing left but a rag." Both men laughed.

"What are you going to do about her?" George asked, smiling lightly. "Something longer term or 'just for now?'"

T.K. Raymond only shrugged. "I expect she'll tell me at some point." Both chortled with male understanding, as coffee arrived.

"So, what's this about, Teke?" George asked, settled back into his chair, regarding his old friend with serious eyes and using the nickname the detective had acquired in college. "Why off the main road, and hushed around Gloria—and Meredith, I assume?"

"Hushed around EVERYONE," said Raymond. He took a long drink of his coffee, set the cup down. "I'm leaning on an old friendship for…support, I guess…information. And assuming pure unmitigated confidentiality…." He looked at his old friend with expectant eyes. George frowned.

"I guess it depends on what we're talking about. I will agree to not talk about this with anyone, but beyond that, what are we talking about?"

"Sterling Music," said Raymond looking intensely at George. The agent's eyes snapped open.

"We represent several of Sterling's recording artists, but I'm not sure what I can tell you about the company itself." The waitress arrived with their food, egg white omelet for George and a bowl of oatmeal and side fruit for Raymond. George picked up his fork and cut into the eggs.

"Here's the scenario, George," Raymond began, picking at his cereal with some disdain.

"Why do you do that to yourself? Eat something that tastes good."

"My kid says this is good for me. I always listen to Will," rationalized Raymond. George shook his head.

"So, I'm on loan to the Feebs," Raymond continued, "to be the boots on the ground, behind the curtain, so to speak, about some kind of an extensive financial...irregularity...at the parent company of Sterling. "

"The feds. Huh?"

"But it's a wide-spread situation since the holding company has tentacles into a lot of entertainment type of companies. Sterling is just one."

George sat back, massaged his brow for a moment. "Is this why Cassie O'Connell visited my wife at her office a few days ago asking about Sterling music and some financial situation there?" Raymond sat upright and cringed.

"Shit! Where'd she get a line on this. Not from Meredith— she had her own devils to fight in New Mexico! Knows nothing about this. Damn."

"Relax. Gloria told Cassie to look somewhere else—and in fact she knows nothing about anything at Sterling. I barely know anything. But here's all I can tell you: one of our artist clients came to me asking about a chargeback his own accountant had found on the bookkeeping statement from Sterling for the first half of the year. It was a pretty sizeable invoice apportioned to all the artists and involved the purchase of some recording equipment. My client—Jimmy Bell—and that's off the record—says the equipment supposedly purchased has never shown up in the studio and no one in the production department seems to know anything about it. Here's the thing: we only handle Jimmy's bookings and his financial associations with the record company. Same as we do for most of our artists, so we didn't have the same books the company had. I said we'd look into it and so far, no one we work with at Sterling seems to know what I'm talking about. The accountant for the company seems to have disappeared, left unexpectedly, picked up a paycheck and hasn't been seen since. That's what I know," George concluded, taking a drink of his coffee.

"Isn't this a little out of your realm, Teke? Don't you usually chase down homicides, stalkers…"

"Since we're off the record, George, Feebs're trying to recruit me for special cases, pulled me into Washington D.C. to work this as a single case. Not much different except—more complex, challenging—and dangerous."

George Masner shook his head. "Well, I wish I knew more, and I have to admit that I don't totally like what you're into. Life here in Tinsel Town is dangerous enough as it is, but mostly we lose face or our good name and income source. It sounds like you're looking at a situation where you can lose your life. What does Meredith think?"

"She doesn't know," sighed Raymond, setting a half-eaten bowl of oatmeal to one side and poking in the bowl of fruit with his spoon. "And I'd like to keep it that way for a while. I was also hoping you'd quietly give me a hand in parsing Sterling."

George sat back, hands in prayer-like position under his chin. A few moments passed. T.K. Raymond watched his friend, an expectant but worried look on his face. "Are you sure swimming around in rougher law enforcement waters is what you want, Teke? You've had an adventurous professional life already—tennis coach, soldier, Hollywood agent, lawyer and cop. I mean, at our ages, it seems like we should be thinking more of distancing away from the daily turmoil...."

Raymond shrugged then shook his head. "Just another branch of the same river. New views, different challenges. Maybe more intellectual adventures?"

George took a thoughtful drink of his coffee, set the cup down and looked intensely at his friend. "Okay—so long as neither Gloria nor my colleagues get hurt. I mean it."

"You're in?"

The nattily dressed agent looked up with an almost wicked grin. "I'm in—but please let's not get maimed or killed, okay?"

CHAPTER 18
WEST LOS ANGELES
TUESDAY MORNING

"Let me look at that once more," Meredith directed Cassie who was adjusting the tape player showing the edited news segment with Meredith on the movie set in Flecha Dorada. Cassie rewound to the point where the camera picked up both the copper blond journalist and Dusty Reed the director.

"*Sunset West's* director Dustin Reed was on the movie location when the young man's death was discovered, originally a helpful shoulder for mother Sonora Hutchinson in her grief. Since then, the two have been romantically linked, but Reed tells us the actress is a rock-solid professional even now…" the interview continued with the tightly built, roughly handsome director.

Meredith blew a sigh and raised her eyebrows. "Well, I did it. I don't like it and didn't make it the lead of the interview, but I figured if I didn't mention that they'd linked up romantically, someone else would mention it and maybe not so nicely. I used it similarly in the column."

Cassie smiled at her. "You're getting soft in your maturity!"

"I think I'm just too close to it. But here it is." Cassie rewound the tape as Meredith returned to her own office. The material would be sent off for use on the twice weekly

Hollywood segment the two produced for several TV news shows. Cassie and Sonia wrapped up production and dissemination of the tape. Sonia went back to her own work. Cassie quietly picked up her bag and called out, "Have a noon appointment, back later. My car phone is on," she added, referring to the newest communication link all now enjoyed.

She quickly got into her car and headed west to Santa Monica and the starkly modern building that housed Sterling Music. On Monday, after some background on the company from her IRS friend in New York, Cassie had looked up the General Manager of the operation and set an appointment, ostensibly for a preliminary conversation in advance of a possible on-camera interview. She was nervous as she approached the reception desk and was escorted to the office of Taryn Manufur. The executive rose to welcome her, extending a strong hand, nails clipped short, and a firm grasp. She was sturdily built, with a no-nonsense air to her.

"What can I do for you, Ms. O'Connell?" Cassie sat down in a plain but comfortable wooden side chair and handed Manufur a business card. The office was also no-nonsense, well-built plain furniture, basic steel file cabinets and a scatter of industry awards and accolades perching or hung on the walls.

'I'm interested in the music business these days as so many aspects begin to change, and would like to write about it, maybe even film some of those changes. So much of what we hear, see and buy today is only the tip of the music iceberg, so much happens behind the scenes. So, I thought we could talk for a few minutes today and explore a more in-depth interview."

Manufur regarded her affably but with some reserve. "Well, I guess we can explore that. First, I'm just the 'acting' manager. Our normal general manager is out on maternity leave and honestly, may decide not to return. So, I'll do the best I can to help you. I'm not sure the general public cares about technology and financial stuff, but sure, let's talk about it." A half hour later, amid a discussion on royalties and contracting, Cassie broached the subject for which she had come.

"Taryn, I seem to remember something about a financial 'irregularity'—or some kind of investigation?" She shrugged. "Someone stealing royalties, padding invoices…?"

"Above my pay grade," said Manufur without changing her demeanor. "There's always something that's rumored to be awry in the music business. I heard someone say the IRS is looking into something with our parent company, and a couple of weeks ago there was an auditor here from headquarters, but they left without any repercussions. You'd have to ask our lawyers about that one. It's an international holding company, and we're pretty well decentralized. Our permanent manager probably knows more about it than I do. It took place around the time she took leave."

"We've also heard that someone had questions about equipment that was on order…." Manufur shrugged. Cassie nodded that she understood, and went on with additional questions, not related. Ten minutes later she began putting her notebook away, reaching for her bag.

"This is a start; one I can explore. Let's see where we go. People are more tuned into the whole music and recording industry now, so we want to have a leg up on it. By the way, how much equipment was involved in that report you mentioned? Worth a lot?"

Manufur smiled slyly and shook her head. "Enough that someone asked about it. Whether it's true or not is a good question." They shook hands, Cassie promising to contact Manufur when she sorted out what direction to take in her story.

☆☆☆

Meredith and Sonia were reviewing items for the day's column as Ito interrupted to say he was going for lunch with a friend. The two women nodded at him and wished him a good meal. He left, checking his notes to find the address in Culver City where he would meet his new friend Mel. After detouring to a hot dog stand near Mel's company, the two made their way to the large stucco warehouse where Quality Fun built and marketed electronic games. Mel escorted Ito through the administrative and business part of the building and through a heavy metal swinging door to the production area. A large open space with sections set aside for specific activities. Mel walked Ito through various work areas, explaining "this is programming...here's where the cases are put together...."

As Mel stopped to talk with a colleague, Ito noticed a small bin loaded with a jumble of stuffed rabbit toys. He picked one up to look at it, turning it over, noticing it seemed limp for a stuffed animal. "Rejects," laughed Mel, picking up another one. He turned it over and over.

"We produce a few electronic 'toys'—mostly little stuffed critters that have been preprogrammed to say something stupid when you squeeze them, but we're just developing this super new product that everyone's talking about—Robo Rabbit. It's different from our usual product line because it really is a toy. It's a programmable stuffed rabbit that you can record you own voice on—with your own message. Very advanced, nothing else quite like it on the market, and it's our great big Christmas product—our great new hope!"

"How does it work?" puzzled Ito, unable to comprehend how a limp fluffy toy could do all that Mel proclaimed.

"Oh—this is just the outer toy casing. We have the technical and mechanical stuff coming in from different places. Circuits, and stuff from San Jose, voice mechanisms from another company here in LA, and the toy rabbits themselves from Mexico. We assemble it all and code it up here. We'll market it from here."

Ito held the soft rabbit, turning it over in his hands and smiling at the animal's outfit of denim overalls and red bandana. "Cute," he said.

"Here, keep it," said Mel. "A memento of your first introduction to Quality Fun! I know you're really fond of computer games—but this'll keep you warm on rainy nights." They both laughed and Ito tucked the toy under his arm. Later, back at his office, he tossed it in a chair next to his desk.

CHAPTER 19
WEST LOS ANGELES
TUESDAY AFTERNOON

Sonia had put the column onto the fax machine by three, making sure it arrived at headquarters in New York. At five, she went through the offices making certain nothing electrical was left on that shouldn't be, and made certain files were locked up. Meredith was at her desk pensively flipping through notes.

"Are you still dithering about ratting out Dusty and the star?" asked Sonia.

"No, I'm trying to figure out more about this whole story. It's really incomplete. Something's wrong."

"Dusty can't have a set-side affair?"

"Not about Dusty. It's about the whole kid thing—and how he died. Maybe the coroner will have the answers if they ever finish the inquest."

"Why are you worried about it? Your story is done, isn't it?"

"If there are still open questions about the whole thing— even if it's about the kid and the movie set—I feel like they should be woven into the final story, Sonia. A story's not done until it is."

"You are so thorough. I'm glad you're here and not there at this point. It sounds like it could be dangerous." Meredith shook her head and laughed. "I have to go," Sonia called as she was leaving the office. "I have a date! A real date!"

"Go get 'em!" Meredith yelled, then added, "not an actor, I hope!"

"Nope. A working man. He owns an air conditioning repair service. He actually does stuff."

Meredith laughed. "Don't let that one go!" Once Sonia was out of the door and quiet settled in again, Meredith refocused on her notes. She kept replaying what she'd heard about the boys from the ranch down the road, Carlton's wish to go home, the co-star's son who did go home apparently to avoid any more interaction with the local boys, the red truck and Reuben's reach for his gun. She opened her drawer and pulled out the card with the handwritten phone number on the back.

"Reuben? It's Meredith Ogden. Could you give me a call, please?" She left her number, then hung up pondering the wisdom of the call. Then she punched in a well-known number always firm in her mind—for CenturySonic Studios. The movie publicist on *Sunset West*, Laurie Shoup, picked up her call. "Working late again, huh?" Meredith and Laurie had worked many films together and had become good friends in the process.

"Oh, most of the photography is wrapping up. Just a few days left with Sonora—when she gets back tomorrow from taking her son's body home to Geneva. So, there's a lot of organization and shuffling around. And, as you know, press demands! Holy crap—the press demands!"

"I still feel like I want to fill out my stories a little more and feel like we didn't do much for Beau Hastings, Sonora's co-star, and I'd like to do a sit down with him for a solo feature."

"He'll appreciate that," said Laurie. "Thanks so much. He's been totally left in the shadows with Carlton's death and all. He's home as of yesterday. Let's see if I can set it up for…?"

"Soon as possible," said Meredith." Both closed with "Ciao." Meredith looked around and realized it was six o'clock. She was alone in the office and a hint of a memory crept into her mind. She'd been alone, late, in the office at Bettina Grant's home when someone attacked her, unexpectedly and violently. Mostly the recollection had faded away, but once in a while it resurfaced. Shaking her head and reaching for her purse, she pushed the thought away. Locking her desk drawer, she hurried to leave, not because of fear, but because for the first time in her adult life, something was more important than Hollywood and gossip. It was date night with Raymond.

CHAPTER 20
OJAI, CALIFORNIA
WEDNESDAY

Raymond and Jerrold pulled up to the small cottage tucked back off a small, winding road a few miles into the hills from the quaint town of Ojai in the mid-coastal area of Southern California. Jerrold unfolded his massive frame from Raymond's sporty car and stretched. "We should've rented!" he grunted. Raymond chuckled. Clumping up the few steps, they knocked on the door.

"This place looks like a fairy tale cottage," snickered Jerrold.

"Yeah and what secrets its inhabitants could tell," said Raymond as a tall, serious-faced man opened the door to let them in.

"How's he?" asked Jerrold.

"Restless, but really focused. Worried, gets whiney," answered the host. Melvin, the accountant from MNS USA corporate had been their guest for three days. His job was to decipher the financial books and records he had purloined from the company in order to help track charges and expenses suspected to be the funding for a continuing operation to bring heroin into the US from Mexico. His own boss had discovered irregularities in the books several months prior during normal work activities, asked a few questions, overheard some rumors as she worked late at night. She took them to the holding company's upper management. A few days later she was struck by a hit and run driver and died a few hours later. But she had innocently already revealed her questions and concerns to her assistant, Melvin Atwater. He quietly collected and copied paperwork and computer discs and was on an airplane from New Jersey to Los Angeles within 36 hours, a guest of the FBI. Now he was ensconced in a hideaway cottage, in the charming vacation Valley a couple of hours north of Los Angeles.

Melvin, Jerrold, Raymond and two stoic law enforcement associates keeping watch over the accountant sat at a large, round kitchen table to talk about the case. Jerrold led the discussion as the senior FBI agent. "Melvin, where are we? Do we have any direct links to Mexico or a Mexican enterprise or…?"

Melvin, a gaunt young man with wavy mouse brown hair, wireless glasses and a heart-shaped mouth scratched his head. "Incomplete," he answered. "I'm finding tracks into several of our subsidiary companies, but nothing big enough yet to suggest a major traffic flow. Problem is, I don't have all the books I need. Just because of the reporting schedules, from the time Martha died and I left, I hadn't received information from Sterling Music which, from what I can see, may have some of the larger connections. Two other subsidiaries also have similar connections—invoices to one or two companies with links into Mexico for products that don't seem visible in the day-to-day operations. Even if we find inconsistencies in those invoices, we don't know that they are linked to drug trafficking. That's the missing link."

"We need Sterling's complete set of books," said Jerrold, looking at Raymond. The Los Angeles-based music company was why he was brought into the picture. He had the entertainment industry contacts and network. Raymond nodded his understanding.

"And we still need the Mexico connection."

"But what do we know about the companies sending the bogus invoices," persisted Raymond. "Where are they? Are they all the same company?"

Melvin shook his head. "The names are the same for each subsidiary company, but different from subsidiary to subsidiary, except in the one case."

"There's another thing," Jerrold spoke up. "All are in or around El Paso or Midland. I guess I didn't know there were manufacturing companies for electronics or the like in those areas."

"Can't we talk to the financial person at Sterling?" probed Raymond, aware that George had already mentioned the absence of the company's accountant and was strategizing entry into the company's inner financial workings. "On or off the record?"

Jerrold shook his head. "He's Terry Tillson, and apparently collected his latest paycheck, quit last Friday and hasn't been seen there since. Headquarters auditors were there the week before—did a really cursory look around. Didn't seem to find anything worth noting."

"We need to visit the financial guy's house. See what gives," Raymond said. Jerrold agreed.

"So, mostly what we need to know now," muttered Melvin, "is more about those companies, who owns them, and what they supposedly delivered—or not—to not only Sterling but the other subsidiaries. I've put a list together."

"Of course you have," snickered Jerrold as the younger accountant handed him the list. "We have some researchers who can dig this stuff out. It'll take a little time, but it shouldn't be too hard. We've got people in other locales working those invoices, but this one seems to be bigger with more frequent purchases."

"I'll have my partner try to find an address for Sterling's numbers guy. When we get back to LA, I'll head to his house."

Jerrold stood up to his full six-foot two stature, looked at Raymond and said, "Not to dismiss your turf, T.K., but you're on loan and you need back-up." Until that moment, Raymond had figured Jerrold as an ancillary player in the drama, an accountant who delved deeply into financial crimes, never a field agent in charge of an investigation. He also never thought of himself as the junior operative. He took a quiet breath and nodded.

☆☆☆

Driving back the 101 toward the LA basin, Jerrold spoke up with solid directness. "I know you run your own operations on your turf here in the sunny Southland, T.K. and I certainly don't want to interfere with that or your general acceptance in so many of the law enforcement agencies here. You have a unique position. But the endgame here is not negotiation or good media coverage or making a bona fide criminal disappear behind the spotlight or find a face-saving way out. The end game is heroin. Brought into the US by thugs, killers, criminals. It kills people in very unglamorous ways." Raymond stifled an unceremonious retort.

Jerrold, tucked into the compact seat of Raymond's car, used the car phone to call his office and request an address for the absent Sterling accountant. "Hope they get back to us by the time we get into the basin," murmured the big agent. Raymond chuckled to himself, figuring that his people could have delivered a simple address with only a few minutes' delay.

The visit to the Tillson house turned out to be easy but fruitless. They arrived at a pleasant neighborhood of well-maintained but humble single-family homes in an industrial city southeast of the Los Angeles airport and made their way to the door of a nicely-presented house. No one answered the doorbell, and soon a neighbor leaned over her porch railing and told them the couple had gone on a long vacation. She had a key but did not know their exact plans. Raymond and Jerrold searched the house without finding any substantive clues as to the activities before the Tillsons left or their ultimate destination.

"They were thorough," commented Jerrold. "We'll turn this one over to the local FBI folks. Take me back to my home-away-from-home, and let's reconnoiter tomorrow." Raymond grinned to himself.

After the large man had unfurled himself from the sports car when they reached his apartment, and Raymond drove toward home, he thought about the case, and about the team. Looking for the absent accountant was one thing, finding bona fide evidence or links to the invoices and their sources something totally different and on his agenda with the case. He phoned George Masner. "Got time for a beer?" George knew from the tone of his old friend's voice that the game was on.

"Gloria's working late tonight, meet at Pete's Dock in Santa Monica?"

"Sure—an hour? Meredith's with Cassie at a late afternoon movie screening."

CHAPTER 21
SANTA MONICA, CALIFORNIA
WEDNESDAY LATE AFTERNOON

"Be careful, George. Investigating is never as easy as it seems," Raymond was admonishing his old friend now co-conspirator in the Sterling case. A comfortable ocean breeze kept Pete's Dock patio pleasantly cool. Both men had shed their jackets and ties, sat back in their chairs and enjoyed a beer.

"So…?" George nudged.

Raymond unveiled the scenario around the questionable invoices. "You told me that one of your artist clients was questioning charges on his own statement about equipment supposedly purchased but apparently never installed. Maybe a different situation entirely, but I have the name of a company, Cortona Industrial, that is currently being looked into. Maybe it's the same company, maybe not. But if it is not, do you have the opportunity to get into Sterling to find out about Cortona, maybe come across a purchase order? If it is the same company, can you get us a copy of the purchase order and the invoice? We need to learn more about Cortona, what they really do and how legit they are—if they are, considering what we know."

"Can't the FBI just subpoena the books?"

"The company passed muster on a very brief internal audit visit last week. We don't want them to be aware of this separate investigation—to tip them off so that they have a chance to bury stuff."

"Well, I do have an in. We have two Sterling clients and since Jimmy Bell has already brought up the charges on his statement, it gives me a good reason to make an appointment and ask the questions. First though I will look at Jimmy's paperwork and his complaint. Part of the answer could be in those."

"You and I are the only ones who can talk about this so we're the only ones who know about your new status as undercover agent."

"And how's your new status? You impressing the Bureau boys and girls?"

"Hardly. They think I'm some kind of a Hollywood toy soldier who goes around fixing images."

"Not so good?"

"Too soon. We're all jockeying for position on this case. The two talked and laughed for another half hour before George looked at his watch. "Better head home. The wife will be there soon."

"Yeah," said Raymond, realizing Meredith would be home soon as well.

"How do we communicate?" George asked as an afterthought.

"Call me at the office or at home and tell me you need to talk. I'll call you back from where it's safe. If you can't talk when I call, just say, 'let's talk later.' We can always catch up at home—or use the car phones."

"I'll look at Jimmy Bell's invoices first thing tomorrow." Together, they stood up and went to their cars.

CHAPTER 22
ENCINO, CALIFORNIA
THURSDAY

Beau Hastings scowled as he trailed his spoon through his coffee, troubled by how to proceed. "Let's just say the kids were playing with drugs." He winced. "This is off the record, right?"

"Oh yeah," Meredith agreed, following the conversation with great care. "You sound frightened by what your son was into—well, what the kids from the ranch were into?"

"Wouldn't you be?" asked the handsome, well-groomed movie actor, co-star of *Sunset West*, sitting opposite from her in the coffee shop. "There were all these kids—bragging about their access to drugs, exposing Trent—my son— and Carlton to them at the ranch—then Carlton dies of an overdose and no one believes he was responsible. We sent Trent home the next day and hunkered down. He went to camp in Florida right away and my wife went to visit relatives. I kept my head down until I came home and then joined my wife out of state."

"Wow," Meredith simply shook her head. "These were the children of the ranch owners?" She finally asked.

"They were visiting, too, apparently for the summer. Maybe you remember that the ranch is only a few miles away from our headquarters, apparently not a regular ranch with fields or livestock. The fly-in air strip is there, and there's some kind of manufacturing warehouse or transit depot—for want of a better word—for some kind of products the father imports. Something like that." Meredith had put her pen down and was totally focused on the conversation.

"The kids invited Trent and Carlton there a lot. One time they were wandering through one of the open warehouses, supposedly just 'fooling around.' A shipment of toys coming in from somewhere. Trent picked up one of them and found a bag of white substance underneath. He asked Frankie, that's the son of the ranch owner, what it was. Trent told me the kid just laughed at him and said. 'Take it home. Your dad will appreciate it.' So, he did. It was heroin."

"Did you call the sheriff?"

"Kidding? Of course not. I don't know what else went on with that gang or at that 'ranch,' but I sent my son home the next day. And looked over my shoulder the rest of the time."

Meredith had requested a sit-down interview with Beau Hastings, reasoning that they'd had no real time to talk while she was in Flecha Dorada. Hastings and the studio movie publicity person joined her at a local coffee shop, and she began her probing. After forty-five minutes of normal interview, she had ventured into the subject of Carlton's death, remembering Bitsy, the wardrober's comments about the kids hanging out together. While she had agreed not to use information about Beau's son Trent, she knew there must be more to the story she'd heard about from Bitsy.

"In spite of the death and all the sadness and chaos, how do you think the movie went? Will it be good or troubled?" The interview continued for another 45 minutes. Meredith collected column material and enough information for a regular weekly feature article on Beau Hastings. He was a nice guy, candid and smart in his answers and remarks. For Meredith, that meant a good story.

The office was busy when she walked in the door. Sonia was on the line, taking notes. Ito was also on the phone. Cassie, busily writing, looked up as Meredith passed her office door. "Good interview?"

"Yep. Got some information on the kids around Carlton Hutchinson on the *Sunset West* set."

"Is there more story?"

"Well, some but a lot of background. Really depends on…." Meredith stopped as she saw a large manila envelope on her desk, rumpled and a little soiled. "What's this?" she puzzled.

"Under the door when we got here this morning," said Cassie. "I figured you'd know what it was."

"Let's see." Meredith ripped open the flap and pulled out an official looking document. "It's the coroner's inquest report from Flecha Dorada," she said. "Just what I was about to allude to." She quickly put down her bag and brief case and sat down to look at the documents. A few minutes later she simply shook her head. "Inconclusive. After all of that. I guess we'll never know how Carlton died."

But she wondered what information trade-off Reuben would want from her. She picked up the phone, extracted the card from her desk drawer and dialed his number. Only a voice mail. "Got the report. Thanks. I'm at the office for the rest of the day. I have some lightweight gossip you might find interesting."

Then she punched in Dusty's number in New Mexico and left a message to please return the call. On a whim, she asked for Fastida. When the Villa concierge answered the line, Meredith greeted her warmly. The woman recognized her and was openly friendly.

"Fastida, what are people saying about the outcome of the coroner's inquest?"

The woman hesitated for a moment, lowered her voice and said, "Honestly, Miss Reporter? They think it's bullshit! Excuse my language."

"Why?" probed Meredith.

"Because no way that boy would kill himself and no one ever saw him doing drugs. His friends? Yes, but not Carlton."

"Were these the friends from the ranch down the road?"

Fastida's voice dipped even lower and became less confident. "Maybe. I don't know for sure. They were around here with him and then they just disappeared. Caleb says their family took them home to the East Coast."

Meredith thanked her, wished her a good rest of the summer and hung up. She barely had time to settle into her desk when Dusty returned her call.

"Hi," she said hesitantly, still feeling guilty about publicly outing his affair with Sonora.

"Good to hear your voice, Meredith," was his answer. "Did you hear about the inquest?"

"Yeah, I was wondering what you thought about it?"

"Well, we all wonder who did the investigating?" Meredith chuckled. "But," he continued, his voice going to a near whisper, "Meredith, he didn't kill himself and he didn't overdose accidentally. Believe me. But even more—he had a ticket to go home to Europe two days later! That was his biggest wish and Sonora gave it to him. It was all he could think about. He hated movie sets and the desert."

"Then are you saying someone gave him the drugs?"

"I don't know. I know that his death wasn't by his own hand or drugs he ingested himself! Everyone has the wrong idea about Carlton. He was eccentric but not a druggie and not suicidal!"

"Damn, Dusty. You know if you tell me this and don't swear me to secrecy, I'll print it! Is anyone investigating it?"

"No, the case is closed!"

"How's Sonora about it?"

"Angry and frustrated...scared."

"Why scared?"

"Think about it. If someone overdosed him, or even just gave him the drugs, don't you think there's some culpability? Someone did it."

"Who'd do that, Dusty?"

"I don't know."

"Aren't you at risk too? Especially if I print anything."

"Print it, princess. Maybe it will force the truth to come out?"

"By sending drug lords down on you or Sonora?"

"Drama. Good copy. And perhaps some reckoning of what happened. Sonora's left, back to LA, I'm here another day. We'll be shooting principal stuff from here on in LA, just the catch-all here with our second unit. You remember second unit crews." He cleared his throat.

"I do, Dusty. In fact, I remember a great second unit director who used to be a stuntman and is now a big-time director. I'm hoping he stays alive through this mess." Silence overtook the line for a moment.

"Here's your bank shot, Merri," Dusty broke through. "Sonora and I are doing fine, become very close as this drama has taken over. We look forward to a good future."

"Got it," said Meredith at the other end of the line. "Thanks for the gossip item. Honestly, I'm happy for you. But Dusty, after all these years, it's my turn to say, be careful. Not just about the romance, but more so about the drug situation there." As they rang off, she felt sad. Dusty was always her voice of reason, grounded and earthbound. Now he sounded like an emerging Hollywood presence and she felt like the reasonable conscience.

"Who wants lunch?" cooed Sonia. "I'm about to head over to the deli. I can pick up for anyone or everyone." She took a pen and her notebook and started taking requests, then left to fetch lunch.

Meredith closed the door to her small office and rewrote the lead for the column going to New York that night. By early Friday morning, LA time, the word would be out across the country.

CHAPTER 23
WEST LOS ANGELES
THURSDAY

As the planning meeting broke up, Sonia noticed the limp but fleecy rabbit toy heaped on Ito's chair. "What? Ito? You into stuffed friends now? There must be a real girl out there somewhere for you!"

He snorted a laugh. "Always a girl out there somewhere! But my friend at the game company gave it to me—it's a reject, torn seams. They're imported here. The game company stuffs it with technology and some kind of a new speaker mechanism you can record. You want it?"

"Sure," said Sonia. "My neighbor has a little boy who'd love this critter!" She picked it up and hugged it, quickly moving into her own office. As she did so, the phone was ringing, Meredith picked it up. Sonia heard her say, "Reuben. I got your package. Thank you for that. Can we talk?"

Sonia idly wondered who Reuben was but before she could ask, Meredith had hung up the phone, grabbed her purse and announced, "I'll be back in an hour. Cassie, are we still hitting the screening this afternoon?" Cassie shouted yes, and Meredith was out the door.

"Who's Reuben?" Sonia asked aloud. No one answered.

☆☆☆

As Meredith slid into the booth at the Charging Frog Saloon a few blocks west of the office, the tall, sinewy, ebony-haired man she'd met in New Mexico came through the door. He walked briskly and seemed on alert as usual, his sunglasses reflecting the lights in the saloon. "Hey," he said as he slid into the cushions opposite her, then smiled his sparkling white-teeth smile, a brilliant contrast to his mocha complexion.

"Look, I have only a few minutes," she said, "but wanted to know if you know more about the inquest report?"

"More? That's all there is. Lots of questions—same ones we both heard over and over," Reuben answered.

"Waste of everyone's time, huh?"

"Mayor of Flecha Dorada didn't think so." They both "tsked."

"This is probably old news, but I learned some things about the kids from that ranch down the road."

Reuben tilted his head and looked at her earnestly. "And?" She recounted the information from her interview. He listened intently as she told the story of the heroin found in the ranch warehouse, and Trent's experience there as told to her by his father. "We've tried to explore that place many times but never had a reason for a warrant other than rumor," Reuben commented, "And never found anything when we've actually had the opportunity to walk through. The report of heroin being actually seen on the premises opens some doors, if in fact it was heroin. "

"His dad says it was—seems to know that for sure. Have you seen the kids from the ranch since I left or since they were speeding down the road shooting?"

Reuben shook his head. "No. The kids were gone the same day you left. Went back to their home in New Jersey with Solver's dad, who, by the way, is rarely ever in Flecha Dorada."

"Beau's son Trent told his dad that there was some kind of manufacturing going on, or products being imported."

Reuben looked out toward the door, scratched the side of his cheek. "Heard that, too. We'll find out what it is. We're on it."

"Well, you have the latest information I have," said Meredith, "and I need to get back. I sure was hoping for more from that damn inquest."

"We all were—but no one was holding their breath. Even the dudes from Albuquerque couldn't figure out why they did it, but it was legal and now the opportunity for a post-mortem is gone. Kid's body went to Europe. But, not my problem. Drugs and the studios—that's another whole thing."

"Where are you next working…um…I mean, driving? What movie will you be working on?" She pulled her purse over her shoulder and moved to leave.

"Mexico," said Reuben. "Can't divulge yet. Studio isn't ready to name their location plans. So, I'm here in LA until we set up." He slid out of his side of the booth, put on his sunglasses and reached a hand to help Meredith stand up.

"Good to see you, Reuben. Thanks for the information. I guess it goes without saying…if you hear anything else about Carlton's death…."

"Likewise. Especially if you hear anything else about the ranch and drugs there." They walked out together. He held the door and, again, seemed to disappear before she had a chance to say more.

CHAPTER 24
THURSDAY EVENING
SANTA MONICA

Country singer Jimmy Bell sat at the console in a small rehearsal studio at the record company and listened to the sound mix on the album he was developing. He scowled here and there and made notes. He glanced up at the clock: six pm. A shot of adrenalin pumped into his body. He rose from the chair, collected his belongings and looked around. He saw no one else in the recording suite. A lone musician or producer wandering the halls was not unusual. Some worked well into the night on a project, but Jimmy scoped out the schedule and figured he was pretty safe for the operation planned. He also knew if anyone saw him with George Masner, his agent, it would be more logical than seeing him with a stranger like T.K. Raymond.

He left the small studio quietly and called out to the guy who managed the production facilities. "Tark?" No answer. Jimmy walked slowly through the maze of windowed rooms, all flush with recording equipment and music materials. And all nearly eerily empty. He knew that Bud, the security guard, seldom made rounds until much later. Finally, the musician walked the long halls, seeing no one, then climbed the steps to the administrative office. Two secretaries were on their way out of the main bullpen that serviced the managerial and accounting offices.

"Hi Jimmy," the younger of the two said to him, an outright flirt. He was, after all, a charismatic and appealing guy, tall, curly brown hair, big eyes, a winning smile and a great body. And a real star.

"Hey, Stacey!" he answered. "Could you let me into Terry's office? I was meeting the temp bookkeeper today and think I dropped my car keys in there." As he spoke, the elevator door opened and the other woman stepped in, holding the door open.

"Hold it for me," called Stacey as she fumbled for her keys and rushed to one of the glassed-in offices, quickly unlocking the door. "Don't tell anyone I did this—and be sure to close and lock the door when you leave. Okay?" She blinked her eyes at the country western star.

"Okay," he whispered conspiratorially and winked at her. She rushed off to the elevator and Jimmy carefully pushed open the door to the office. He waited a few minutes, looking idly at papers stacked on the desk then put a paper jam into the door as he walked quickly out and down the stairs, making his way through the studio maze to the small back employees' door. He cautiously opened it, and let George Masner into the building. The two of them walked quietly back through the maze and up the stairwell to the executive offices. George was playing the role of ninja burglar well, shirking his usual designer suits and shoes for black jeans, a black shirt and windbreaker. He wore Walmart sneakers and a fraught look on his face. Real-time breaking and entering was different from the scripted stuff.

He looked around as they passed studios and then offices. He knew this place mostly as a VIP collaborator, meeting around the business of his clients and the music company's artists. Jimmy moved the paper jam out of the way and quietly pushed open the door to the accounting head's office. George swallowed hard knowing he was now officially breaking the law, but remembered the goal. The file cabinets were locked, but Jimmy touched his arm and whispered, "No problem. Keys in the desk drawer." He retrieved them. Together they began to explore the files. George had prompted Jimmy on the documents to look for, especially invoices from the Cortona Industrial. It took only fifteen minutes before they found them.

"Copy machine?" asked George almost silently. Jimmy pointed to the corner of the bullpen space. George made his way to the bulky copier to duplicate the handful of papers while Jimmy straightened up the rest of the office. Originals back in their proper files, drawers closed and locked, the two quickly left the offices, locking doors and making certain there was no detritus of their visit left behind.

As they exited the back door, Bud, the security guard came around the corner, nearly bumping into Jimmy. "Hey man," said Bud, "working late?"

"Always," sighed Jimmy. "This is my agent, George," he quickly introduced the two. Bud nodded congenially. "Well, you two have a good night," and unlocked the back door and entered, the door slamming with a "bang" after him.

Jimmy and George looked at one another and both sighed with heavy relief.

"I owe you," said George down the street from the studio.

"Just get my books straightened out with these dudes," Jimmy answered. "Make me more money! Oh—this was kind of fun. Can we do it again, dad?" They both went to their cars and drove off.

George headed to the deck bar at Pete's Dock, only a short distance in Santa Monica from Sterling Studios. Raymond was waiting at a table, off to the side of the patio. The air was warm despite the breeze—it was August in LA—and George stripped off his windbreaker. "You auditioning for a role as a Bel Air ninja?" chuckled Raymond.

"Hey! Hey!" barked George. "I just broke and entered for you!"

"And what did you find?" George handed Raymond the sheaf of papers he'd collected. Raymond quickly looked at them under the scant lighting and whistled. "You got it, George. Wow. Get this man a drink," he said, signaling the waiter. George quickly added, "Dry martini, no olive."

Both men scanned the invoices and purchase orders on the table. "What did we actually get?" asked George. "Something that gives up the ruse?"

Raymond shook his head. "No—but we have everything we can get to slice through the bureaucracy. Find out where these folks come from. Someone has to go there, though, to see if they really do exist or are just a post office box, or not even that. Someone's back bedroom."

"And that's your job?" queried George.

Raymond shrugged. "It says here that Cortona Industrial Corp is in Midland, Texas. Probably someone closer than me to the source in Texas. But…my case, so…." He folded the papers, put them in the satchel at his side. "I need to get out of here— it's my night to cook. Good Chinese place on the way…so, how will you explain this get-up to Gloria?" He pointed at George's dark wrapping.

"I won't. I'll change it right here in the bathroom when we leave!"

CHAPTER 25
BRENTWOOD
THURSDAY NIGHT

"Who's the source?" demanded Raymond. "Are they credible, not just rumormongers?"

Meredith couldn't tell him the identity of her DEA contact, but said simply, "some on-the-scene studio people with nothing to gain." Raymond scowled, running a hand through his thick dark hair, the sprinkling of silver picking up the soft patio lights. Tension was in the air in the Brentwood condo even though Raymond had delivered on his promise of "cooking" for the evening. The conversation had strayed into work and Meredith's latest information about the New Mexico drug death had been casually revealed. She swirled a finger in a partially-consumed martini.

"I think you know that you and your story-chasing pals are crossing a bunch of 'Hollywood news' lines," the detective went on. "You all should be asking yourselves just who you want to be at this point. Glamour-chasers, story-tellers-for-the-stars, or investigative warriors. You saw the repercussions of it with the Joey O'Neal story a couple of years ago. And just being in the shadow of Bettina's murder. Instead of unhappy celebrities or studio execs that need placating, you have drug dealers and murderers without scruples and no interest in being outed in the press—sorry for the lecture." His voice had tapered off, now slightly embarrassed. It was not a new subject.

Meredith had filled him in on her interview with Beau Hastings and then her quick meeting with Reuben, who she named as only "a source." The Hastings interview by-passed interest—an every-day activity in Raymond's mind. But the rest....

"Well," sighed Raymond at last. "Living here, at least I don't have to assign officers to guard your door twenty-four-seven."

Anxious to change the subject, Meredith ventured, "What's keeping you so distracted and preoccupied these days?" He described a hillside search for a weapon used in an attempted burglary of a celebrity by a trusted friend, and plans to restructure his office's relationship with the various law enforcement agencies. Meredith listened and idly began to stack used plates.

"Will you teach me to shoot?" she asked suddenly.

The tall detective stood up and began to collect the dinner debris from the table. "Tomorrow is your filming day and you have big news to tell. Let's table that discussion for another day."

☆☆☆

Across the massive LA basin, Sonia sat back happily in the comfortable leather chair at the upscale Italian restaurant on Ventura Boulevard. She smiled at her date, Art the air conditioning shop owner, always well-pressed and pristinely dressed, his muscular thick body was wrapped well in a stylish pullover and khaki pants. Relaxed as well, he looked at her with a large grin.

As they talked, an older couple approached the table, "Art? How are you?" asked the woman, a comfortably-presented woman of about 60, her husband tall, slightly stooped, but with silver-grey hair and an electric sparkle in his icy blue eyes.

Art practically jumped out of his chair with delight. "Sonia, this is Don and Irene Sanderson. They run the *Valley Chronicle*. I'm one of their advertisers!"

"Oh, come on, Art. More than just an advertiser. We've worked with Art for years. He's one of our favorite friends," said Irene. "And he tells us you're a writer. A Hollywood columnist, no less!"

Sonia flapped her hands quickly. "No, not quite. I'm an editorial assistant to a couple of columnists and TV reporters, but I write some pieces for them, research a lot, and write a question/answer column. It's pretty plain vanilla."

"Nice job," affirmed Don, nodding in a gentlemanly way.

"You two come over this weekend and we'll grill something good and get to know you," smiled Irene. "Bring your bathing suits...oh and bring the kids. I understand you have a teenager around the same age as Art's." And they were gone.

Sonia wondered how much better it could get.

☆☆☆

Ito, sitting on the sparse deck of his Venice beach apartment, pondered the puzzle on the table in front of him. He'd taken a confidential call from the Media Syndicate's boss, Russ Talbot, a few days earlier, with an accounting question that Ito relished the opportunity to solve. In the past year, more and more of his work was focused on syndicate issues, which was a perfect blend with his duties at the Hollywood Dateline offices. From the setup of the organization, nearly three years before, Ito's job was split between running the small editorial group and working with the media syndicate headquarters in New York to sort out financial elements dealing with several operations on the west coast.

The overhead light on his patio illuminated the spreadsheet in front of him and he wondered why Russ Talbot at the media syndicate wanted him to come to New York for "some training." He wondered how much Meredith or Cassie or Sonia knew of the situation. Exciting, but curious.

☆☆☆

"Cass, you have nothing but great horizons out there. Why are you complicating it?" Cassie and husband Bob sat on a low cement wall on beachside walkway at Manhattan Beach and carried on a serious conversation. His arm was draped over her shoulders. Darkness was nearly total, a small shaft of light along the horizon, the lights of the pier soft but alive, the gulls long since quieted.

"I'm not. But everything else is."

"You're whining, Toots."

"I know. I feel like I've hit a huge fork in the road and don't know how to navigate. I kind of started this whole newsroom idea and now…well, it's not working for me."

"If there ever was any doubt about the affair with Dusty and Sonora, there certainly isn't now. You made that clear," huffed Cassie with a chuckle. She and Meredith breezed into the office about 10:30 after a taping session at the local studio where their five-minute programs were produced.

"But I'm a little worried about the certainty Dusty and Sonora have about her son's death and how they disagreed with the conclusion on the coroner's report."

"Well, you made no specific allegations on anyone—just enough to advance the story and the theory of foul play."

"Geez! What's Ito's been into?" barked Sonia. "Looks like he had either a salt spill, bad dandruff or a talcum powder leak!" Meredith and Cassie both came over to the chair and looked at it curiously. She had noticed the side chair to his desk where a small white substance—granules or powder—was sprinkled lightly across the seat on the floor in front of it.

The door opened and T.K. Raymond bumped his way in carrying a bulging brown grocery bag. "Hi! A former victim we helped just dropped off a huge load of citrus to our offices this morning. Thought you'd all like some...." He looked at the puzzled faces and joined the circle. "Make up? Or powdered sugar—donuts?" He asked and they all snickered at the cop reference.

"We don't know. It just kind of appeared this morning. Ito went to the bank and the stationery store before coming in, so we don't know what happened here," Sonia explained.

Raymond set the bag down on the floor and tapped his finger into a small sprinkling of the dust, looked at it closely, put it to his tongue then scowled deeply. "Stay away from this! Unless I've lost my sense of taste analysis, this is heroin, or something like it. Where'd you or Ito get this?" The three women all shook their heads, eyes wide with surprise. Then Sonia slapped her head and squealed.

"On my God! Ito had that funny little stuffed animal—the rabbit—he tossed into this chair. He brought it back from the game company he was at yesterday. It was torn, or somehow messed up and discarded. His friend gave it to him. He told me to take it and I did. I don't think either of us saw this stuff, though! I was going to give it to my neighbor's kid. Thank goodness I haven't yet!"

Raymond continued to study the sprinkling of powder, trying to imagine how heroin landed in the office chair of this group. "Leave it there and don't touch that chair," he told the three women who were staring as intently as he was. "I'd like to talk with Ito when he gets back. I can't see him doing drugs and absolutely wouldn't bring them into this office. He's a little too careful. He doesn't smoke and he seems like a health nut."

"So how did it get in here? I don't think anyone broke in here to do drugs," chuffed Cassie. Raymond shook his head.

"It's the bunny," piped up Sonia. "He tossed it into that chair when he came back from lunch Tuesday and it sat here all day Wednesday and Thursday until I took it home last night. He left at the same time I did. I doubt that he even saw the powder."

"Have him call me when he gets in. I should be in the office," said Raymond turning to leave. As he did so, Ito came into the office, carrying the packages of office supplies he'd bought. His face lit up.

"Ah, T.K. Raymond. How good to see you. It's been a while." Then he noticed the rest of the office staring at him. "What?" He dumped the packages on his desk and looked at the assembled group. Sonia pointed at the chair with its dusting of white granules.

"Someone ate a powdered donut?" has asked, breaking the tension.

"It's heroin," said Cassie with a steel voice. "How'd it get there?"

Ito shrugged. "I don't know. Whose been sitting in the chair? Some celebrity interview? Janitors? I've never even seen heroin before. Is that what it looks like?"

"Your stuffed rabbit was the last bottom to occupy that chair," snuffed Sonia.

Ito's eyes flew open. "It's a toy! I saw a bunch of them at the game company. They stuff them with technology so parents can say silly things to their kids—forever. They don't stuff them with heroin!"

"Back up," soothed Raymond. "You brought it in, put it in the chair and didn't touch it until you gave it to Sonia last night?" Ito nodded, trepidation in his eyes.

"I had been trying to learn about the accounting practices at Sterling Music and its subsidiary— Quality Fun game company. Trying to help Cassie with a story she's working on." Cassie rushed to explain, Sonia started telling about her research and the cacophony goaded Raymond into calling a halt.

"Hey!" he called out. "Cassie! You started this with digging into Sterling Music's accounting?" She nodded defiantly.

"Let's all sit down and make sense of this," he directed, turning Ito toward the conference room. Everyone followed. Cassie explained how she heard about the "federal investigation" of Sterling from her agent friend, thinking it was IRS, and recounted her unproductive meeting with the "acting" general manager. "She did confirm there is something going on but wasn't involved because she wasn't in the manager seat yet. I think there's a lot more."

Ito explained his probing into the accounting work through his social friend Brent and the contact he had made with the subsidiary company's financial person, Mel. He described his own nonproductive visit to the company and how he ended up dragging a toy rabbit to the office. Sonia added her research into Sterling's artists, undertaken at Cassie's direction. Raymond ran a hand through his hair and looked hard at Cassie, then at the group. Meredith was smiling inside. She knew the lecture that was to come—glad she was not part of it. She had not been involved in this issue.

"Why do you think there's a lot more, Cass?" Raymond asked in controlled combination of ire and curiosity.

"Because Taryn Manufur, the acting manager, called me just before we discovered the powder...heroin...and you came in. She wants to meet me here in a half hour. She sounded...well, stressed."

"Tape it," said Raymond. "Can't use it in court, but it gives you confirmation of whatever she's going to say."

"She could tell me to fuck off."

"She could. And that brings me to another familiar mantra. You have to decide who you are. When you dig into issues like this and end up with heroin in your office and possible drug dealings, you better be prepared to harden up a little. No, a lot! It's well beyond Hollywood happenings and deep into the realm of the police, or FBI or more! If you are playing with the tough kids, you better understand the stakes and choose to work with them." He looked both angry and resolute, thought Meredith. She hadn't seen him quite this adamant before. Cassie glanced at Meredith and they caught each other's eye. It was a lecture he'd delivered before half-jokingly. He wasn't joking anymore.

"If there is anything to what you're chasing," he admonished, "you'll have Police or FBI or even DEA on your doorstep. They'll want to know everyone you ever talked to, how you came across this story, what trail they can follow that you've already forged. And, there are others who'll be interested, too. But they won't ask questions."

"I'd never give up my sources," murmured Cassie, a sly grin on her face. "I've always wanted to say that." Raymond let out an exasperated breath and Meredith rolled her eyes. "And Raymond, don't Cassie—and her source—become your sources—who you can't give up, either?" Ito and Sonia were both looking at their hands, eyes cast down. The room was silent. Soon the tall detective stood up and went into the small kitchenette and poured himself a glass of water. Everyone else remained uncomfortably at the table.

"So, no matter how lightly you take this warning, you do have heroin on your office chair, and someone has to figure that out."

"What if I called my friend Mel at the game company," suggested Ito, "and tell him I gave the bunny to your neighbor's kid and the brother wants one, too. Is there another I could have? We could get another look at one of the stuffed animals, see if it, too, has that substance. And if it matches the one in the chair."

"Good thinking. ASAP. Possibly this afternoon? And I'll go with you—but I'll stay outside when you go in to pick it up. I want to see the place," Raymond quickly continued. "Cassie, meet your contact, probe. You're good at it and you know how to get around a confidential issue. By the time we get back, we should know more. I'm taking samples of the powder, and the new rabbit with me. Sonia, may I have someone pick up the other one from you."

"No need. It's still in my car. I had a...busy...night last night and didn't even remember to take it into the house."

CHAPTER 27
WEST LOS ANGELES
FRIDAY MORNING

Taryn Manufur whisked through the office door a few minutes later, escorted by Cassie through the back door of the cottage into the tiny conference room. The congenial journalist offered coffee or water and invited her to sit and be comfortable.

"What's on your mind today?" Cassie began the conversation. The music company executive looked warily at her, then pulled a sheaf of papers from her large purse.

"You had asked about an investigation into our accounting practices."

"Yes. Following up on a rumor, as I mentioned," answered Cassie. The squarely-shaped woman dressed in a black pantsuit slumped back into the chair.

"Where'd your information come from?"

"Several places, actually," responded Cassie. "Seems to be general but ghost knowledge. Awareness but no detail."

"Yeah, well.... Here." Manufur handed Cassie the papers with a sigh. Cassie frowned as she sifted through the pages.

"What are these?"

"Memos—confidential between our holding company corporate VP of finance and our own Sterling Controller, Terry Tilson. The guy who left in a rush last week. I see why now."

"Where'd these come from? How'd you get them and why give them to me?" Cassie persisted.

"Let's see. They explain why we have obscure and unfounded charges we've paid, pretty well suggesting we're flushing money through our company to pay for something but not what is on the invoices. Maybe drugs, probably out of the country, if I read between the lines. I got them because we have the hands-down stupidest secretary who was cleaning up Terry's desk just before he left. He wasn't much smarter. These were under his desk blotter. She put them in a folder with other things for him to review later, but forgot to tell him. He did a very clean sweep of his office the night before he quit, but she left this stuff on her own desk and he never knew they were there. She came across them—never read them, thank God— although she probably wouldn't have understood the contents— but dropped them in my in-box the beginning of the week. I didn't bother to look at them until yesterday. And, it just so happened it was the same day that the corporate VP visited our offices to clean up the mess Terry left behind and meet with the rest of the staff. I realized that the situation was explosive and as the general manager of Sterling, even the 'acting' one, I would be in everyone's direct line of fire from all sides. So I took a leave of absence early this morning. My mother is ill, and I'm going to visit her in the Northwest later this afternoon."

Cassie widened her eyes and let out a "Whoo." A minute later she asked, "But why me? You're risking a lot—going to the press."

"You asked. And I know you. I don't want to be the one stepping into the jaws of law enforcement, although I know it's eventually inevitable. I don't know or want to know any more than what's in those documents, but you seem to be focused on the situation. You can do the digging." The stolid woman seemed to wilt at that moment. "And I trust you."

Cassie took a deep breath. "Can I use your name in association with them?"

"God no!" gasped Taryn. "I hope I'm alive to even read your story."

"Can I help you, Taryn? Will you be okay?"

"I hope so. I feel like someone has lied to and manipulated me and I'm shocked, resentful, and frankly scared." She slumped even further back in the chair and dug at the thumbnail on one hand.

"Do you want to go over these with me? I won't divulge you as a source."

"No." Taryn stood up, reached for her purse. "I'm out of here, but I may or may not contact you when I've landed. I know you'll probably have questions, but I doubt that I'll have any answers. Here's the real general manager's home phone number. She should have those answers." And she left as briskly as she entered, leaving Cassie looking at the memos.

When Ito opened the office door, Cassie jumped up and ran to him. "Is Raymond still out there?"

"Sonia's getting the rabbit from her car for him, and then he's leaving." Cassie ran out the door, documents in hand, shouting at the detective.

CHAPTER 28
BRENTWOOD
FRIDAY NIGHT

The snarky huff of the cat wakened Raymond. He looked at the clock—three a.m.—and settled back into the covers reaching for renewed slumber. A soft rustling from the floor below interrupted the process. He glanced over and saw that Meredith was curled up in deep sleep next to him. The rustling came again. He thought at first it was Paco, eating kibble, or jumping from his usual perch on the fridge. But the slightest creak of the hardwood floor told him differently, Paco wasn't that heavy. Another rustle and creak.

He silently slipped from the covers, pulled on his sweatpants and instinctively reached for his back-up pistol under the nightstand. He listened again. Only the slightest creak. Soundlessly, he moved around the bed, bending over Meredith's relaxed body. He gently shook her and when her eyes flashed open in surprise, he placed a hand carefully over her mouth. Terror stiffened her body and her face. He put a finger to his lips then lifted her shoulder. She got his message and slunk from the bed as Raymond pointed her toward the master bathroom.

"Lock the door," he mouthed, indicating same with his hand, then "Call 911, say b&e then get dressed. Hide." He ran his hands over his body to indicate clothing. Meredith slipped into the bathroom, noiselessly closed the door. He heard the minute click of the lock. There was a phone as well as the walk-in closet in the large bathroom area. He picked up the gun from the bed, unlocked the safety and moved stealthily into the hall and toward the steps.

Meredith followed his directions, terrified with no idea of why the sudden nocturnal drama had unfolded. She punched in 911—whispered a request for help, giving the address. Pulled on the shorts and T-shirt she'd left on the floor from the night before and burrowed into the closet behind the floor length dresses kept for formal events. Then she began to shiver.

She heard nothing for a few stressful minutes, then shouts, thumps and clunks, finally punctuated with the sound of two loud gunshots. Then nothing. Where were the cops she had called? She waited. And waited. Finally taking a series of silent deep breaths, she talked herself back to a centered calm. She quietly slid from behind the gowns, gingerly unlocked the door and padded softly through the bedroom into the hall at the top of the stairs.

In the darkness, a large figure loomed near the top, his back to her, pointing a weapon down the stairs. She could not see Raymond and the only sound was the form in front of her breathing heavily. A large bronze bust of Nefertiti sat on the floor just outside the bedroom door, a souvenir from one or another movie set. She picked it up, raised it and without a second thought brought it down heavily on the head of the man two steps below her. He groaned so she hit him once more. He toppled forward down the steps.

"Raymond!" she yelled.

"Here," he barked, standing up from behind the kitchen island across the living room, facing the staircase. He flipped on the light and was holding his arm. She could see a dark stain running down his hand, dripping onto the floor. "I'm okay," he called. "Only a graze." She picked her way down the steps and around the figure on the floor. "Good aim," huffed Raymond. He noticed the red dripping down his arm. "I'll clean up the tile later." At that moment, lights and voices from cars outside told them the police had arrived.

"They won't arrest me for assault, will they?" she whimpered.

CHAPTER 29
BEVERLY HILLS
SATURDAY AFTERNOON

Cassie made her way through the halls of the Beverly Hills police complex, quieter than normal on a weekend. She had been summoned to a meeting with law enforcement after the break-in at Meredith's condo the night before. She suspected it was all about drugs and stories and had projected what questions were coming and how she might answer them. She'd talked with Meredith early that morning after Meredith and Raymond had returned home from the emergency room. Cassie wasn't completely sure of all that had happened in the Brentwood townhouse, or why, but she suspected Sterling Music was involved. Such intense legal scrutiny was new for her. Over the years there had been angry responses to her stories by actors, studios or agents. She'd faced a couple of depositions in lawsuits filed against her publications, none of which came to fruition. But never a "sit down" with the law. A uniformed officer directed her to a conference room and opened the door to admit her.

Inside the long room, centered by a no-nonsense wood conference table and solid brown wooden chairs, Meredith and Raymond sat on one side, a stocky older man with his back to all poured coffee from a glass pot into his mug. He turned to see

Cassie, his face reminding her of a tough old dog who'd seen a lot of sidewalks. A shock of steel grey hair hung over his forehead.

"Anyone else?" he asked holding up the pot. Everyone declined including Cassie who moved toward the back of the room.

"Cassie O'Connell Ainsworth, this is Tom Beltrom." Raymond made the introductions. "Tom's in charge of the special units, part of the joint task office on crime here in LA County." The older man only nodded. Cassie, already miffed at giving up her Saturday, wasn't about to take a dismissal so easily. She walked forward, held out her hand assertively and said, "Tom, good to meet you." He shook her hand and said, "Yes." She looked at Meredith and Raymond, surprised they both seemed fairly alert and pulled together, considering the night they'd had including two hours in the emergency room. Raymond's arm was held close to his body in a sling. But looking more closely she could see that Meredith, especially, was weary, probably to the bone. Yet, here they all were.

"We have one more person to join us," said Tom. And as he made his way to a seat at the table, the door opened and a tall, slender red-haired woman entered, dressed in a crisp black pantsuit and black blouse, sensible loafers and a heavy leather bag over her shoulder.

"This is Margo Flaherty, special agent with the FBI," Tom introduced her. The lithesome redhead, hair pulled into a severe bun at her neck, shook hands with each of the others as they introduced themselves. She looked mischievously at each one as though sizing them up one by one.

"T.K.," she smiled warmly. To Meredith, she said, "Hello," holding her gaze as though assessing her, then nodded to Cassie.

"Damn," thought Raymond. Cassie saw something predatory in the agent, noticed Meredith on somewhat defensive alert as well. Both idly wondered why any woman, even an FBI agent, would wear a heavy black wool suit in Los Angeles in August. They all wondered what, specifically, was the objective of this meeting.

"We're all here to talk about Sterling Music," Tom Beltrom began in his raspy voice. "Everyone at the table seems to have a shovel in the dirt. Ms. O'Connell, you seemed to have pried up one of the rocks which is why you and Ms. Ogden have been invited to attend." Cassie mused at the word "invited."

Raymond picked up the discourse, logical because the case involved Hollywood journalists and an entertainment industry company. "We need to find out exactly what we collectively have and where it goes from here. As you three know," he said, nodding at Meredith, Cassie and Tom, "something came to a head last night at my home. Given the involvement of all of us in this elusive case, we aren't sure who was targeted by the intruder—myself or Ms. Ogden. She and Ms. O'Connell included a blind mention of Sterling Music's 'investigation by the fed' in a column a couple of days ago. On the other hand, as you know, Tom and Margo, I've been asked by the FBI to assist in learning more about the financial situation at the company. As far as we can tell, that's all anyone other than ourselves knew last night."

"But we're not really sure that the Sterling case has anything to do with the b&e last night," continued Tom. "It's hard to imagine that anyone outside of this room and a couple of other people knew that T.K. was involved. So, I'm thinking the target was Miss Ogden. Here's what was printed in her column," said Tom, handing out copies of the brief item about Carlton's death in New Mexico in the column from several days before.

"But the work on the Sterling story has been all mine," asserted Cassie, sitting upright. "Meredith wasn't even in town when it all started."

"Yes, but the column carries both of your bylines, and Meredith has the reputation of deep investigative digging," said Tom.

"And she's so visible," Margo added. "Lots of public attention."

"Wait a minute," interrupted Meredith, leaning forward on the table, folding her hands and sitting forward aggressively. "First things first. Who was it that broke in last night and shot Raymond? We spent two hours going over this stuff in the early hours while your detectives pulled everything apart and went off to ID the guy. Who was he? That's one good clue on why he was there!"

Tom looked uncomfortable. Margo seemed totally remote. It was clear she had no stake in, nor knowledge of the predawn activities. Raymond clenched his lips and glared at them both. Cassie caught Meredith's eye and they exchanged a knowing collaborative glance. Their work carried the irony that show biz journalists were often chided as the least credible and respected, still they abided by and were governed by the same legal and ethical rules as the rest of the news field. And they covered some of the most sought-after stories by the public. Yet, people tended to discount them. Silence lingered in the room.

"It seems to me," Meredith finally continued, "that out of courtesy or at least integrity, you'd tell an assault victim who assaulted them. Someone want to step up?" She looked intently at Tom and then Margo and finally at Raymond. Cassie slumped back in her chair and shook her head in shared frustration.

The older man finally cleared his throat and said, "We don't know, Ms. Ogden. His fingerprints, face and other identifying factors don't show up in any data base we have right now. We've put the word out to other law enforcement, international and domestic, but have no response so far. And he's not talking."

"He can talk?" probed Meredith. "I think that says I didn't kill him." Margo's eyes sprang open as she re-entered the conversation.

"She has a hell of an arm!" murmured Raymond.

"No," Tom continued. "You didn't kill him. But even with a huge headache and people monitoring him, he isn't saying a word. "

"So back to the original discussion," interjected Raymond. He mentioned the suspected heroin powder found in the rabbit from the Sterling subsidiary, Quality Fun. "The lab is currently testing that as well as another bunny from the company, but so far there seems to be no connection between that toy and the larger Sterling Music case. And we haven't really explored financial issues yet. So, let's consider what we do have on the investigation and where it goes next." Background spilled out from those involved and information was knit together.

"Where do we go from here?" asked Margo. "What's your next move, Cassie?"

"There isn't one from me," Cassie answered with a shrug. "At least until my source decides to contact me again if that ever happens. I've beaten every bush I know, and this is as good as it gets."

"We may need your contact's information, Cassie," Margo said. The journalist said nothing. Silence reigned.

"So," Meredith took the conversation, "Let me sum this up. You have memos from the parent company, copies of invoices linking payments to nonexistent companies, rumors of irregularities in the finances of both the parent and music companies, a mysterious hit and run of the original discoverer of the irregularities in New Jersey, the surprise disappearance of the financial guy at Sterling. And a heroin-sprinkled bunny from another subsidiary. I think you want us to reveal from whom Cassie got her information, but I also think you know that we aren't likely to do that at this point."

"For us, the story is still open and up for expansion—when and if my sources return with more. But if I give them up now," Cassie added, "none of us would hear from that source again. Worse, he or she might be in danger…judging from last night's shooting soiree at Meredith's."

"I think the next move is yours," Meredith said. "I, for one, am done here. I wasn't involved. I understand how someone could misconstrue that I was with the double by-lines, as you explained, Tom, but you guys owe Cass some protection. Us, too, since Raymond isn't up to his usual protective mettle, a one-winged eagle so to speak. I have other stories to research and I'm going to work." She stood up to leave. The others around the table looked at her, surprised. "I'm tired. As for your collaborative efforts and request for more, I already gave at home."

"Since you have everything I can tell you at this point, I'm going, too." Cassie announced, also rising to leave. "Meredith, I'll drive you. I think these guys want to hash this out more and we have nothing else to add."

"Can you drive?" Meredith asked Raymond, pointing at his injured left arm.

"Yeah, and it's not far."

"Good to see you again, Meredith," said a chastened Tom Beltrom. They had met at several social events in his official capacity as Raymond's boss. She smiled and waved tiredly. Both she and Cassie tossed icy glances at the red-haired FBI agent.

"Who's the femme fatale-feeb?" Cassie asked rhetorically driving toward Meredith's Brentwood townhouse.

Meredith shook her head. "Don't know. Never saw or heard of her before. But then, I heard a bunch of stuff I never heard about before either. Like the fact that Raymond is on loan to the FBI on this case." Cassie thought about the call from Raymond, familiar sounds of the Malibu surf in the background, but claiming to be in D.C. while Meredith was in New Mexico.

"Sounds like it's time for a serious dose of truth-or-dinner with Raymond," suggested Cassie.

Meredith literally snarled. "Oh yeah!" She sat quietly rubbing her hands together and scowling. Cassie allowed her the time to seethe.

Finally, Meredith breathed deeply and sighed. "But knowing Raymond, this is tough for him, too. Neither of us are in the most transparent professions, except at the end of a project. Some detritus left behind in the road along the way. I guess it is time for some street sweeping and maintenance." Cassie laughed at her friend's use of imagery. It was one reason why she was a good writer.

"Remind me how you came on the Sterling Music story anyhow?" Meredith changed the subject. "I feel really distant from that story."

"It was a slow news day," chuckled Cassie. "You were in New Mexico. I went to lunch with a good friend who works for my book agent. She sometimes has a little bit of news stuff about a celebrity author who's doing something interesting. Turns out they have authors who are musicians and on the Sterling label. Totally happenstance. The happenstance turned into a major collision with this big drug case." Meredith nodded.

"You've been nose-to-the-grind-stone since you returned from New Mexico. What are you working on?" Cassie asked, changing the subject.

"AIDS in Hollywood. I've lost some good friends and colleagues. And Queen's AIDS concert last year opened up some awareness doors. Lots of focus on San Francisco gay community, but it's taken a real toll here in Hollywood as well. I just finishing a special feature on it."

"I'm glad Russ went for it. I have a friend in San Francisco who's the main correspondent there for a major news syndicate and they've turned her down over and over about extensive coverage of the disease."

"It's time," murmured Meredith. "The first non-gay cases have started to develop from transfusions and stuff. I don't know how we can ignore it. I found some great resources—one of the public health specialists who concentrates on 'Hollywood,' a church that has started a support group. I went to a meeting and wow, how enlightening. One of our favorite old TV actors was willing to talk about his disease and how he's dealing with the inevitable. Good stuff.

"But speaking of stories, you and I haven't really sat down and planned for a long time, either," Meredith added. "We haven't caught up on how the office is running these days, or what you're up to or me, either." Cassie nodded in agreement. They decided to lunch together the next day and update each other. Cassie happily acknowledged the plan as her colleague and friend stepped out of the car and left with a "see ya."

☆☆☆

As she opened the front door to the townhouse, Meredith took a deep breath and let it out slowly. The police hadn't made too much of a mess as they arrived at her 911 call during the night. But remnants of the attack and the investigation that followed were unmistakable, not the least of which were the swipes she'd made on the counter and the floor to clean up the blood from Raymond's arm wound, a clear shot—almost a simple crease but also creasing the top corner of the fridge behind him in its trajectory. Lodged in the wall above, police had dug it out and taken it as evidence. Absently Meredith was amazed the intruder got the drop on Raymond and must have shot from low near the floor. A few stitches and two hours in the emergency room took care of the arm, it would take more to remedy the appliance or the reason behind the crime.

Paco was back on the top of the refrigerator, looking at her as though it was she who had committed the crime. His domain was sullied. There would be treats. Meredith thought about priorities, and although a shower and a nap seemed imminent, she first went to the phone and called her housekeeper. Could she come on Monday?

☆☆☆

Raymond entered the house clumsily from the garage, compensating for his disabled left arm. Driving had been easy. Juggling keys, briefcase and getting the door, not so easy. Meredith heard him and came downstairs to help. It was after five by then and she had slept for a while, taken a long cleansing shower and had dinner preparations underway. Raymond looked melted, unusual for his stoic, strong and tall demeanor.

"Hard day," she said.

"And night," he sighed. "I need Ibuprofen and a drink."

"I don't think you're supposed to have them together," offered Meredith.

"Don't care. I also want a shower and yes, I know I'm not supposed to get this thing wet, either. I'll be careful."

"You need some help?"

"Normally I'd jump to have your help in the shower. But tonight...," he shook his head. She smiled.

"Yell if you get in trouble."

"A beer with dinner?" He asked. She huffed but agreed.

Sitting at the round dining table in the kitchen alcove he was glad to have mostly finger food which he could maneuver with his right arm. "I'll be out of this thing," he said, looking at the sling, "very quickly. Only a day if that." She nodded and smiled.

"How about telling me about the meeting after I left, and what is going on with this case you're chasing...the 'loan' of you to the FBI and," she hesitated, "the redhead who seems to be working with you now."

Raymond scowled and took a slow drink of his beer. "Margo." He said simply. "She's a top of the line agent. Smart. Tough. And a little crazy. And, she's lead on this case, and yes, I'm on loan and have been working it. But...I'm tired. I'm beat up. And I don't feel like going into all the details tonight. I'd like to get some sleep and run the beach in Malibu tomorrow morning, then talk about a lot of things. Could we do that?"

Meredith thought about it for a moment then smiled. "Lots to talk about for sure. So, in the words of someone I care about, 'Done.'"

CHAPTER 31
MALIBU
SUNDAY

Wet white froth tickled Meredith's toes and ankles as she stood in the surging surf in front of Raymond's house in Malibu. Hot in the city, the beach-side weather was refreshing, and a diamond blue sky painted an energetic frame around the day. The wash of the waves and incoming surf lightened the blithesome young woman's spirits. She'd risen early in Brentwood, only 45 minutes away, rushed to the early aerobics class at the nearby spa, and returned home to the townhouse in time to fix pancakes and eggs for Raymond as he finally emerged from a much-needed night of sleep. She'd decided his usual healthy oatmeal-and-fruit breakfast wasn't important today. Then, per his request, they had driven to his own home on the water to take a day of…discussion, reconnoitering…regeneration…? The purpose was elusive but assumed, the outcome uncertain. Even frightening.

She watched Raymond in an unusually slower jog than normal, injured arm clenched to his side, as he ran up the sand toward her. "Need a lot more of this," he panted. "Used to do it every day." Small doses of guilt wrapped around her brain as she realized his decision to live with her in Brentwood most weekdays had significantly altered his own comfortable habits.

More fodder for her paranoia. They settled on the patio with large mugs of coffee. Meredith pulled her shoulder-length copper blond hair into a pony-tail and snapped an elastic band around it. She pulled an oversized Queen t-shirt over her bathing suit and sprawled into a lounger. Raymond left his shirt off but wound a towel around his neck, crouching into a cushioned chair. A gull called overhead.

"I have stuff to say," he said. "and some things I can't." She nodded and sipped at her coffee. He told her of his loan-out to the FBI, how he was being briefed in Washington D.C. two weeks earlier. "There was no conference, so that's why you could never find me at the hotel." He explained the simple basics of the drug-empowered financial case they were investigating that involved Sterling Music—and many other subsidiary companies—careful to keep most details out of the conversation. Most of this she had intuited from the meeting the day before. But it helped to make things clear. He did not tell her of being recruited from the LA special cases team. He still had too many doubts about it himself and was not yet ready to discuss options.

Meredith listened intently, nodded and asked a question here or there. When he wrapped up, she felt calmer but not satisfied. The air was quiet for a few minutes, then Meredith asked, "What else, Raymond? There's a bigger story. I can see it. And who's the redhead? Where does she fit into this equation?"

A slight breeze ruffled the detective's dark hair and the sun highlighted the blush of silver in it. He folded his hands and stared at them, reminding Meredith of her fascination with them from their first meeting—their strength and firmness. "Margo is nothing for you to worry about. She's a highly-valued agent with the FBI and she's in charge of this case…now you know almost as much as I do about her."

"She seems comfortable with you and a bit condescending toward me and apparently Cassie as well." Raymond shook his head, puzzled and somewhat sad.

"Look," Meredith said quietly, "lots of very credible people seem to bat us around for our association with the glamor life. But you know something?" Raymond looked at her. "Most of them would love to be in our shoes! Even yours. You do live in a hyper-lit world, all on your own. I don't help."

"I'm sorry. I've not been candid with you. I've felt guilty for sliding around the truth these past few weeks. But I could not, and should not, be telling you as much as you already know. Cassie kind of stumbled into our case and now you're both involved."

"Knowing Cass, she's probably negotiated exclusive coverage from Tom by now," chuckled Meredith. "I would have, but it's not my story."

"And what is your story?" Raymond asked, looking at her warily. "I'm not the only one who's been distant lately. What went on in New Mexico? I know about Dusty—of course— you've always been forthcoming about him. But you seem anxious, antsy. What else?"

She shrugged. "Most of it you've read. The rest of it—some I can talk about, some I can't. Carlton's death, well, there's still a lot of story left. But it's in New Mexico so keeping up with it has been...," she fought for words, "challenging." Raymond looked at her curiously. "It involves drugs, too," she explained, almost hesitantly.

"The kid overdosed, I know that," Raymond said.

"It's how he overdosed that's never really been fully explained. And despite the inquest that couldn't come to a determination, lots of people who were there, have a different opinion."

"Why do you think it's up to you to find out the truth? Couldn't you just report it when it comes out?"

Meredith fidgeted, uncomfortable in her seat, and looked toward the shimmering horizon, watching a gull float effortlessly against it. "I kind of jump-started the process," she said quietly. "I wrote what Dusty believed and I'm afraid...," she hesitated, her throat constricting, "...I'm afraid that's what the home invasion was about night before last. Not your case here with Sterling Music." She looked down at her hands. Raymond stared at her, but he had no words.

"What's worse, I'm afraid for Dusty and everyone else I've interviewed. Even before my involvement, some of them were already slinking off, distancing themselves as soon as possible from the movie, most 'just in case,'"

"Just in case...of what?"

"All I really know is that whoever owns the lavish estate where the movie company headquartered, also owns a private ranch and airfield a few miles away. Carlton and a couple of the other movie kids hung around with the sons of the owner—kids who came in just for the summer when school was out at home—somewhere on the east coast. The movie kids talked about seeing drugs and how the ranch kids were always boasting how they and their dad could get them anything they wanted. Drugs, booze, etc."

"And you printed that?"

"Not exactly. I just quoted Dusty saying that he was positive Carlton's death wasn't suicide or an accidental overdose. He didn't take drugs and was leaving to go home—what he wanted—two days later. Then, Dusty said someone might talk to some of the local kids who were hanging around the movie set with Carlton and others—I didn't print that but the fact that he said it means it's out there already."

Raymond ran a hand through his hair and blew out a long breath. "Don't take this the wrong way, let's hope people assume gossip columnists mostly print a lot of rumor."

"There's more, but I can't give you specifics. I have an agreement. My 'source' is a federal agent in New Mexico, and he's directed some of his own investigation on the information I've been able to provide. And given me some good stuff, too." The tall man stood up and walked to the railing, turned around and leaned against it. He looked hard at Meredith.

"I ask again, who is this agent. What's the organization? Where's it headquartered?"

Meredith shook her head. "That's the confidential thing I can't say. He's a source. Just like yours." Raymond thought for a minute, sat down next to Meredith and placed one hand over hers, but said nothing.

"Are we okay here?" she asked. He shrugged.

"We've never exactly been the Cleavers," he sighed. "Think about how we met and what we went through just to get to the other side of the drama of Bettina Grant's murder. The drama, itself, was bonding. Maybe we both seek it. Adrenalin, puzzles."

"Or maybe we are only now coming out of it and into a new phase, Raymond. Life's been pretty status quo for us both until the last year or so. Honeymoon time, now it feels like real life is revving up. I'm restless in my work. Indifferent about pure gossip now. You obviously have new ground you're covering. We've been tightly and safely ensconced in the townhouse, dutifully doing our work and coming home to the cocoon. Even that seems to be a little constricting. You say you miss the beach."

"Well, a leather reclining lounger, larger screen TV and a dedicated closet hardly constitutes a full-service home, and none of them is why I'm there," smiled the detective. "You are. But I think there's a broader world out there for us. Can we talk about it?"

"Sure." The conversation followed them to lunch at the Sea Shack, an afternoon of swimming and sunning, among other things. After dark, sun baked, relaxed and toting take-home shrimp po'boy sandwiches and cole slaw, the duo returned to the townhouse.

CHAPTER 32
WEST LOS ANGELES
MONDAY MORNING

"...and Meredith—stay away from New Mexico. That was a truckload of...well, you know." Russ's deep voice across the line from New York charged her nerves and made her smile. She grunted agreement. "Your article on AIDS was excellent, by the way. I always admire your think-pieces and our editors appreciate them as well. They get positioned in the papers like the politico opinion pieces which makes us all look good." She thanked him and promised to consider more depending on availability of topics that were appropriate.

"Russ, Ito is scheduled to meet with you in New York next week. He's nervous. We're curious. Can you give us some idea so we can calm him down?"

"Oh, hell, Meredith. I'd like to show him the ropes here and let him get some training on the new computer systems. A lot of upgrades and changes going on. Best he sees it firsthand."

"Thanks Russ. We'll settle him down. He probably thinks he's getting fired." Russ snorted and closed off. Meredith smiled as she hung up. After the long Sunday discussion with Raymond, she had some upgrades and recharges planned for herself. She thumbed through her Rolodex and called Allan Jaymar, her now-mentor and advisor, retired super-manager of highly successful show business luminaries. Allan had helped her maneuver into the shoes of her late boss Bettina Grant over much competition albeit co-bylined with Cassie O'Connell Ainsworth. Nearly three years later, the experiment that knit their skills and abilities around Hollywood gossip was established and ready for assessment. With many moving parts to the organization they had forged, Meredith felt the need for guidance.

Lunch was set for three days later and Meredith set to work on lining up interviews for the next week. She firmed up a set visit on a new film, lunch with the long-time star of a day TV soap opera, and meeting with the union chief of a craft union that served the film industry and held a great deal of sway over how production took place.

Cassie, meanwhile, prepared for the next morning's TV shoot; script, graphics, production schedule with the TV studio to be used. She planned out tentative stories for the next two weeks assuming no "breaking stories" interrupted the plan.

☆☆☆

"Sonia has a boyfriend," chuckled Meredith. "It may be serious."

"Good for her. She's worked so hard and grown well. She deserves a good life," Cassie said, buttering a slice of warm sourdough. "And Ito's going to New York."

"Russ says he'll be trained on new computer systems that will be introduced in our offices soon," Meredith explained. Cassie groaned. The trendy Italian décor of the legendary restaurant was rustled with the sounds of busy diners, mostly in deep conversation about contracts and deals. A few well-manicured matrons out for a nice lunch. Servers in crisp black and white tended to the tables with much-acknowledged efficiency.

"Are you planning a follow-up on the Sterling Music story?" she asked Cassie. "There's a lot to say from the other day. How are you going to handle it?"

"I got that we shouldn't be saying anything right now, didn't you" she asked rhetorically. "I'm thinking we wait until we have some definitive action to write about. You know we'll have the first break. Tom promised me we'd be the first call."

"I figured you were negotiating with him," smiled Meredith. "I hope you're bugging him often just to make sure we don't miss anything." Relieved that retelling the story of the break-in would not be part of the ongoing chronicle, she quickly changed the subject to upcoming events that needed news coverage. Network introductions to the season's new and renewed shows, national and international press—many who carried the Hollywood column, and the Emmy awards.

"Spouses? Significant others?" asked Meredith. They talked of the social plans and set calendar dates. "Emmy Awards—six weeks out. Any thoughts about who we should prepare to feature, who might get awards? The usuals, of course—Golden Girls, Cosby...."

Cassie scowled deeply. "Someone else will have to interview Bill Cosby, if he wins. That 'beloved' TV father and 'funnyman' was one of the meanest interviews I ever had. Completely different from his public persona." And the conversation continued.

As the waiter brought the check, Cassie casually mentioned her book. "Mort says the publisher is high on it and we expect publication in the fall, probably November-ish." Meredith enthusiastically congratulated her on another good win. Then Cassie added, "I'll be doing a month-long press tour in late October or early November, so we have to think about that."

Meredith felt a mental jolt. She said nothing until she could figure out what to say and how to say it. "Well, we have a lot of advance work to do then. That's one of the biggest and most active times of the year. We'll set up interviews with the new series people in September for use later. Generic column items for later. We can get Sonia up to speed on some phone interviews and...and...." Cassie was collecting her purse and starting to get up before Meredith had finished.

"We'll get it worked out," she said and waved a dismissive hand.

"Hey, Meredith Ogden," came a deep-voiced call that interrupted their conversation. Meredith looked up to see Renn Burton, Dusty's mentor, as he walked over to their table. With him was a familiar face, Hank Torbin. No surprise, thought Meredith. Renn's petite blond wife, Angelina, was also in the group. A massive amount of hair was piled on top of her head, her pixie face made up to the max, she wiggled two tiny fingers at the women and whispered, "Hi."

"How goes the continuing saga of *Sunset West*?" boomed Renn Burton. "Dusty's got his hands full!"

Meredith smiled as she commented blandly, "Like all movies, Renn, it goes like it goes. Every day's a new adventure." Burton nodded, chuckling.

"How'd that set visit go, Meredith?" Torbin spoke up, "Solve the mysterious death of the teen yet?" She waved him off with a friendly smile. Everyone murmured a perfunctory acknowledgment as the group bid one another goodbye.

"He's pretty but seems kind of pushy. You two have background?" asked Cassie.

"I've worked hard to avoid it," snickered Meredith. "Met him on that football movie at one of the universities back east— one of Renn's big movies. He hovered around outside my hotel door one night. He's seems…well, on the prowl. Maybe it's me. Or testosterone. I've always liked Renn. He's always seemed pretty straight forward, not a lot of hype. Interviewing him has been very satisfying. But his entourage…."

"Well, Angelina's sure no angel. I guess that's why you don't see her very often with Renn," Cassie growled. "She chased and chased him after she met him when she was a walk-on player in one of his westerns. But he's kept her around for a long time. She pads after him like a caretaking little pet…." Meredith smirked at Cassie and murmured, "Meow."

As they left the restaurant, Meredith continued the business conversation. "We'll have to tape shows in advance, too, or hire someone to produce/direct in your place," But Cassie was already hailing the valet and it was clear that discussion was over.

Ito was waiting for them when they returned to the office. "What did Detective Raymond learn about the toy rabbits and drugs?" he pestered. Meredith explained that she had no information yet but would let him know when there was some. Ito seemed disappointed and anxious.

☆☆☆

The morning at the Special Investigation Department was taken up looking at the progress and possibilities of current cases. The unit had been established six years before to provide more personal, "concierge-style" law enforcement service to members of the entertainment and surrounding communities. The aim was to help them avoid getting lost in the vast LAPD system, to create a friendly and collaborative relationship with visible and vocal popular public figures, and especially to avoid unnecessary press attention. Potential felony cases from burglaries to stalking to spouse or family abuse to homicide filled the "active" board on the office wall.

"Jerrold and I are going to Ojai to wrap up—we hope—with our whistleblower/ accountant," Raymond explained to his partner Marty. "We'll leave later this afternoon and probably stay over one or two nights, depending on the status of the situation."

Jerrold let out a loud gasp at the other end of the phone. "Jesus, that's a lot of driving. Are we taking the tiny jewel box you normally drive? Isn't there a company car?" Raymond only snickered.

"Pick you up about three. Maybe we will beat the traffic our of LA!"

Then he called Meredith to let her know he'd be away for a day or two.

CHAPTER 33
HIGHWAY 101 EN ROUTE TO LOS ANGELES
WEDNESDAY

The tedium of road travel had set in between Raymond and Jerrold returning from Ojai, and they were within an hour of LA when the car phone rang. Raymond answered to an intense, tight-voiced Meredith, blurting out, "Raymond, something's happened to Dusty! He never got back from New Mexico. The studio has been all over the country with police and sheriff's department, and he's just disappeared. I knew I shouldn't have printed his comments...!"

Raymond blew out a breath and said in his command voice, "Slow down. Breathe, Merri." He waited for a moment or two, then spoke up again. "Now start from the beginning and tell me what's happening. I know about the article and about Dusty's comments. I know you feel the assault the other night had to do with that, now tell me the situation right now." He pulled to the side of the road, into a roadside truck stop to listen carefully.

"I got a confidential call late yesterday from the movie publicist on *Sunset West*. She's a friend and it was on the QT. She wanted to know if I had heard from Dusty. He was due back on Monday evening and in the studio yesterday morning but never showed. They started calling him at home, at his ranch, any place they thought he might go. The house manager at the

Villa in Flecha Dorada said he left mid-morning Monday, expecting a twelve to thirteen-hour drive. No one's seen or heard from him since."

"You're sure he left?"

She whimpered, "Yes. He'd never miss a day on his own set. And if so, he'd let SOMEONE know. I talked to Steve Bankleman, the producer, who said they expected him Tuesday, he'd called in Monday morning as he was leaving. No idea what might have kept him. Now they have...what do you call it...BOLOs out for him in three states."

"Well, at least they have the authorities on it. Do you happen to know who was the lead law officer in New Mexico? I'll call him."

"Wouldn't you be the lead out of California?" she implored.

"Not necessarily. My jurisdiction is really the LA area. But I'll check it out if you can get me the contact person where he left from."

She breathlessly agreed and hung up. Raymond looked at Jerrold. "Never a dull moment," he smiled, then phoned Marty and sent him to Meredith's offices to hand hold the entire situation. He pulled the car back on the road and punched it all the way to West LA.

Delivering Jerrold to his rented apartment, he said, "Call me if something comes up from the Coast Guard and let me know what's next with the fake invoices and their source companies." Jerrold agreed and Raymond made a fast trip to the editorial offices. He arrived, road-weary, a two-day stubble—unusual for the usually fastidious detective—and both curious and wary of the current drama. It sounded serious and real.

Meredith wasn't in much better shape. She wore guilt heavily and it contorted her bright open face. He walked past Sonia and Ito who nodded at him, waved at Cassie and went into Meredith's office. He shut the door, then made his way to her, lifted her gently out of the chair and hugged her. "Not your fault," he whispered. And was surprised she was focused, if shaky.

"I just don't understand why he felt he should tell me the things he did, and then tell me to print them. He said, 'print it princess!' Why? He knew it would be trouble. I should have known but was too involved in the drama, and excited about the revelations I thought I heard." Raymond walked her to the small sofa in her office and sat down with her.

"How was he doing with the movie? Was it really going okay?"

She shook her head. "I don't think so. The fact that he was foolish enough to bring me in to 'cover' the murder? And I was foolish enough to do it. I should have done a phone interview. I think the studio was already on him for that. He used the company plane to take me there!"

"But you got good stories. And I thought you felt you had helped with Sonora's image. And a lot of attention for the movie."

Meredith snorted. "Oh yeah. Put Dusty right in the cross hairs. Lover to the star, observer and wise man to her kid's problems. And put you and I both in danger."

"Meredith," Raymond counseled. "You did your job. You did the job Dusty asked you to do. He wouldn't have told you the things he did, or tell you to use them if he didn't have a reason. Come on. He's a good, sweet, raw guy. But he's not stupid. I suspect there's more going on there than either of you realized. Didn't see the unexpected consequences. Any chance you found out the name of the lead investigator in New Mexico—or Arizona?"

"No. I tried, but didn't know where to start. I just hope Dusty's alive and okay," she said, close to a snivel, something Raymond rarely saw from Meredith.

He took her hand and urged her from the couch. "Can I take you to lunch or take you home?" She shook her head.

"I need to focus. I have a lot to do and we tape again tomorrow morning. God, I hope I don't have another murder story." Then she looked at the detective and her eyes opened. "I'm sorry, I forgot you've been a victim, too. How's your arm?"

He did a queen's wave and smiled. "Ducky."

"Then get back to your own case and let me collect my wits here and figure out the next step. And no, you can't help— now—at least. We may call on you for direction later." And just like that, Meredith was back. Raymond said goodbye to everyone and he left, nearly loping down the sidewalk to his car, problems of his own to deal with.

CHAPTER 34
SOMEWHERE IN THE ARIZONA-NEW MEXICO DESERT
MONDAY AFTERNOON, TWO DAYS EARLIER

Dusty Reed looked around at the scant cluster of trees, skinny, water starved, ugly, but providing a small amount of shade. He mused that he and Meredith had once, long ago, debated on how many trees it took to make a copse of trees. She said "a few." He said, "Several dozen." He was right. But it made no difference. The emaciated collection at least gave him some reprieve from the searing August sun in the middle of the New Mexico desert, he wished he knew exactly where.

He took deep breaths and exercised the calming techniques he'd learned decades before to settle and focus himself before jumping into the rigorous stunts for which he had become known in the movie industry. He felt a familiar and deep twinge on his left side and knew, from past experience, he probably had broken at least one rib. He was glad he had worn his wristwatch—and that it had survived the pushing, punching and final dumping he'd taken— and reminded himself to check the time often. Knowing how long he had been in the sun and the sand helped him stay grounded.

He had packed up his Jeep and left Flecha Dorada midmorning, anticipating about a twelve-hour trip to Los Angeles, the aloneness a pleasant thought considering how many people he'd juggled for weeks on the movie set. He stopped for a break about three hours later and sometime after that a brown van overtook his quiet reverie from behind, forced him off the road. Two tough thugs dragged him from his car into the back of the van, where a third took pleasure in hitting or thumping on him. Another hour or so later, he estimated, he felt the car leave the roadway asphalt and onto less firm ground. Then they stopped in the middle of the desert and tossed him out of the car, blindfolded, wrists bound together. He only heard the vehicle leave, then felt the hammering rays of the sun almost immediately. He worked the blindfold off with his bound hands and with a great deal of grit and teeth gnashing, worked loose enough of the knots on his wrists to free himself. His stunt training served him well.

But there was no road, only a few tire tracks left and no shade. He realized he had been left to die. But why not just shoot him? He struggled to recall a face, voice or accent of his kidnappers, but realized those recollections would come later. His first need was to survive. It took an hour of hoping he was following the tracks he thought he saw. But dehydration and heat made him question his own mental acuity. Then he spotted the scrappy set of trees toward the horizon and he tried to judge geometrically the angle from which he strayed for the path he had chosen. Under the lacey protection of the trees, he took deep breaths and looked for a water source. There had to be one if vegetation could exist. His strong, muscular build gave him some physical and willful strength many might not have enjoyed.

He thought about why he was there. Stranded, abandoned, and presumably left to die. It obviously had to do with the overdose death of Sonora's boy, the stories that had run about Dusty's relationship with Sonora—and his opinion that the kid didn't suicide or accidentally die. He thought about the poor, shy kid. Unhappy. The director had tried to engage him in tasks around the set, but it never worked. He'd spend lunch hours with him, hoping to bring a connection that would prove some satisfaction for the boy. Didn't happen. The connection with him was merely a passing acquaintance with little notice of the growing relationship between his mother and Dusty.

Then, obviously, someone assumed Dusty knew too much about the drug flow around the isolated movie location. But he wondered what he really did know. Nothing. He only knew that Carlton was not a druggie, no longer had a reason to be unhappy, and wouldn't have killed himself. And then there was the equipment shipment back to LA....

Closing his eyes, he meditated and worked to calm his heart rate and body stress. Techniques he'd learned as a kid working with horses on his dad's ranch. Later as a horse trainer and rodeo rider. Then as a movie stuntman. The mental discipline had served him well and had been perfected over the years as he parlayed his abilities into movie work and beyond. Saguaro cacti speared the landscape here and there and he called on his reading of western comics and novels, remembering how thirsty heroes had sipped and sucked moisture from cactus leaves. He ventured out to a regal looking monarch plant, long spines threatening even a simple approach. He wrapped his hand in his blind fold and used his belt buckle to carve off a small and messy piece of flesh from the plant. He found some minute amount of liquid, but enough to be promising and found himself carving more. Hands scraped, pierced and bleeding, he made his way back to the trees and settled in, not exactly sated, but more optimistic. He checked his watch. The sun would be setting in about two hours. Both a relief and a concern. No escape in the dark and leaving the cover of the trees meant morning sun with no reprieve.

Thinking this may be his last opportunity to visualize life, he thought about his father and the ranch where he'd honed his own eventual career skills. Originally a working ranch with some agriculture and livestock, over time, pieces of the land were sold off for development and other uses. The livestock was gone and now the stables were used only for boarding other people's horses. One caretaker did it all—with the help of part-time high school kids. Dad was in his seventies and retired, waiting for Dusty to come back and "build the place up again." Dusty cringed at the thought. It would never happen. The younger generation had all moved on. Maybe someday....

Priscilla's face came to mind. His ex-wife, a high school cheerleader and rodeo queen, perfect foil to a football and horse champion. He studied ag in junior college, she home economics. They married young and were already heading to Hollywood when the first boy arrived. The second came two years later. In another two years, Priscilla left with the boys for an insurance broker from Long Beach who promised her a house on the beach. She liked that the broker was home all the time, liked socializing with prettier people, and not on the road in remote, gritty locations. Dusty had seen his now-late teenage sons only a few times a year in the past few years.

But his path in Hollywood had continued, as did the remote locations. It all began when a movie stunt producer had seen a young Dusty in an exhibition rodeo near Phoenix and approached him about a movie to be shot there soon. He was notable because of his similar build and coloring to the film's star, Renn Burton, a famous and popular action film actor. For the next ten years Dusty advanced in Renn's wake. First as his personal double in the daring-do action scenes, later as the guy who organized the stunt work for Burton's films and eventually other western and action productions. Dusty began directing the stunt segments of films and the "second unit" or background and secondary action segments. *Sunset West* was his big break, Renn was one of the producers and trusted Dusty's eye and direction.

But Dusty knew very quickly he was in well over his own head. Not so much in the creative direction, but in the management and administrative parts. Renn occasionally stepped in to help, but it seemed to Dusty that an important step had been missed in his training as a top-class director, negotiator and manipulator. Now, he figured he'd be lucky to live long enough to keep the job or even hear the bad reviews.

He dabbed at his cuts and punctures with his shirt tail and made his blindfold into a small bag to hold pieces of saguaro. With a deep breath and small prayer, he followed his reckoning back to where he thought he had seen the van tracks, figured they came from a road somewhere. The indentations in the sand and scrub brush were a little more obvious in the higher sun. Helpful. He concentrated and worked his way slowly along and his mind again meandered, this time thinking about Meredith Ogden.

A chance meeting on a movie set where he was directing stunt work, she landed next to him at the lunch line during break. Once introduced, she showed a definite interest in his work and asked a lot of questions. They lingered and agreed to meet up in LA for a drink. She had energy, liked to laugh, and was always engaged in whatever he had to say. And had plenty to say, herself, which was always fascinating to Dusty. They were a good partnership in the events of the entertainment industry. Her community overlapped his and being seen in hers was good PR for him. She was comfortable with his courteous demeanor in the limelight and his sense of fun out of it. But schedules kept them from any kind of commitment or even an expectation of it.

She had visited the ranch twice, two times more than any other woman since Priscilla. Their individual careers advanced well. Their personal liaison not so much.

Then Bettina Grant died, Meredith was hyped into career super-gear and T.K. Raymond walked into the room. When Dusty got the big break with *Sunset West*, he met his own super star in Sonora Hutchinson. Now, he was lost in the desert with little prospect of living.

As Raymond headed for his car, Meredith quickly picked up the phone and punched in the numbers on the card she kept well hidden in her desk drawer. "Call me now!" she commanded. Then phoned CenturySonic Studios' VP of Publicity Lou Marquand. Not surprisingly, he seemed to have expected her call.

"Meredith? I actually was about to call you," he answered with his usual raspy avuncular voice. "We just got word that Dusty Reed has been found! He's alive, but barely. Kids illegally riding ATV's in the desert saw rocks he'd tried to use to spell out 'help.' He was unconscious under a very small outcropping of rock, the only shade I guess in miles."

"Thank God, Lou. Where is he now?"

"Taken to a hospital in Phoenix. Steve Bankleman is flying there now."

"What happened?"

"All we know is that he disappeared Monday. His car was found off the road by a state trooper Tuesday afternoon. Thought it was abandoned. But that's the only way they knew who he was. His studio picture ID was in the car. A passing motorist said they saw someone 'escorting' him into a rust-colored van. Obviously abducted."

"Will he still be on the picture?" she asked, feeling suddenly embarrassed about her less-than-humane question.

"Meredith, I don't think we'll see Dusty on any project for quite a while, if he even makes it. I HEARD—and I emphasize that. I don't KNOW. But I heard he hasn't regained consciousness yet and no one knows what the state of his mind will be when he does. So, as a good friend, I'd say let's be sensitive to that. But the studio is already reviewing options for a replacement for the rest of *Sunset West.*"

Sadness struck her heart. "Sonora?"

"Don't know. She finished her photography Monday, and no one's heard from her since."

"I guess it goes without saying—call me when you know something, Lou. You know I have a really focused interest in this. If something's off the record, say so, but keep me updated, please?"

"I get it, Meredith. I will."

"Reuben for you," Ito called out to Meredith as she hung up. She punched in another line.

"Where are you?" she demanded.

"Hey! Meredith. What's going on? I'm in New Mexico. Why the angst?"

"Do you know anything about the abduction of Dusty Reed?" She heard silence and some long-distance background noises.

"Yes, I do," answered the deep, controlled voice. "And you don't want to get involved."

"Did I cause this with my story?"

"No. Well, just say it was a catalyst but something like this was inevitable."

"Why?"

"Mercy, mercy, Miss Merri," Reuben chided, lightly.

"Don't placate me, Reuben. You chose me or maybe I should say recruited me. Now level with me."

"I will be in Los Angeles tomorrow afternoon. I can't tell you anything right now and not this way. But I'll contact you about two tomorrow. There are updates you should know about. Ok?"

"If that's the best you can do, sure. I'll make sure I'm in the office waiting for your call. Or…," snarled Meredith, reciting her car phone number, then hanging up and wondering why she was so pissed off at Reuben. She turned to her keyboard, pulled up a new file on her computer screen and quickly began writing.

Half an hour later she called to Sonia, yelling to Cassie as well, "We have to get this lead on the column going out this afternoon. Only two paragraphs, push the rest down and save the soccer item for tomorrow. Quickly. And, I have a fairly brief news special to fax to New York immediately about Dusty Reed's kidnapping! Cass, this should be incorporated into our TV script for tomorrow, too." When the pace, anxiety and angst in the offices settled down, Meredith quietly gathered her belongings, straightened her desk and announced, "I'm going out. I need some air and to think about all that's going on. Call me on my car phone or at home."

"Want some company?" asked Cassie.

"Nope, I want some clarity."

☆☆☆

A slight overcast shrouded all of the LA basin including the normally-verdant Bel Air hillside community, dimming its genteel sparkle only slightly. Meredith maneuvered her auto along the slender streets and their well-designed curves until she came to the address on her notepad. The house was a large, but not ostentatious, modern Tudor, hedges and landscaping obscuring most of the structure from the road. She parked across the street and sat back in the familiar confines of her long-loved red Mustang. She doubted that Sonora would even be home, but still planned how she would handle any conversation that might occur. Before she had worked the concept, a limousine pulled up in front of the house and Sonora came out the front door, a stylish paisley over-filled duffle over one shoulder and purse over the other, a helper toting two suitcases to the car. Meredith rushed across the street to Sonora. The actress looked up sharply and then recognized the young woman.

"Meredith," she gasped. They looked at one another hesitantly and then Sonora sighed, "We weren't very good for him, were we?" Meredith shook her head.

"Where will you go?" she asked Sonora.

"To Phoenix, of course," said the face so familiar to so many. "I only got word a while ago and I'm there. This is all because of me but I'm hoping we can get beyond it. It's a huge hope and God knows where we'll get the strength."

"So, this thing is real?" asked Meredith, shyly because for once she felt like an intruder into someone else's deep personal life.

"Oh yes, but who'd ever believe it? The movie star and the stunt man."

"Director," Meredith corrected gently. Sonora smiled, fumbling with her bags as she moved toward the limo. Several items spilled from the open duffle. Meredith reached down to help, as even more spilled and there was much scrambling to reassemble the bag. Meredith took a deep breath and pushed the conversation. "Stranger things have happened than a real love developing on a movie set, Sonora."

"It was almost magic..." the raven-haired woman said, thoughtfully, then told Meredith more story of the romance.

The limo driver tapped his watch. Sonora seemed determined to make certain she was believed, so the two women stood on the street in Bel Air and talked about relationships. With the urging of the driver, Sonora finally realized she had a plane to catch, an important flight.

"Will you please tell Dusty, when you can, that I'm thinking of him and so sorry," Meredith implored. "I should have thought more deeply when he talked to me and gave me the information he did. I did ask him and he said to print it. But I should have thought about the consequences."

"I'll tell him," said Sonora, readjusting her purse. "I think we all need to give each other a break. Who knew? I'll be away for a long time, I suspect. I have a lot to process and heal about. And if Dusty makes it through, I need to be there for him. And I need his solace. It's hell losing a son."

"What about *Sunset West*? Do you know what's happening with it?"

"They have insurance—on just about everything and everybody. But I expect it will be released and I intend to see that Dusty gets a fair deal from it."

"Thanks," murmured Meredith. "For more than you can imagine." Sonora stepped into the limo and it drove off. Meredith clutched her own catch-all bag to her chest and hastened to the Mustang. Now she needed some time to think.

CHAPTER 36
BRENTWOOD
WEDNESDAY NIGHT

A sigh escaped Raymond's lips, one he'd be embarrassed to be noticed in public, as he collected his bag and belongings from the car parked at the townhouse home. He nodded to the police car idling at the curb in front, duty protection of the residents after the break-in and its possible consequences. Similar drive-bys were in effect at Cassie's and Ito's apartment buildings. Favoring his now sling-less injured arm, Raymond wrestled himself to the door, and entered with an increasing feeling of solace.

"Hey," he called out, once inside jettisoning bags, briefcase and jacket onto the sofa. Meredith called, "Hey!" back to him and came downstairs, towel drying her hair, and wearing slightly faded but definitely comfortable pajamas laced with images of Mickey Mouse.

"Uh oh," Raymond had to laugh. "Mickey Mouse pajamas and fluffy slippers. It must have been a really bad day."

"Well, it wasn't my favorite one," she countered. "But turned out a little better than it started. That's for sure."

"Dusty?"

"Not dead...yet...." She looked at his road weary face with his tired eyes and changed directions. "I'll explain in a few minutes. First, you've been on the road from…Ojai? Had a half-hysterical woman on your hands and finished the day juggling bad guys and different bosses. Go shower and put on something comfortable."

"Yes, ma'am." he practically sprinted up the stairs, duffle banging against his legs.

Meredith had stopped at the exercise spa on her way home and taken a high-energy aerobics class. She kept an exercise bag in her car, stocked and ready for action at any time. After the class, she sat in the steam room for a while and parsed out all the situations and inputs she'd processed over the past few days. Feeling refreshed and less stressed than she'd felt in days, she stopped at La Croque and put together a real dinner—coque au vin, mélange of fresh vegetables, rosemary rice and lemon chiffon pie. All richer and heavier than usual, but deserved, she reasoned. She unpackaged and sorted the various menu dishes, organizing for a tasty and quiet meal.

Raymond came downstairs a few minutes later, running shorts and a T-shirt over his tight, tall body, barefooted. "A gourmet meal!" he exclaimed. Then handed her a thin, long, triangular package. "I brought you a present to help soothe your day. I wanted to get some elegant gourmet chocolate, but I didn't have time. But Toblerone is good and this is the dark chocolate you like." He smiled almost shyly. She accepted the candy and grinned at him.

"Thank you—you're such a romantic, Raymond. I'm lucky. But first things first. Have you heard anything about who broke into our place? Anything at all?"

"No," he said with a sigh. "Lots of assumptions we've already talked about, but the shooter in custody won't talk at all. Has no lawyer of his own and won't talk to a public defender. There's no real forensic evidence linking him to anyone or any particular case. We can only assume it had to do with either your story and your connection to the *Sunset West* chaos, or someone knew that I was investigating Sterling Music. Neither situation seems vital enough right now to merit attempted murder. So, we're still at the starting point on that." He shrugged.

Meredith shrugged, resigned. "Well, I have a present for you." She went to her carry-all to retrieve it.

"The Mickey Mouse pajamas are a pretty good gift in themselves. And look, a real meal. One of us should learn to cook. But what a treat."

She tossed him an exaggerated frown and handed him an object in a clear plastic bag. He took it, looking at it puzzled. "Be careful, Raymond. You may want this for some kind of chain of evidence, I think you call it. But there are probably a million fingerprints on it. It's been around a while."

He held up the bag and then opened and peered into it. A small stuffed animal looked up at him. Familiar. But different. It was a bunny, not at all unlike the one Ito had brought to the office, but unlike Ito's, fully stuffed and complete as a toy. "Where'd you get this?"

"Sonora Hutchinson. It was among her son's belongings. She found it when she packed up everything to come back to LA. I met her today—long story for later—but she dropped her carry-on, it opened, and it spilled out with a bunch of other things. I asked her about it, and she agreed to let me keep it, for you, but I had to promise to return it. "

"How'd the kid get this? Where?"

Meredith shrugged. "She doesn't know. Never noticed it before. But it has the same little overalls and bandana we saw on the bunny Ito had. It's just a whole toy, stuffed. And not with electronics like Ito's was destined to be." Raymond held it up, examined it from all sides, then set the bag down.

"I'll take it to the lab and see what's going on. Maybe the game company where Ito got his rabbit is using the same basic design as the original toy company?" He pondered it.

Meredith stood on her tip toes and pecked his cheek. "Presents are fun and so is dinner." The rabbit sat dismissed as they prepared and enjoyed a "real" meal. Meredith unraveled her conversation with Sonora, updating Raymond as much as she knew about Dusty.

Later, finishing the kitchen clean-up, Raymond asked, "What's on your agenda for tomorrow?"

"Eight a.m. in the studio with Cass. I'm on camera tomorrow. Then writing the column with her, phone calls and…" she almost murmured, "I'm going to Allan Jaymar's house for lunch and a catch up. He is my agent."

"You just want those two lovely people to pamper you."

"You bet. Almost no one better, almost," she grinned at him. Paco looked down from the top of the refrigerator and closed his eyes. The corner of the appliance still carried the deep scar from the bullet that blasted through Raymond's arm, and the ceiling needed repair from where it was extracted. "What about you, detective? What crimes are you chasing tomorrow?"

"I'm not sure yet. First thing, I have to be at the Beverly Hills Police Department for a meeting with the honchos from the regional Bureau of Investigations. Tom, of course, is part of that, but even his boss, Bernie Bristow, will be there. Not sure what's up. Hope it's good."

"You aren't in trouble for this loan-out to the FBI are you?" Raymond shook his head.

"And my counterpart, Jerrold Munsen, called me just before I got home. Right now, the Sterling case is waiting for more input from the onsite office where Sterling is headquartered, and Washington State."

"You have to go to Washington?"

"Nope. The Seattle office got the hand-off for now. Margo's up there shepherding it. I think my involvement with that case is over. Good riddance." He didn't provide details about the accountant in the Ojai safe house and that once the source of the Sterling's bogus invoices—and their further network—was unraveled, he would likely be pulled back into the scene. It was all part of his test exercise to show his mettle to his potential new law enforcement home. It was also his case, technically, along with Jerrold. But he now had completely unrelated questions about the various rabbit toys. Something seemed too coincidental.

Unspoken, Meredith was pondering the same questions. Later, lights off as slumber was near, she turned to him. "You never answered me—will you teach me how to shoot?"

"No," he said, kissed her on the nose, turned over and was asleep immediately.

CHAPTER 37
BEL AIR
THURSDAY

Bettina Grant's former home, gracefully spread over a small carpet of well-manicured grass, had a totally new look since the days when the gossip queen and her staff, including Meredith, had occupied it. A subtle new addition on the back, bright contemporary color scheme on the exterior and redesigned landscaping helped Meredith drink in the sight, one she'd viewed only once since moving away more than two years before. Bright Leaf Lane sparkled, as always, even in the shroud of summer smog, and she stole a quiet moment from her schedule to look at the professional home she'd known for a decade. Good friend and nominal "agent," now-retired super-agent and manager to dozens of successful and prominent celebrities, Allan Jaymar and his partner had lived across the street from the house for decades, and had been kind and comforting, and then instrumental to her career in the wake of Bettina's murder.

Meredith left her car and made her way to the stately portico of Allan's charming home. She smoothed her hair and adjusted the yellow sleeveless cotton sundress that displayed her well-toned figure and arms. Allan's partner Potty, former well-known character actor from several TV series, opened the door and hailed her. "So glad y'all decided to lunch here. I don't get much chance to see your shining face and catch your news! Thanks for coming." She hugged his pear-shaped form and they moved into the house hand-in-hand.

As always, the ambience welcomed her like a rich and calming bunting. She immediately felt the world melt away. Allan came from the kitchen, walking briskly through the dining room and into the living room. He held out both hands to her and she took them.

"How's our star gossip princess?"

"Tired, Allan. Always tired. But good otherwise. You look wonderful! What's your secret?"

"Good life. Good love. Good friends. All you need." Meredith looked around at the classically genteel surroundings and added, "...and good digs."

Lunch was typically elegant, simple, and delicious. Cold crab salad with ripe, succulent tomatoes, piping hot whole wheat bread with rich creamy Brie cheese, lemon sorbet with cinnamon crisp wafers, a light, summery white wine. They ate on the back patio overlooking the pool and back yard, a verdantly designed landscape lifted from the English countryside. Potty kept busy, using his love of plants and the outdoors.

The conversation was as light and airy as the meal, with some discussion about Raymond and how the relationship was going. Meredith had asked about a mutual friend she had not seen in a long time and Allan's face clouded. "You don't know? He passed two months ago from complications from AIDS. Just one of four friends in the past year." Meredith squeezed her eyes shut and shuddered.

"So many of our colleagues and friends. I just finished a long special piece about AIDS and Hollywood for the syndicate. It's getting a lot of play."

"I guess Potty and I are lucky that we've been in a monogamous relationship for a long time now," said Allan, shaking his head. Silence took the air as the trio toyed with their dessert.

"So, tell me," said Allan, smiling and perking up, looking at the attractive journalist enjoying the summer garden. "How's the gossip network going?"

Meredith settled back in the colorful, heavily tufted patio chair and took a deep breath. "It's going as well as it can, Allan, considering we were band-aiding together two people's careers, and salvaging a super successful gossip train to keep it on its forward moving track."

"But…," interjected Allan.

"Even in two years, times have changed dramatically. Partly because of Cassie and I and partly because of the Hollywood news market. My assessment is that our favorite editors still carry us because they like us, and people do read about Hollywood. But between *People, Entertainment Tonight* and the myriad talk shows now swarming around what used to be 'gossip,' our value is diminishing. We aren't on the inside front cover of newspapers' second sections any longer. We're on the back pages and often edited down. When we have seriously breaking stories, we get attention, but the day-to-day columns aren't valued so much. And, neither Cassie nor I are Bettina Grant. Not in style and not in name. Our TV shows are growing—slowly— in subscribers but the talk shows themselves have their own Hollywood experts now as well." She took a breath and watched Allan fold his hands on the table and lean forward. The sun glimmered off his silver-white hair that framed a bald spot, larger since Meredith had last seen him.

"So, you're worried that your job is in jeopardy, again?"

"No. I think that as long as there is a column to be had, we're the best there is, and Russ will always tend to keep 'us,' whoever that may be, around. My worry is that writing about what's left of 'traditional' gossip columnist gossip today is really unsatisfying for everyone, even the readers. There's so much of it—in the supermarket aisles, on TV, everywhere. Allan, you know that from the start, my aptitude has been in more traditional journalism and longer form articles and stories. But I forged forward and then linked up with Cassie to hold on to the top spot in the column and gossip field. Maybe Bettina's passion and verve for it made it stellar, or seem so, or maybe even she would be unsettled with it by now. Both Cassie and I thought this would be like it always used to be. Lots of meaty interviews, explosive exclusives and drama in stories, good deep journalism. There's drama in the entertainment industry. Trust me, the last month has driven that point home for me. But the essence of the drama is everywhere, exploited in the rag weekly tabloids, on TV talk shows, even local newspapers carrying their own versions of the stories."

Allan regarded her curiously. "What happened in the last month?" he asked. Meredith exuded a deep sigh and Potty excused himself to fetch iced tea. By the time he returned, Meredith had begun her narrative of the entire *Sunset West* saga from the moment she received Dusty's three a.m. call to her discussion with Sonora the day before.

"And, a really terrifying nighttime break-in by someone who seemed intent on shooting one of us. No one seems to know who he was, why he was there or whether T.K. or I was the intended target."

The shimmering tea glasses were on their second filling and Potty was settled into his chair, spellbound, as she went on to describe the strange encounters with the drug enforcement agent. "I'm so paranoid now I even asked Raymond to teach me to shoot a gun!"

"And what did he say to that?" mused Allan.

"No. Emphatically. But every turn I take seems to be laced with crime, mostly drugs of some kind." She explained about the music case Cassie had happened onto and Raymond was actively working, about the heroin and toy rabbits, "and of course drugs are apparently the engines behind the break-in and shooting at our house, Carlton's death, Dusty's abduction…."

Allan chuckled. "Well, the entertainment industry has always loved a great rallying point around a trendy sin. But it should be good fodder for an investigative journalist. I can see a bunch of stories that usually would have you salivating. What's changed?"

"The death in New Mexico, an intruder wounding my…my…whatever you call him…." Both men smiled at her stumble.

"What do you call him?" chided Potty.

"I don't know. We're too old for boyfriend and girlfriend…beside the point."

"I think the question here," Allan interjected, "is 'what do you want to do, Merri?' Who do you want to be? You've had a taste of the summit of the peak. You and Cassie are the most widely syndicated Hollywood gossip columnists. It comes with all the pomp and glamour, but also with some mandates. Bettina wore the mantle well. She loved the trappings, the spotlight and the acclaim. And the timing was perfect in so many ways. It might not be so now."

"I like some of it. Not all of it. I love the good introspective and investigative work. I feel a little insignificant visiting daytime TV sets and asking actors what's new?"

"Here's an exercise," said Allan, standing up and pacing on the flagstone. "With all the danger and assaults on yourself, friends and family, ask yourself—what are the three most important elements in your personal life—for whom or what you would risk another assault, or even take a bullet. Your personal life. Think about that while I use the loo. I'll be right back."

Meredith wrinkled her brow as she worked to process the challenges Allan had posed.

Potty reached over and placed his hands on one of hers. "Merri. Don't get addicted to the sugar on the grapefruit." She looked at him puzzled. "Lots of meat and juiciness in show business, but hard to get down to it sometimes because of the treacle surrounding it."

Allan returned carrying a piece of paper and a pen. "Have you decided? Here, write down the three. Writing sometimes embeds a commitment more fully. It helps when confusion threatens." She wrote a small list without hesitation.

"One: My own integrity. I want my family, friends and colleagues to know I'm a good and true person, one who cares honestly...about everything. Allan, Potty, you're part of that. Two: T.K. Raymond," she hesitated a moment then added, "and maybe along with him, my cat Paco. Three: My passion for writing and the ability to follow it."

"See how easy that was," said Allan. "Now remember those three elements as you make decisions moving forward. But here are three more, and then we have to let you go back to work. Of your work, what three things are the most satisfying and enjoyable."

Meredith thought for a few moments and then thoughtfully wrote down, "Writing well about good material, respect and acceptance of my colleagues and peers, and making a good income that rewards my value."

"Well done!" said Allan. "Does that help you?" Meredith nodded her head slowly, looked up at him with a wide grin. "Now, get out of here so we can clean up the dishes and get our nap. But I'm thinking I'm due a call to Russ. Haven't talked with him in a few months, not since the last time he was out here. Just checking in on the progress. You need to do the same thing with me, Merri. Keep me abreast of how things are going and what changes you see coming."

"I'd like to meet your detective," Potty offered at the door. "All we've ever seen of him is in crisis. The day of Bettina's death, your assault in the office. How about a small backyard barbeque on Labor Day?" Allan enthusiastically agreed. Meredith promised to call them with an answer later that evening and left feeling more grounded than she had for a long time.

Pressure, indecision, even anxiety rested heavily on Raymond's shoulders as he left the Los Angeles Commercial Club, following an older tall, slightly bent man providing continuing narrative of the Club's history. A traditional old-school professional dining and social establishment, LACom, as it was known, had for decades, hosted executives, politicians, bankers and lawyers, even a variety of white-collar criminals in a leather and wood ambience as fashionably patronized in the 1950s as the 1980s. Truthfully, Raymond could have cared less. In fact, he wanted to escape back to the less imposing confines of the West Side. And he had work to do. But Bernard Bristow was the big dog of the Special Investigative Unit under which Raymond worked. He was Tom Beltrom's boss, and a lot of people's boss. And he had dropped a sack-load of decision on Raymond.

The early morning meeting in Beverly Hills had been short and succinct and offered no insight into the break-in of the townhouse. Raymond suspected the incident was pushed to a back burner in the case load simply because no one had any handle on its source. But the meeting did result in Bristow asking Raymond for a ride back to downtown headquarters. He couldn't really say "no." On the road, Bristow had put forth the real reason for the meeting: Reorganization of the unit, no surprise as it had been announced at the earlier briefing. But what that reorganization meant was significant to Raymond and to his younger side-kick Marty Escobar. The special cases duo would join two other uniquely focused detective groups to form a larger "Special Cases" Unit. It would report directly to Bristow who now reported to the chief of police. T.K. Raymond was invited to head the Special Cases Unit. His current supervisor, Tom, would be retiring.

"It's your choice, T.K.," said Bristow, a long-time colleague of Raymond's, one he valued and enjoyed, but also knew to be an eccentric task master. "But it comes with some reservations for a guy like you." Raymond's curiosity was piqued. "You won't be so much of a field cowboy. You'd have a bunch of hot shots working for you and some in specialties not your own. You'd have to wear your grown-up suit at least once a week for briefings and you'd have to play nice with the Chief of Police, the D.A.'s office and the governor." Bristow looked over at Raymond, who was deftly maneuvering his sleek car through LA traffic.

"Field cowboy. Huh. Location? Travel? Salary?" Raymond ticked off his questions. "And what happens if I say 'no?'"

"Last first. We'd find another slot for your grade and talents, or you might want to work for whoever the new guy turns out to be. Then, the new guy would probably have a large say in where the offices are located. All of the investigators who would be included live all over the LA basin right now and I doubt anyone is moving. We don't have room for you all downtown and wouldn't want you there anyhow. So, that's up for negotiation. This position is an executive one so there'll be some travel. What and why? Don't know. And salary. Well, if you're interested, let's talk more when you're ready. What else?"

The conversation continued over lunch, then Bristow asked to be dropped off on a corner in downtown LA, saying he wanted to walk a few blocks back to the office. Raymond headed west to his own headquarters. FBI field cowboy or "High Profile" exec? He found himself wondering what profile would work best with Meredith. But then he wondered what profile Meredith would be wearing at that time.

☆☆☆

Meredith was also in her car, parked on a street off Bright Leaf Lane in Bel Air. When she left Allan's house it was two o'clock and the car phone brought her upright. Reuben was on time. "Where are you?" he asked.

"In Bel Air. About twenty-five minutes from my office this time of day."

"I'll wait for you at the Frog Bar place then." He hung up.

When she slipped into the familiar bar she saw Reuben in a corner booth again. She sat down quickly and said, "So, tell me something I don't know."

"Well, you probably know your friend Dusty was found and is recovering in the hospital." She nodded.

"And...," she prompted. "Who took him, why? What's this got to do with Carlton's death? You're supposed to be the drug expert, the investigator's investigator on all drug things around *Sunset West*."

"And that's the issue," Reuben spoke up, pulling his sunglasses from his smooth face and looking her intently in the eyes. "I'm assigned to the movie company. That's my jurisdiction. I'm not a homicide dick. I have another assignment. You led me to some interesting sidelines. They might tie in, but my focus is on the movie company and how drugs relate. Not on recreational games with substances."

"I'm confused," Meredith shook her head. "An overdose death on the movie set which you cover isn't part of your jurisdiction as a drug enforcement guy?"

"The MOVIE COMPANY is. It's a bigger pond than the set." He said the words slowly and distinctively. She screwed up her brow and thought about his words.

"So, the studio, or the crew or company on *Sunset West* is what you are protecting?"

"I'm not protecting. They have security guards. We're investigating drugs and a film company."

"So, are you saying the movie company, or maybe the studio, is involved in drugs—the use of them or the trafficking of them?"

"Users aren't my pond. Not big enough. How do you think these vastly expensive movies get made, Meredith?"

"Investors, production companies, banks, wealthy producers and even sometimes actors…."

"A movie that cost over a hundred million dollars, who are the investors and where do you think they come from?"

"Oh. Cartels? Drug syndicates? Huh."

Reuben smiled a placating smile. "I always said you were smart."

"But what are you doing down in the weeds with the crew? A driver? Will you find the level of involvement there?"

"Connections show up. Especially on *Sunset West*. There are so many missteps and some links that may or may not be significant. You've handed me some possible clues."

"Is one of the linkages Dusty Reed? Or at least his attempted murder?"

"That's a theory."

"And nothing to do with Carlton Hutchinson's overdose?"

Reuben shrugged. "Don't think so. But what I can tell you is that Dusty apparently saw something and reported it just before he left to drive back to LA. He disappeared a couple of hours later."

"What did he see and who did he report it to?"

The tightly built young man straightened up his slender body and picked up his sunglasses. "Working on it." He looked at her, his dark eyes pools of dangerous intent. "Don't print anything else of substance right now. You could say Dusty is recovering and the incident is under investigation. Then let it go. If you think the break in at your home was messy and uncomfortable, you haven't seen anything. And, for Dusty's sake, leave it alone for now."

"Who did break into my home?" Meredith demanded.

"Your local police folks know more about that than I do. It's not my territory, but walk carefully around all of this, Meredith. It has the smell and feel of a larger crime web. I know the symptoms. Don't test it without a lot of help.

"I can tell you something new, though—quid pro quo. Sonora's ex-husband, Merit Sturgiss, was incensed at the poor quality of the Flecha Dorada's coroner's investigation of his son's death. So, he had the body shipped to Switzerland and autopsied there. They found more than the advertised, obvious chemical cocktail in the mix. There was an indication of some other drugs as well. I'm not sure what all they were, but it has caused some raised eyebrows over there in Europe."

"Who knows about that? And what will it mean to the investigation here in the US?" implored Meredith.

"You, me, a bunch of folks in Switzerland, probably Sonora, and probably the authorities in Albuquerque but so far, no one has been willing to undo the closed case in New Mexico." Reuben slid his glasses onto his face and stood to leave.

"You'll have a good story when it does finish. Probably not before." He held out a hand to help her up. At the door, she turned and waved to the bartender. Turning back, Reuben was gone.

"Whew, what a maze! And what's it all mean?" Cassie breathed, scratching her head. She and Meredith stood in front of the large whiteboard on the conference room wall, a network of marker lines and paper snippets.

"Let's land on the locations," suggested Meredith, erasing the marking and starting the process over. "Other than two similar toy bunnies, nothing else seems to be linked." They focused on the movie set headquarters in Flecha Dorada, outlining a whiteboard column for it. Meredith taped a sticky note with "Villa" in the middle. Next to it, she taped a different color for the fly-in ranch located a few miles from the Villa. "Owned by the same people. Used by the studio for its truck parking. Carlton overdosed in the Villa but was playing with kids from the ranch. They boasted they had drugs. Beau's kid saw an obvious bag of drugs at the ranch. Dusty was headquartered at the Villa, left there to drive home and was abducted and left to die. The movie crew and cast were staying at the Villa, a narc was monitoring them, suggested drug suppliers involved with the movie financing or production or…?"

In the Villa column at the bottom she also added, "Drug rabbit found?"

Cassie created a second column next to the Villa/ranch information, and placed in it a sticky note, "Sterling Music and Quality Fun (subsidiary)." At the bottom of that column she wrote, "rabbit drugs suggested."

Centered underneath both panels, she placed a note, "rabbits," and with the marker drew arrows to both panels. She drew a line from the game company to the Villa.

"Someone—Dusty, Reuben, Bitsy the wardrober—told me that there was some kind of manufacturing or 'assembly' work that gets done at the ranch, just occasionally. But it sounds like something mechanical or technical."

"Who owns those two properties?" Cassie asked. "Some movie mogul?"

Meredith shrugged. She picked up the folder of notes from New Mexico and began thumbing through the pages. "Reuben told me the owner was Bert Solver, lives on the East Coast somewhere and has a ranch manager who oversees the operation. His kids—and probably their friends—came out for the summer. Acted like typically spoiled rich kids whose dad owns the summer playground. But we should know who he is."

"So, where's the link between the bunnies, the drugs, Carlton, Dusty—and how did a bunny in drug-filled-Oshkoshes end up with cousins in Culver City?" Cassie scratched her head.

Meredith opened the door and called out to Sonia. "Did you ever find the owners of Sterling Music?" Sonia came into the room with a notebook in hand.

"I did the best I could, but this stuff isn't easy to dig up. Ito helped a lot. It looks like Sterling is part of a multi-company set of affiliates or subsidiaries of a holding company, MNS Inc., headquartered in Switzerland, with US headquarters in Pennsylvania. And switching subjects, you need to know that I just came in from a set visit to that nighttime soap, 'Day to Day' and I had a surprise set visitor." The two other women scowled, puzzled. "John Harmond, the head of studio security. He was very cordial but asked that you please consider the *Sunset West* story wrapped up and they will let you know if there are any other details. I kind of understood there might be repercussions if we don't."

"Not a good sign," said Cassie. "Wonder what they're covering up?"

"Well, let's wait to see if there are more details—probably just worried about the already trembling reputation of that movie," Meredith murmured aside.

Cassie was drawing arrows on the chart, linking Sterling and Quality Fun to MNS Inc. "We need to find out more about those folks." She looked at Meredith knowingly. "Raymond? He's been investigating them." Meredith quickly called to Raymond's office and caught Marty who answered the line.

"Cut it out," Raymond admonished Meredith when she told him what they were doing and the information they needed. "Two days ago you were weeping because of the trouble you caused Dusty and me by what you printed. You're only adding heat to the flame. Why don't you let the professionals investigate this? It's what we do. And when it develops and there's something to write about, you'll be the first to know!"

"But Raymond, amongst us all, the information we've charted shows us where the holes are in the logic. It could be helpful—and it's clarifying for Cassie and me. We've all had a stake in this. And I've had some ideas about the rabbits. It might be helpful if you could take a look at this." She heard a rustling behind silence at the end of the line.

"I'll be over at five. Involved in things here until then. Work for you?"

"Sure. I also have some information about Carlton's death that is interesting," she said, repeating the words to Cassie and Sonia. Both agreed to hang out.

By the time the detective came through the office door, he brought news along. The lab had identified heroin in the stuffed rabbit from Sonora's bag. Ito had joined the other three, and all studied the white board. Two additional sticky notes were added to the landscape, both under the fully-stuffed rabbit from New Mexico. The first said: Loaded with heroin, in Carlton's backpack, not noticed until the day Sonora left NM. The second: Accidentally forgotten in Dusty's room, never seen by authorities, found by Sonora the day she packed to leave.

The star had phoned Meredith earlier in the afternoon to update her on Dusty's condition. "Guarded." But she answered a few of Meredith's questions.

Raymond's mood had lifted by the time he worked through the chart. "We still don't know, though, where the rabbit came from in the backpack." All pondered the question.

"Here's a possibility to check out," said Meredith. "*Sunset West's* co-star Beau Hastings' son was in Flecha Dorada with Carlton for a while and was privy to some of escapades at the ranch. Maybe he knows where the bunny came from? But Raymond, you'll have to follow that lead. It's, as the saying goes, 'above my pay grade.' We can give you the studio contacts for Beau—or you probably have your own."

"But does this have anything to do with the kidnapping of the director?" probed Ito. Everyone studied the chart, but nobody answered the question until Meredith spoke up hesitantly and said, "I've heard that he didn't like something he saw in the equipment shipment before he left for LA and reported it to the studio. But there's no connection anyone has mentioned to the toy rabbits."

"And, Detective T.K. Raymond," said Cassie, perched on the edge of the conference table, "since you've been investigating Sterling Music and its parent entity and subsidiaries like Quality Fun, who owns MNS Inc.? There has to be a link somewhere unless these fluffy bunnies are just coincidentally fashion clones."

"I can find that out," said Raymond, suspecting a connection as well. The question Meredith continued to wrestle with was whether Dusty's abduction was in any way connected to the rabbits. Reuben's words, "…don't test it without help…" sat heavily in her mind. "Meanwhile, let's go home, all of us." Her suggestion was greeted enthusiastically by all.

The last to leave, Sonia was bothered by a name she found familiar. Just before she closed and locked the door, she returned to her desk and pulled out a sheaf of papers, the press materials for *Sunset West* from when the New Mexico story began and put it in her purse.

CHAPTER 40
WEST LOS ANGELES/BRENTWOOD
THURSDAY

"Let's go home and take a run," Detective T.K. Raymond said to Meredith as they headed for their cars.

"Okay, but remember you have much longer legs than I and you'll have to do more of a jog than a full-out run. Otherwise, I can't keep up with you." Raymond gave a thumbs up and went to his car.

Later, as the sun's glow was waning, the two trotted through the pleasant Brentwood neighborhood. Meredith realized how long it had been since she'd actually explored her own small village. Ultimately, sweat wrapping their bodies and breathing hard, they came to a small park and slowed to a walk. Raymond pointed to a bench under a group of trees and a streetlight and lightly grasping Meredith's elbow, guided her to the rest spot. They sat.

"So, Sonora's bunny was packed with heroin," Meredith murmured as she gulped for breath.

"And," Raymond added, "it tested at about the same grade as the powder we found in Ito's rabbit."

"So there is a connection? What's next?"

"I'll know more early next week."

"Well you should also know, Raymond, that Bert Solver, the owner of the Villa and ranch, is also one of the producers on *Sunset West*. Sonia came up with that late today and said she thinks he is also associated with the production company actually funding and making the movie. Going to research that. Also, did you know that Carlton's father, the Swiss banking guy, took his son's body back to Switzerland and had an independent autopsy done? They found more than the heroin in the system. Nothing was mentioned of that in New Mexico."

"And the beat goes on," Raymond sighed, then cleared his throat and began again. "We had this long conversation last week about our professional futures, but also about our lifestyle." He worked to sound grounded and logical. In fact, he was more nervous than he expected. "We talked about the possibility of moving to Malibu, changing up our cocoon life that we only punctuate with glamourous events on special occasions." He looked covertly at Meredith who was sitting back against the bench listening closely. "There are some things you should know right now about what's happening in my work. You've probably noticed changes and I know you have questions about the FBI 'loan.'" Meredith nodded, on alert.

"More than a loan, more like a test—for them and me— They're recruiting me to join the company. That comes with a big change in work styles, projects…all of it."

"Like? Where will you be headquartered? What kind of work? How much danger? More than now?"

"In the order of your questions: Probably here in Southern California but maybe not. More field work, cases like the Sterling Music case. And danger? Probably lots more. The cases are bigger with a lot more violent criminals than aging matrons whose gardeners have stolen their earrings, or a twenty-something bimbo whose older producer has locked her out after smacking her around. The murder and mayhem opportunities I see right now are not particularly major unless you consider Bettina Grant's death." Meredith continued to listen impassionedly.

"More diverse types of cases with lots of research and fact finding. Probably across state borders. More spur of the moment travel."

"Hard to see you in that role," Meredith said, looking up at the stars. "I know you'll be good at it. You're always focused and thorough. But it sounds like a game for a much younger man, Raymond. And I don't mean energetic or vital. I mean someone who doesn't understand what risk means. You seem to have outgrown the 'cowboy' role."

"Well, there's more." He settled against the bench, arms stretched out long against the back, one hand touching her shoulder. "On the other side of coincidence, the LA department has decided to expand the unit I work in. The plan is to add 'special investigators' in highly-visible areas other than show biz. Finance, sports, high tech. Tom is retiring, and I've been asked to head the new operation."

"Same questions: where would the office be located, kind of work? Dangerous—more so or less so?"

"No determination on office location, but if I accepted, I would have a say. My work would be more oversight, higher level strategy, guidance, 'administration'—a nasty word. Probably some field activity and attendant danger, but not a daily dose. More danger from the higher-ups than the criminals. Ironically, the department chief said I'd have to give up my 'cowboy' role. Am I a cowboy?"

Meredith snickered. "Maybe more a heroic super-guardian who can and does step off the cliff, guns drawn, from time to time. But not as a normal course."

Raymond chuckled softly. "I've been called so many things in my life: smart, stoic, dumb ass, resourceful, foolish, courageous, intuitive, clueless, and my all-time favorite— detached."

"I get that," Meredith murmured. "You are the most conscientious engineer of the most dependable train I've ever known. Not that you don't offer surprises from time to time, but your steadfastness is the real surprise for me. I've never seen it so profound before. It's as though you know in advance exactly the right thing to do or say without drama or conflict. And with real commitment."

"I don't think I'd go that far. And what makes that work? Meredith, you live in your head much of the time. No, not all of it. You have an amazing ability to surprise in ways that are sometimes breathtaking. In your work and much of your life, you just move ahead of what needs to be done and somehow you've managed to survive it."

"But I'm good at what I do," she insisted.

"No argument there."

"So what do you want to do with your job choices?" Meredith redirected the conversation.

"I'll let you know as soon as I know," he answered. "And what about you? What did you intuit or decide after your afternoon with Allan Jaymar? Insight on your future?"

"He asked me what I valued most in life, what I would take a bullet for. I told him first, integrity—the respect and love of my family of friends. Next, T.K. Raymond...and in addition, of course, Paco the cat. And finally, my ability to write." She leaned forward, elbows on her knees. Raymond was silent, taken aback.

"That should help me define how to proceed," he murmured, his arm around her. He pulled her closer. She nestled against him, both facing the night in thought. "We're getting awfully close to the 'L' word, Meredith."

"I know that word, Raymond, and I feel it, but I'm terrified by it," she said.

"What's so scary?"

"L has so many wonderful parts to it. But the other side of 'L' for love is 'L' for loss and I've seen the letter switch from the happy side to the other side so often. Parents, fiancé, friends, boss...I'm 'L' shy now, I guess."

"Hm. I understand—completely. I just have to make sure there's no reason for you to be afraid. Maybe be a cowboy, after all." They stood up, arm around each other's waist, and walked toward the townhouse. "Bernie's Burgers and Dogs is a block away. Hungry?"

"Sure," Meredith answered. "Just don't get killed in your new role, whatever you choose, Raymond."

"What's on your agenda tomorrow?" asked Raymond, dropping to the bed's edge, pulling off a sneaker.

Meredith bit her upper lip and answered in a quiet voice, "I'm flying out at eight to Phoenix." Raymond shot a worried glance at her, puzzled.

"Sonora called and said Dusty would be happy to see me. He's weak but talking now," Meredith responded.

"Why are you doing that? After the studio has warned you off any more back story coverage of the movie? And all the drama you've already had from it?" His body tensed and his dark eyes were hard and determined.

"Because I owe it to Dusty—as a friend. And I'm not going out there to get a story. I'm going to satisfy my own confusion, and guilt. I'll only be a couple of hours there and back by five tomorrow night."

"Then I'm going with you," the detective said, standing up and moving toward the phone.

"Why? Don't you trust me about this decision? About my ability to watch out for myself? I've been doing it for a lot of years."

"Yes and no. I trust your judgment. And your determination. But it isn't you I distrust on the issue of taking care of yourself in the presence of people who are extremely good at creating deadly chaos. In simple terms, I have a gun and can use it—and take it with me, to be blunt. I have some other detecting skills, too." Meredith couldn't help but smile. She read off her reservation information as he booked a seat on the same flight.

☆☆☆

Raymond stood outside the room, pacing restlessly. A young, apple-cheeked security guard looking as though his uniform was borrowed sat in the hall next to the door. The trip had been uneventful so far. Raymond's own work was quiet enough to give him the break, but he knew there were big enough projects looming in only a few days. Jerrold, Margo and even he and Marty were on edge, anticipating the impact of them. And he hoped they were still planned out far enough past Labor Day that he wouldn't have to disappoint Meredith in accepting Allan Jaymar's invitation for a Labor Day barbeque. He'd like to know the man better, considering how important he was to Meredith.

And besides, raids usually happened on weekdays. Well, usually. And he needed the break.

Inside the hospital room, Meredith sat gingerly and subdued next to the technology-laced bed where Dusty held court. Sonora, sprawled in a large soft chair on the other side of the bed, was wrapped in a roomy red and black shawl. Her famous eyes shone with concern, but her face was void of the usual flare and makeup. All around, the typical symphony of medical monitoring beeped and hissed. Dusty looked drained. His cheeks were sunken and deep circles drooped below his normally flinty eyes. The tightly-strung, usually smiling and zestful guy seemed like a poorly crafted silhouette of his usual dynamic action-figure self. Meredith had apologized about the printed story that she worried caused his abduction.

"You can let go of that bombshell, Merri," said Dusty. "Had nothing to do with what happened to me. Really." She looked at him skeptically. And shook her head. "I just got myself into a mess over something totally different," he added.

"Bad enough to get you killed?"

"That." He affirmed. She looked at him in total confusion.

"Look," he murmured, glancing around the room. He looked at Sonora who nodded her permission. "It was a simple mistake in wisdom. Do NOT print this, it's a nonstarter. But I was looking through one of the big equipment trucks getting ready to head back to LA. I was making sure they had included a couple of things I'd asked them to take. I stepped into the truck bed and was shoving boxes and crates around when I knocked over a crate unbalanced on top of another one. The top fell off and I saw it was basically full of what I know was bricks of…well, I'd guess heroin or cocaine. Probably Mexican brown. I put everything back really fast, but it bothered me. How was it on a studio truck, from our movie set?" Dusty reached for his water glass. Sonora quickly moved it closer to him on his movable table. He took a sip through the straw. Meredith was just staring at him.

"So, stupidly, I got in my Jeep and called one of the producers. I thought I was being a good citizen. He sounded shocked and angry and told me to get the hell out of Dodge—New Mexico—and get back to LA. Call him when I arrived. But one of the truck crew must have seen me, maybe didn't know how much I found, but knew I was in the cargo and had been digging around. I got about two hours down the road before I was overtaken."

Meredith took a deep breath, her large eyes like deep molten moons of concern, her hands to her mouth. Reuben had been right and probably knew a lot more. "On my God, Dusty." She shook her head. "What does that mean?"

"It means you don't write about it, you walk away and write about the Bobbsey Sisters in the movies, kiddo. Leave it alone."

"But who did you call, Dusty? To take it that far must have meant someone higher up than a truck driver was involved."

Dusty sighed and hunched down in the bed. "Renn."

Meredith clasped a hand over her mouth. "But he's your best friend. Your mentor. He's producing your movie. Would he really do that to you?"

"Someone would and he's the 'higher up' I called."

"Have you heard from him since, has he come to see you?"

"He sent flowers," Dusty smirked, nodding toward the bank of arrangements and bouquets on the sideboard.

"His tag-along Hank Torbin brought them in person. Renn was busy. How Hollywood," sniffed Sonora.

Meredith mused at the mention of Hank Torbin. "Hank—did he offer lots of disingenuous sympathy?"

"He pulled me out of the room and asked if I wanted to have lunch," chuckled Sonora. "Said I could tell him what Dusty had to say about how and why he was abducted. I turned him down, said I'd already eaten and quickly wished him a good trip home." She visibly shuddered.

"Have you talked with Renn since?"

Dusty shook his head. "He's out scouting a location. Hasn't picked up his calls yet."

"Don't forget that his wife Angelina called me and passed along a sweet message of condolence," chuckled Sonora.

"Have you talked to the cops?" Meredith pushed forward.

Dusty nodded wearily. "A lot. But I don't know what's happening. I don't really want to know. Too much to process right now." Meredith murmured something and stared at the floral cacophony. "Hush, Merri. I'm tired and you have nothing to feel guilty about. But don't do something that gives you a new reason to fear for your life. I'm tired. Why don't you send in your detective friend who's chilling outside. Let me meet him in person and then you all go to lunch with Sonora. How about that?"

Meredith and Sonora looked at one another and both nodded. Meredith kissed Dusty on the cheek and told him she'd see him back in California. Sonora squeezed his hand. Outside, Meredith told Raymond that Dusty would like to meet him and he entered the room, emerging only a few minutes later. He wore a discreet smile and said, "Ladies. Let's find a nice place and have some lunch."

On the plane back to Los Angeles, Meredith asked him, "What did you two talk about?"

"I'd like to ask you the same thing, but he told me not to. But mostly he told me to take good care of his girls."

CHAPTER 42
LOS ANGELES
LABOR DAY WEEKEND

"Damn! Dusty had another attempt on his life," Meredith reported to Raymond, agitation in her voice and a shake of her head. "He was lucky. The nurses had him up and walking around the halls when a guy dressed as a medical assistant came into his room, started fiddling with the equipment. A nurse walked in and didn't recognize him, asked his name and demanded his ID. He ran. She yelled and two cops went after him and caught him on the driveway outside. And no, I won't run off to Phoenix again, but I will print what Sonora told me. I have her permission. They have her under police watch." The call from Sonora had come as Meredith and Raymond had returned from a Labor Day pool party.

The day had been hot and smoggy in the coastal areas, but Allan and Potty had hosted the entire news office for a leisurely day around their pool and for a gourmet dinner from their grill. It was a rare treat for the entire group with spouses and dates to spend social time away from work. No one turned down the invitation.

His wise consideration of the group convinced Potty to invite their own new neighbors; a family recently arrived from Japan with an eye-catching college-aged daughter. Ito, arriving single, had a full plate for the day. Barbecued salmon and scallops and beef kabobs were served with limed rosemary rice, a mango drizzle, fat, fulsome garden vegetables seared on the grill, steaming corn bread, and ice cream sundaes topped with an entire scope of choices for dessert.

The day dawdled by, everyone relaxing, pool and alcohol dipping, chatting casually and personally. Potty had cornered Raymond, determined to know more about this man who had captured their Merri's time and, apparently, heart. Allan circulated, the perfect host. Then sat down next to Meredith on the end of the chaise where she stretched out. "How would you feel about going to New York in a couple of weeks?" She sat up and tugged off her sunglasses. "When? And why?"

"I had a brief discussion with Russ this week after our lunch, and I think he might like to spend some time with you."

"Am I in trouble?"

"No. Not at all. But I think you two might have some common subjects to discuss." She looked at him quizzically. "As you put it, Meredith, the last two years have been a transition time and as he said at the start of it, an experiment. I suspect some fine-tuning should be done."

"Should Cassie come along?"

Allan shook his head. "Not now. It's early for that."

"I hope we can hold off until next week—it's new TV season time and the Emmys are just around the corner. I'm swamped. I'll have to squeeze in a very quick trip."

"You know how to do that better than anyone I know," smiled Allan. He patted her leg and stood up to fetch a drink.

Once home, as Meredith processed the update on an attempt on Dusty's life, Raymond had a call from Jerrold, pulling him into reconnaissance duty in Sacramento, a short plane ride away.

"You're under police watch so please don't hesitate to whistle to Marty for help if you need it. I will be on the road tomorrow and probably for the next two days on the FBI case. Jerrold and his team are going into a company up in the Central Valley. Similar raids going on other places in the country. That's all you need to know." He looked distracted and Meredith got it. The weekend leisure was over. Half an hour later, as Raymond showered and readied himself for the next morning's seven a.m. pick up by Jerrold, Meredith called and checked in with Cassie.

CHAPTER 43
FLECHA DORADA, NEW MEXICO
TUESDAY

"A place I thought I'd never come back to," Meredith said in a whimper. "Thanks for coming along. Don't think I could have done this alone and I sure hope this isn't a wild goose chase, or worse."

"Remind me why we are doing this?" Cassie implored. "It seems either unnecessary—or incredibly dangerous." She tilted a water bottle and took a long drink, letting out a large gasp afterwards. "Hot and dry."

"I'm trying to wrap up a story that I can't seem to finish—get my arms around. It started out here with a young boy's death and it hasn't ended with a resolution. Instead, people have disappeared, been assaulted, shot, and events knitted together throughout the entire evolution. But we still don't know why Carlton died. I know the beacon of all happenings in the Villa—Fastida. But she won't talk with me on the phone. She seems to trust me, but when I reach her she says, she's sorry, she cannot take personal calls. I can tell there's more."

"Dangerous?" asked Cassie.

Meredith shrugged. "Probably. Considering the things that have already happened. But for us, maybe not if we're smart or careful. Since no one knows we're here, gut instinct tells me to move quickly and quietly, in and out."

"Well, it's good that both Raymond and Bob are out of town after all their lectures about danger and overstepping our Hollywood gossip boundaries." Both women snickered. "Hey, little ladies, wanna party!" Cassie mimicked a biker who had accosted them a few years before in one of their first partnered investigations.

"I hope that's all the 'danger' we find here," said Meredith. But she was still skeptical. She'd called Cassie the night before and proposed the quick trip to interview Fastida, the house manager at the Villa where the *Sunset West* crew and cast had stayed. "But I'm not stupid," she had told Cassie. "I need savvy back-up. A second set of smarts when mine get fuzzy."

Overnight they had churned out a column for Wednesday, alerted Sonia and Ito they'd be away on an out-of-office retreat, booked air to Albuquerque at eight-thirty the next morning. The flight would take about two hours, the drive to Flecha Dorada about ninety minutes.

"Wow," said Cassie as they pulled up to the Villa in their rented Toyota. "Nice digs for a rustic movie location."

"If those walls could talk," muttered Meredith, pushing the gate buzzer. She gave her name and the gate opened. They approached the luxurious white stucco portico. A young Latino man came out and Meredith explained they would only be a short while. They were directed to an open space along the brick driveway's curb. Inside, Meredith looked around the open and airy entrance lobby. It was mid-morning and the place seemed deserted. Probably no films shooting or retreats in session. "Fastida?" She called out. She moved around the large space and called twice more.

Out from one of the hallways came the rapid steps of the squarely built woman, an apron around her middle and her dark, silver-peppered hair pulled back. She looked at Meredith quizzically. "Miss Reporter! What bring you back here?"

Meredith went up to the woman, clasping her hand in both of her own. "It seems quiet here today. Hope you're getting some down time after the *Sunset West* drama." The older woman just sighed and rolled her eyes.

"We were at the Elephant Butte resort place and I thought we'd take a quick drive down here to say hi and satisfy my own curiosity about something that's bothered me since I left. This is my friend and colleague Cassie O'Connor Ainsworth." Cassie reached forward to shake the woman's hand.

"Can we talk for a minute?" Meredith asked congenially. Fastida looked around as if to check on who might be in the area. Then she turned to the women.

"Would you mind meeting me down at the Crossroads Center—about five miles back the way you came. There's a restaurant there my hermana—sister—runs. Best menudo in the area. In one hour, I'm off duty until tomorrow. It would be easier." Meredith and Cassie readily agreed.

"Do we have to eat the menudo?" Cassie asked, wincing at the idea of cooked livestock stomach.

"I'll bet they have more on the menu."

After prowling through the nearby gift shop at the Crossroads, they found Fastida at a table in the dark paneled dining room. Mexican ranchero music played in the background. "They have good margaritas, too," said the Villa house manager. It was one o'clock and a margarita sounded good.

"I'm an old friend of Dusty Reed," Meredith began the conversation. "I don't understand what happened to him. Why he was abducted, kidnapped, and left in the desert to die, and who would do that?"

Fastida looked down into her food and shrugged. "He left us in the morning and we never saw him again. We heard about the...crime, later."

"But we've heard that the movie company and its producers of *Sunset West* always stayed at and filmed near the Villa for most of their westerns. We've also heard stories that somehow the company is involved with drugs—moving them—maybe selling them or storing them or...?"

"We are only a short way away from Juarez. Lots of drugs pass by us."

Meredith chewed on a tortilla chip and looked up at Fastida. "But Dusty? He's such an innocent. I can't believe he was part of anything illegal."

"He's a nice man and he was so good to everyone and Miss Sonora, especially when her son...was...died. But he asked too many questions, I think."

"What questions? And of whom?"

"The executives—Mr. Bankleman, movie producer who works here, and I guess the other producers. He didn't like the schedule they set up to ship the equipment back to the Los Angeles studio. He fought them on what equipment should be rented from local companies in Albuquerque and the stuff they insisted to trucking out here." Fastida took a drink of her margarita. "He liked to be more than the director. He said he was used to being on the 'front lines' of movie 'technologies?' and couldn't understand wasting money for unnecessary props and equipment—and people—and having to drive it back and forth to California."

"What about the ranch down the road from the Villa?" Cassie interjected. "What's the story with that?" Meredith looked at her warily.

Fastida again shrugged. "It's owned by the same man who owns the Villa—Mr. Solver, Bert Solver. A few cattle, the air strip which is used mostly by guests at the Villa. And some kind of...," she searched for the words. "...maybe importing. He brings things in from Mexico and then sends them to stores in other part of the country, I think. That's what someone told me."

"What kind of things from Mexico?"

The woman shook her head. "I stay away from all of that, I don't know."

"But you're right in the middle of it all, Fastida," said Meredith. "As house manager, you probably see everything that goes on."

"But I'm not stupid," she retorted. "The day I came to work Caleb told me, 'Do not know anything but what our guests need and how to make them comfortable.' He said to stay away from the ranch. It was 'off limits' and could get me into trouble if I didn't pay attention to his words."

"Who is Caleb?" Cassie persisted.

"My boss. They call him the 'El Jefe' as a joke. It means the "chief" or 'the Boss' but they aren't kidding."

"'They' meaning the owners of the Villa and ranch?"

"Also, the producers who make their movies from the Villa."

"I met him when I first arrived on the set visit," Meredith explained. "Were you here when Carlton was found?" Fastida shook her head.

"No, they called me in right away. I got here about an hour later. Out of my night's sleep! Mr. Bankleman met me and gave me instructions to stay away from the 'scene' and keep everyone but the authorities away as well. The whole pool house was off limits."

"Is there a list of who came and went at the Villa during the work on *Sunset West*?" Meredith asked, scooping up a dollop of salsa on a crisp browned tortilla chip. After much hesitation, Fastida nodded.

"Is there any way we could get a look at that list?" Fastida's eyes slid down and to the right, gazing at the cluttered table.

"I can't…would be afraid to…."

"To help Dusty out, did his friend Renn Burton visit the movie location or the Villa the last few weeks?"

"No. I never saw or heard about it," Fastida said with apparent confidence.

"How about the owner, Bert Solver? Do you know him?" Meredith asked cautiously. Fastida shook her head. "I've met him and seen him. The only time he's around is when the MEGAWATT, the company producing *Sunset West*, made other movies here." Meredith and Cassie looked at one another. Sonia had dug out the fact that Bert Solver was one of the producers in MEGAWATT. As lunch ended and they thanked Fastida, she looked seriously at Meredith. "Be careful, reporter lady. Don't let something happen to you like it did to Mr. Dusty. Please tell him I'm happy he survived."

"I thought this was the first movie Dusty had made here. But I'm a little confused. The producers included Renn Burton, his mentor, and Bert Solver. Hasn't Dusty been a part of most of Renn's films?"

"Yes, but as I read it, Renn is one executive producer. Bert Solver, another. But Bert is actually part of the overall production company that filmed the movie. Renn, apparently, from what Dusty explained, was just one investor/producer." The two sat in the rented Toyota for a few minutes.

"The ranch?" Cassie asked as they pulled away from the restaurant. Meredith bit her lip and then nodded. "Yes. I think so. But God, let's be careful. It's not what I envisioned of this trip."

A gusty wind kicked up grit and dry brush as Meredith pulled the car off the road into the shadow of a group of tired-looking trees, forward and away from the entrance to the ranch parking lot and apparent office. "Let's be casual and curious, not aggressive," she said as they walked through the empty lot. The front building looked like a large commercial ranch house but a high, chain link fence surrounded the rest of the property as far as the eye could see. Barbed wire atop. Behind, to the left, was the hangar area. One sleek private jet was parked close by. The runway extended as far as the fencing, both far out of sight. To the right sat an industrial-looking building, seemingly a warehouse. But no activity and no evidence of a human presence. Meredith pushed on the entrance door, but it was solidly locked. They looked through the fencing.

"Hey, hey, what are you doing?" a voice suddenly struck the air. A large, heavy set young man ran toward them from a side door. "Who are you and what do you want?" he demanded.

"Got a story ready?" asked Meredith. Cassie smiled.

"We're interested in the airfield. We didn't know there was one around here. Is it open to the public?"

"Not really, ma'am," said the burly man. "You'd have to talk with the manager."

"Is he here?" Cassie persisted.

The man shook his head. "Not right now."

"I'd like to talk with him. I'm thinking of holding an event in a few weeks. Could I have some guests arrive by air—here? Is that possible?"

"You'd have to contact our manager when he's here."

"That jet is really something," Meredith piped up. "I've never been this close to a private one—so sleek. Who owns it?

"I'm not really allowed to give out that kind of information."

"Is that building over there the terminal?" she continued.

"No terminal. Just part of the maintenance operation," said the guard.

"Do you meet celebrities?" Cassie inquired.

"Sometimes," said the guard. "Lots of movies made near here."

"Who have you met?" The youthful arrogance of the guard suddenly came forth and he blushed. He offered some names and the conversation began. Soon, Meredith discreetly changed the subject.

"So, movie stars and rich folks come and go—cool gig—but is there ranch stuff like cows, too? What else goes on around here?" Slightly on alert, the young man mentioned some livestock and agriculture and some occasional "truck stuff." Both women laughed and looked curious.

"Truck stuff? Like alfalfa or crop farming or…."

The man shook his head. "Nah. Not really, and only occasionally like when one of the movie companies is working. Production companies park their big trailers and vehicles here and I think they help with moving equipment around and sometimes bringing some stuff in from across the border."

"Stuff? Like cameras and all?" Meredith probed.

"Don't know," said the kid, wide-eyed. "I'm only here when they need me, and three days over weekends when nothing else is going on."

Meredith began to pace slightly, nervously, and finally spoke up. "I'm so sorry. I just finished lunch with two giant glasses of water and a margarita. Is there a bathroom I could use?" The thickly set young man stared at her, confused.

"We're not allowed to let anyone in the building or the yard."

Meredith wrung her hands and said, "Oh gosh. Please."

"Hey, we'll stop by the side of the road up a ways," Cassie said with assurance. Meredith squirmed and nodded, but the guard relented.

"Make it quick. It's against the rules. I'll have to walk you inside, myself. I'll stay in the hall in case anyone comes in or asks." Meredith murmured her thanks. They walked briskly into the main office, through it and down a dingy hallway. Cassie stopped in the office and looked around, noticing what she could. She quickly noticed a three-month calendar pinned to the wall; notations jotted periodically on the grid. She pulled out a cigarette pack and slipped out her tiny Minnox camera, snapping two photos of the spread, tucking it back into her bag as an angry voice came through the door.

"Who are you? Where's Julio?"

"Is that the nice young security guard?" minced Cassie. "My friend and I stopped to look at the jet—I'd never seen a private one up close, but she has a bladder issue and had to pee. The large security guy is standing guard by the bathroom so no one does anything they're not supposed to." She introduced herself to the slight, older man, grey hair a bit too long for his angular face, flinty eyes that were, in themselves, frightening. As he studied Cassie and assessed the situation, Meredith and Julio came into the office from the hall.

"I know you," the older man said to Meredith.

"Caleb isn't it?" she asked. "This is my friend Cassie Ainsworth. We were up near Elephant Butte for a conference and I wanted to show her where *Sunset West* was headquartered when I visited the set. Then we saw the jet and..."

"I know who you are, Miss Ogden," growled Caleb. "And I've read your ongoing coverage. Why are you really here?"

"We were in the area and I guess we were curious about the airfield."

"Why?"

"Nature of the beast," she shrugged. "I never got a chance to see the 'ranch' but sure heard a lot about it, so we were nearby and I was curious to see more. Just personal curiosity."

"Too bad about that," he said. "None of this is personal." He pulled a revolver tucked in his back belt and pointed it at Meredith. "Julio," he commanded, reaching into the bottom drawer of the nearby desk, "Pay attention! Take them to the warehouse—back room." He tossed another gun to the younger man who checked it quickly and pointed it at the women. The foursome trudged through the hall toward a back door opening into the enclosed yard. One hundred feet away stood a large metal building.

"This is ridiculous!" Meredith spat. "We're on our way through and made a quick stop. We aren't a threat to you—this time, truly, just sightseeing." He nudged her on with the firearm. "We're on our way out. Ask the young man—we've only been here a few minutes and are happy to leave now."

Caleb snorted a scornful laugh. "Really, Miss Ogden. You underestimate me. I've read your work. You're relentless. This is one story you don't get to write."

"What story?" she implored, turned around, hands on her hips, standing firm. "I didn't realize there was a story here to write."

"Here's a story," he murmured as she took a step toward him. He struck her hard on the side of the head with the gun butt. She stumbled, falling against a splintered wooden railing, feeling splinters rip along her arm, biting into her palms as she grabbed to keep from falling. Don't show weakness, she reminded herself. Don't beg. She'd read that somewhere about being a captive. "This is such a mistake," she insisted as Caleb pushed her through an expansive dirt covered yard and toward a large corrugated metal building.

Meanwhile Cassie had stopped, turned and stared at Julio. "What's wrong with you?" she spat out. "You'll get sent to jail for nothing!" He pushed her away. She stumbled and fell, her ankle twisting and sending a shaft of pain all the way up to her brain. "Ow," she seethed at him as she righted herself, wincing. He pushed her forward, following the path of the other two. "Bully!" she sneered. He kicked again, connecting with the troubled ankle. His gun never wavered from its aim on her.

CHAPTER 45
FLECHA DORADA, NEW MEXICO
TUESDAY

"Well, another fine mess!" mocked Meredith, gently shaking her head, trying to get clear vision back again. "We turned into Lucy and Ethel."

"We know better than this. We ARE better than this," sneered Cassie as she watched her own ankle begin to swell. The two men had jostled them through the dirt yard, into a large open metal building that obviously served for some activity involving vehicles. In the very rear of that cavernous space, they were pushed into a small, long-unused gritty utility room. Caleb and Julio forced them down in two rusted metal folding chairs and tied their hands behind them. Caleb scooped up their tote bags and rifled through them. Shook his head. "Nothing but extra clothes, and some make-up bags. Wallets, tickets and cigarettes." He tossed the bags onto the floor.

"Tape their legs and their mouths?" asked Julio as he pulled more prickly twine from his pocket.

"No, I don't have the time right now and they can't go anywhere. Only two doors out—both locked— and no reachable windows. No one can hear them out here. I have to be in El Paso in two hours—but you need to check on them often, I mean it! And also keep alert out front. We don't know who knows they came here or might be looking for them. Keep your gun handy," Caleb instructed Julio. "I'll be back before morning. We'll take care of them then." He turned to the younger man with a stern stare. "Keep a close watch." They locked the door to the room, then the women heard the clunked securing of the outer door to the outside. The women were left in the dim afternoon light with only grimy slats for windows high up near the ceiling and no way to reach them.

Meredith's head ached deeply in a way she had only experienced once before—from an assault long ago. Blood snaked down her cheek from a cut above her eye. It blurred her narrowing vision. "Cassie can you stand?"

Cassie fumbled in her seat. "I could…but, you know…the chair."

"I'm going to try something," Meredith suggested, her self-anger held in check. "Maybe this will work." She slid forward in the creaky folding chair, standing up, knees still bent and pushed against the seat with all her might and with her butt. After two or three tries, she managed to find an angle and the chair tipped far forward allowing her to open her elbows wide against the wrist restraints. The chair legs slipped off the floor, the metal back scraping her spine and waist but falling down and away with a clatter. "Ow," she cried out, standing up, startled that the strategy had worked. "So. You can do this, and it might hurt your ankle. But we have to make it work." Taller than Meredith by a few inches, Cassie had a more difficult time of it, but Meredith kicked at the chair legs and together they managed to free her.

"Had a Tetanus shot lately?" snarked the tall brunette, looking at the condition of both chairs. The women backed up to one another and began an unspoken task of working to untie each other's bindings. "Those fuckers are strong," said Cassie.

"And they tied a hard, hard knot. But where's my tote? Did they leave them with us?" The two looked around and spotted two bags discarded on the floor. "I have one of those utilitarian pocket 'tools' in there. If we can get down to it. It's in my small cosmetic kit. I don't think Caleb found it. Or the camera—but if I can get to the knife…."

Together they worked their way to sitting positions on the floor and scooted across the dirt and gravel-covered floor to their bags. "Someone should call housekeeping to this hovel!" Cassie snickered. On the floor she managed to reach with tied hands under the flap of her bag, Eventually, she felt the zippered cosmetic bag, then identified the tool and dug at it, pulling it onto the dirt-covered cement. She worked the components with her fingers, finally managing to open the knife portion. Back to back, wrists to wrist, the two women worked at the straps on their hands. Cassie finally slipped the blade under one of Meredith's bindings and with all her strength, and Meredith also pulling against it, frayed it. A few more thrusts up and the strap broke, then unraveled. Unbound, Meredith cut Cassie's wrist bands and the two went for the door, shaking and rubbing their hands.

Cassie anxiously tested the ancient doorknob. Like the rest of the room, it was tired and splintery, but the lock held. Meredith pushed hard on the door and heard it creak. She looked at it for a few seconds, putting a hand to her throbbing eye. Finally, she turned to Cassie. "Is there a screwdriver in that tool thing you have? We're inside this door—it's locked from the outside. I think there's a way to unhinge the door."

Cassie fumbled with the tool, pulled out one small arm, a screwdriver. "We had to remove a door in our place once in New York. We took off the hinges. I think I remember how to do this." She examined the door mechanisms and looked closely at the hinges. Twisting and prodding the screwdriver, she pried the small round hinge top off the middle of three on the door. One by one, she wrestled each out. Meanwhile, Meredith was deep in thought, pushing aside her understanding that this was no casual or forgiving situation where someone would just shrug and let them go on their way. Her focus was on the next steps and the way out of the property. Probably the way that would save their lives. But time was critical. She knew that while Julio could not see them from his usual post in the front office, he was charged with checking on them. That could happen at any time.

As Cassie freed the last hinge and asked Meredith to help her swing the door open, Meredith began verbally mapping out their escape. "The office is on the left side of us, open field on the right. Hidden from office view by this warehouse building we're in. Getting out of the warehouse is our next big challenge." Cassie grimaced as she moved into the massive interior of the building, now empty of any apparent current business or trucks. The two women slung their bags over their shoulders and moved cautiously into the expanse.

"That kid's an idiot!" whispered Meredith. "He locked the door on the left—the one toward the front office—but left the door on the right-hand side wide open. Let's move!" Cassie scrambled limping and grunting as they went toward the opening.

They crept along the building wall as far as possible until it ended and they calculated how to cross an open field about fifty feet to the fence and the road where their car was parked. But the fence was at least four feet tall and topped by spiraled barbed wire. The remnants of the woodshed were overtaken now by large bushes against the fence. The overgrowth had broken down the fence to only about two feet off the ground, but the barbed wire remained intact. It was still the only opportunity they could see to cross over out of sight of the office windows.

Meredith dropped to her knees and began crawling across the opening, Cassie following closely, relieved she didn't have to stand on her ankle. Burrs and rocks cut into their arms and knees. They hardly noticed.

"We'll have to go over that fence to get to the car. That's sure going to hurt my ankle but…." Meredith put her arm around Cassie's waist and they hobbled the last few feet to the clump of bushes and the dipped fence. The afternoon was growing dim and they hoped the brush and overgrowth would hide their escape and that Julio or anyone else would not be nearby to notice them. Using a discarded piece of moldy horse blanket they had stumbled across, they pushed the fencing down hard and covered the rusted, sharp barbs. Then, each one rolled herself over, backward, landing with a hard thump next to the roadside. Clothes ripped and arms scraped, ignoring other injuries, they crabbed to their car on the side of the road out of the direct sight of the office. They heard the distant sound of a televised baseball game coming from the front office, but no sign of life otherwise.

"Where can we go and be safe?" Cassie asked.

"Straight to the airport," Meredith whispered. She could feel her blood surging with adrenalin, visions of Caleb swinging his weapon and worse.

"Don't you think that's the first place they'll look for us?"

"Let's just hope they don't find out we've gone for a while. There's time on our side. Caleb told Julio to keep watch from the office, no one would hear us or find us, and he won't be back for several hours. I'm guessing Julio'll probably be absorbed in that game for quite a while. We need about ninety minutes. We can call the police or whoever from the airport. Not much between here and there."

Her left eye vision narrowing with swelling, Meredith slipped into the driver's seat and motioned to Cassie to quietly climb in. Slowly backing up to avoid dust or tire crunches, she then pulled out onto the road and drove cautiously out of sight of the ranch. Once past, she broke every speed limit all the way to Albuquerque International Airport. Both kept watch behind them to make sure they weren't being chased.

"This wasn't our finest hour," Meredith murmured. "We're lucky to get out of it—if we do."

"Now I really feel like Lucy and Ethel."

"But we did get some evidence. Your photos and I snagged a little bandana that looked like the one the drug bunnies wear, scrunched in a corner by the door we broke open. I grabbed it to wipe away blood and it looked familiar. It's in my bag." Neither said much for the rest of the trip but breathed deeply and sighed often.

Meredith dropped the car at the curb of the rental kiosk without checking it in. Hurriedly with heart still pounding in panic, she yanked a scarf from her tote bag and pulled it around her head, then slipped on her large round sunglasses in hopes her burgeoning eye and face would not be too distracting. From the water bottle left earlier in the car, both women cursorily splashed off obvious blood and dirt, trying to look pulled together as they arrived at the airline counter and changed their flights from the following day's reservations to the last one of the evening, thankfully heading to LA.

They upgraded to first class and moved directly to the VIP lounge. In the powder room each washed down as much as possible, grime, grit and fear circling down the drain, blood and sand wiped from scratches, hair slicked down. Both breathing quickly and nervously, saying little. Clothes were changed into the fresh garments tightly packed in their over-the-shoulder bags and intended for the next day. Soon a glass of white wine was in hand. Cassie talked herself into calmness and held an ice pack from the bartender on her ankle. Meredith was on the nearby pay phone, hard anger on her face, eye swollen nearly shut under the dimness of her sunglasses.

"Reuben you call me back right now. I'm on a pay phone at the Albuquerque airport and I've been beat up, tied up and fed up. You wanna know what I know? Fine—tell me what you know, or I'll print, happily, what I know." Realizing she was grasping for clarity and help, she left the phone number for the Club provided by the concierge. But by the time they had settled into their flight seats and the aircraft was taking off for Los Angeles, no call had come in. Meredith's heart was still hammering from the close call, the adrenalin surges during the escape and the fear of what might await them. Caleb knew who she was and since she was so publicly well known, she'd be easy to find. Someone already had a couple of weeks before in the night. Cassie tried to sleep.

At LAX, they quickly deplaned, captured Meredith's car and pulled out of the airport. "Do you want me to take you home or back to your car at my place?" Meredith asked Cassie.

"Since both Bob and Raymond are gone, would you think me a wuss if I asked to spend the night at your house? I'm not feeling all that courageous right now and don't feel like being alone."

"I get it," said Meredith. "And I can call Raymond's partner Marty and ask for cover if we feel it's necessary. Damn, I wish Raymond had been willing to teach me to shoot. But then I have no gun—unless he left his behind. But I doubt it. Yes, let's go to my place and scope out our chances. We put in extra security stuff after the break in so we should be safe. And boy, do I know the cops around the neighborhood. And we should have your ankle looked at. God, what a long day!"

Cassie sniggered. Meredith looked at her curiously. "You're rambling," said the brunette, "and you should see your face and eye. We ought to have that looked at too. I hope it doesn't hurt as bad as it looks." She fell silent for a moment then asked, "How did you figure out the chair release anyhow?"

"Saw it in a spy movie," answered Meredith.

CHAPTER 46
BRENTWOOD
TUESDAY NIGHT

"Oh, Oh. There'll be some 'splainin' to do!" murmured Meredith. It was 11 p.m. when she pulled the Mustang into the townhouse complex driveway. Cassie's car sat in a guest space, but Meredith saw Raymond's BMW as the garage door opened. "He was supposed to meet Jerrold at the office early this morning to go to Sacramento!" She hesitated before pulling in, but her headlights had already shone in the front window. And she couldn't think of another alternative. She knew there would be an immediate conversation about crossing boundaries.

"Maybe I should head home?" Cassie suggested.

"No. And you shouldn't drive or be alone! And, the good news is that we now have on-site police protection." She pulled in and parked next to the BMW and then helped Cassie out of the car, grabbing both bags. As they opened the door into the townhouse they heard voices. They lumbered into the living room to find Raymond and Reuben sitting on alert, watching the door.

"Ladies," said Raymond standing up. Meredith could tell he wasn't happy and Reuben, the least expected guest in her home, scowled with concern.

"What are you doing here?" she looked at Reuben, then started to say something to Raymond, but he noticed her face and swollen eye. He rushed over to her and gently moved her head around. "My God in heaven," he gasped. "What happened to you?"

"I got hit in the face with a gun butt and pushed down, tied up and left to simmer."

"Told you," said Reuben.

"How do you two know each other?" Meredith demanded. "Just met," said Raymond as Reuben came over and looked at Meredith's eye and cheek with Raymond. "Emergency room now," Raymond declared.

"I hurt my ankle," piped up Cassie who stood, hobbled, in the shadows. Reuben went to her and guided her into a chair, examining the now badly swollen ankle. He grimaced.

"Hi, I'm Reuben," he said to her, "and Raymond, this one needs to go too."

"But how are you here, Reuben? How did you two meet up?"

"Talk in the car—but let's get these Injuries cared for," Raymond's firm voice took control. He turned Meredith to the door, Reuben helping Cassie to her feet.

"My car," said Reuben. "It's bigger and easier for these two to be comfortable."

"UCLA Med Center's the closest ER," Raymond barked. Into the large SUV they piled, ladies toting their bags with them. The conversation was fast and erratic as they sped to the medical center.

"Why did you go to New Mexico?"

"How did you know Raymond?"

"How do you know Reuben?"

"Why aren't you in Sacramento?"

"Could you call my husband Bob on your phone and let him know what's going on?"

"Our Sacramento case wrapped up in three hours and we flew home."

"Sure, what's his number?"

"Didn't know each other but when I got your frantic call and you were apparently already flying home, I drove to your house, rang the bell and got Detective Raymond."

"This must be the mysterious unnamed contact in New Mexico."

"We went so I could talk with Fastida. She knows all that's going on at that movie location and trusts me. But I knew she wouldn't talk on the phone."

"You got a fax a couple of hours ago from a restaurant in...I forget the town...with what looks like the guest log for a hotel."

"The Villa. I knew she'd come through." And they arrived at the emergency room of the UCLA Medical Center. At midnight, there was an eerie hush in spite of the presence of an elderly man bent into a painful slump, his wife sitting next to him holding his hand. A small boy clutched his swollen elbow, tears running down his face, his mother with an arm around him. All waiting. The foursome stopped talking and sat down to await their turn for attention.

After front desk paperwork formalities, Meredith sat calmly in the curtained treatment room as the gash above her eye was being carefully stitched, the doctor trying not to disrupt her smooth youthful face as much as possible. "There, now when this all heals up and the swelling goes away, you'll barely be able to see the scar," said the physician, a guy with buzz cut hair, agile on his feet and built like a stevedore with big, firm hands—yet ever so gentle. "It'll add just a little character to your otherwise fine face."

"Well, I sure won't be in front of the camera on Thursday morning. Cassie'll have to take the anchor chair again." The doctor looked at her, amused. He spread a large dressing over the injury. Feeling like a mummy, she imagined herself at a luxurious spa, and treated to a grand mud facial. With pain killers and a mild sedative, the illusion dulled, but her imagination held on as long as possible.

She looked at Raymond, who seemed to regard the process with mixed puzzlement, concern and just the littlest bit of annoyance. Other scratches and contusions were treated and the doctor beckoned Raymond outside the privacy curtain. "I don't know the whole story on this injury and since you are the police—I won't have to report it— I'll let you figure it out. But this woman is probably well into shock now and likely has more to come. Keep her warm and let her sleep. I've given her a light sedative and here are additional doses for tonight and a prescription for that and antibiotics for tomorrow. She should have her eye checked by a vision specialist. She's strong willed, isn't she?" Raymond could only laugh.

In the waiting room, while Cassie's ankle got attention, the silence between Meredith and Raymond was palpable. "Tell me," he finally said without affect. Meredith was surprised—and amazed—at his calm and lack of ire. It was the stolid Raymond she'd always known but did not expect in this case.

"The whole thing with the producers—Renn, Bankleman, Solver and the MEGAWATT Production Company—had me confused. Renn wouldn't hurt Dusty. I know that. And I knew there were connections between the movie, the Villa and the ranch, but I couldn't figure out what they were. I hoped Reuben could figure it out, but his focus is more on the movie company itself. So, I thought Cassie and I could make a visit to Fastida to see who was around on the important days. Maybe even have a nice overnight at a world class resort nearby."

"And did you get what you wanted?"

Meredith smiled. "There's a bunny bandana in my bag I got from the ranch—some blood—mine—on it. And the rest came in by fax a while ago. I hope there's something telling in it."

"And then...."

"Well, the kids had told so many stories to people about the ranch and drugs, we hadn't planned a full-out dive in. Just a quick toe in. But, well...." She told him the saga of Julio and Caleb, the escape and the terrifying drive to Albuquerque and painful trip home. Silence again took the room as Raymond relived the words and story, hoping to regain some kind of grounding. Cassie and Reuben came in, the usually buoyant brunette now quiet and subdued in a wheel chair, her ankle wrapped tightly and elevated.

"Just a bad sprain and bruising. Whew. No break. We can go home now," she sighed.

"Cassie's staying with us until Bob gets home," Meredith said, then yawned. She looked at Reuben. "There's a couch in the living room."

"I'm good," he laughed. "Family in the area. Raymond and I have notes to share tomorrow."

"Oh," gasped Cassie. All eyes went to her, on alert. "I forgot." She asked Reuben for her tote bag, reached inside and pulled out the tiny camera from the cigarette pack. "There was some kind of an extended calendar schedule on the wall of the ranch office. I think I got some shots of it before the sky fell in. I'm not sure, but I think they might be in focus and maybe helpful." She thrust the camera at Raymond.

"Correction," said Reuben, "I think we need Meredith and Cassie with us in that discussion."

Meredith's eyes fluttered shut.

CHAPTER 47
WEST LOS ANGELES
WEDNESDAY

It was a short night's sleep for everyone, especially Raymond who not only had a long list of "first thing" phone calls he'd compiled for the morning but was kept from falling asleep quickly due to ponderous thoughts about the entire episode. About three a.m. he was awakened by what he assumed was Meredith mumbling in the midst of a bad dream, but it turned out she was sobbing—half asleep—mostly awake. He held her close for a while as she murmured, "So afraid," repeatedly, until she drifted fully to sleep again.

Early Wednesday, from his car phone in order to maintain quiet in the house, he caught Sonia at home to apprise her of the previous day and night's activities. She gasped at his news. He assured her both Meredith and Cassie would be in the office— but later. He'd see that they slept as late as possible. Meredith would call her to pick them up—neither should be driving. Sonia agreed to set up the conference room for about six people at two that afternoon. He called Bob Ainsworth at his hotel on Eastern Canada's Prince Edward Island, and explained the situation more fully than Cassie could do the night before. He called Bernard Bristow and asked to delay their meeting at Raymond's office for a half-hour, giving him time to drop off the film Cassie brought from Flecha Dorada at the lab, and to make copies of the list that arrived from Fastida by fax the evening before.

Then he phoned Jerrold Munsen and invited him to the two p.m. meeting. "What's in it for me or the FBI?" Jerrold asked.

"Probably everything you've been looking for."

"That's good," snuffed his colleague. "Because between Melvin, me and our forensic accountant in D.C., we think we have a thread into or through a bank or banks in the Caribbean, and into Mexico. We think. But we don't have the next connection—from Mexico banking to drugs coming in the U.S."

"Huh," Raymond said. "Well, come in the back door. Park at the burger shack around the corner. Low profiles necessary. And no turf chest-bumping." He hung up, took a quick two-mile run around the neighborhood, picked up croissants, orange marmalade and hard-boiled eggs at the nearby deli, showered, grabbed a pastry as he set out from the townhouse at eight-thirty, leaving a large piece of notebook paper on the master bathroom counter for Meredith. "Call Sonia to pick you both up for work. Breakfast on counter—eat some protein. Yogurt in fridge. Make an eye appointment." He'd drawn a small red heart at the bottom.

Heading to the door he felt a presence behind him and turned to see Paco the cat standing on the kitchen counter staring at him. "Okay, okay. I forgot you." He dropped his hefty briefcase, went to the fridge, dumped cat food into the dish that sat on top of the refrigerator, slammed the door shut and left.

CHAPTER 48
WEST LOS ANGELES
WEDNESDAY MORNING

Slumping back in his chair at the office, Raymond looked around and was surprised to see several colleagues already at work. His tiny two and a half person "high profile" division—himself, partner Marty Escobar and a shared secretary—was wedged into the quarters of another special unit. Each group worked independent of one another, although the full resources of the Los Angeles police units were available to them. Raymond sipped coffee from the paper cup he'd brought in and studied the Villa visitors' log. The venerable Deputy Chief of Police Barnie Bristow was on his way to meet with Raymond and would likely want an answer to the job offer proposed a few days earlier. Raymond, however, wasn't ready with a decision, and anyway, wanted Bristow to attend the debrief meeting he'd set up later in the day. It would take some convincing.

An enlargement of the case grid from Meredith's office was pinned to the board next to his desk and he pondered it as he reviewed the Villa log. It was nine o'clock and he felt comfortable calling the news office. Sonia, of course, answered. "Any word from the infirm?" he asked.

She chuckled. "No sir. Not a peep. What anyhow?"

"I'm sure they'll tell you better than I can. Get a cup of coffee ready for yourself and them. It's a long story. In the meantime, do you think you could find out what other TV or movies MEGAWATT Productions has filmed in and around New Mexico?"

"Sure," she answered. "But I can tell you that one of their TV series, *Donaldsons in the Desert,* a sappy family off the grid storyline, shoots near Las Cruces. In fact, their whole cast and crew will be here next week kicking off the new season. I'll check to see what else they might be doing."

He thanked her and went to the next item on his to do list. "Hey, Detective Raymond," Ito greeted him, "just on my way to work. What's up?" Raymond made his request and Ito quickly agreed to make a phone call. "I leave for New York this afternoon, but I'll call Mel right now before I go to the office."

Deputy Chief Bristow walked into the room and looked around. "Been a while," he mused. "Small digs, lieutenant." Raymond shrugged, stood up and shook the older man's hand.

"It's what we got and it's enough."

"I hear there's a good coffee spot down the block. Probably a good idea to do that. Better coffee. Some privacy." Raymond agreed. The two men walked the few blocks into a more commercial district and sat down at an outside table. "Love spending time on the west side," said Bristow. "Air seems cleaner. I know it isn't, but the attitude makes it seem so." Both laughed as the waiter brought out their drinks.

"What makes you think this whole thing is connected?" asked the senior lawman, after the second refill on his cup. Raymond pulled out the photo of the case grid and laid it on the table. Using a well sharpened pencil, he worked Bristow through the linkages. "Some pretty big gaps, lieutenant." Raymond figured Bristow kept using "Lieutenant" to remind him of the promotion being offered.

"Yes, but right now there are investigations going on to tie those up. And we think we can do it soon. I'd just like you to be on hand to provide your insight and counsel. It's certainly a combined effort. When we're ready to pull the plug on it, your approval will be necessary anyhow. You might as well understand the whole complex web."

"Take the appointment I'm offering if I agree?"

"Blackmail," winced Raymond. "I promise I'll have an answer this week. How's that?"

"Look, son. I know the Feds are rushing you hard. I don't blame them. But we can do better for you. And surely better for your health and well-being. By the way, how's the arm?"

Raymond shook his head. "Never was enough to make a thing about. And I'm too old to be your son, Barnie!"

"Then how's the spectacular young woman you go home to?"

"Now she's something to make something of," murmured Raymond. "You don't really think of me as a cowboy cop, do you?" he asked impulsively.

Bristow regarded him across the table, looked down at the case grid, then back at him. "Up to you. You get to choose what you want to be, lieutenant." He rose, reaching for his cup and one last drink before leaving. "By the way, if anyone's looking for me, tell them I had appointments in the area. I'm going to the beach just to breath the air. See you at two."

Sonia feared what she might find with her two bosses after their ordeal as she pulled up in front of Meredith's door. Raymond had given her a scant account of their previous day and she expected the worst. But when Meredith opened the door, ready to head out to the office, aside from the paisley covering over her left eye, she looked fresh, alert and determined. Cassie came from another room, bolstered by a crutch and a flesh-colored compression bandage on her ankle, but also looking professional and ready for bear.

"Oh! Oh!" thought Sonia. "These two are angry. It'll be quite a meeting."

In the car they told her the entire story of their ordeal, down to the last admonition from the doctors in the ER. "So, you're not mad at Raymond or me? "

"Oh jeez," snuffed Cassie. "No one could get mad at Raymond after last night. He and Reuben got us through the ER stuff with as little drama as possible. We left yesterday morning at eight and got home from stitches and crutches at one a.m. With flights to and from New Mexico, beatings, escapes and terror between the two. And still there was a bed made up for me, breakfast for us this morning, and you here to pick us up. What a concierge."

"I expected a whole lot more consternation, actually," said Meredith.

"Reuben? The mysterious Reuben?" Sonia asked.

"You'll see," said Meredith. "It's all reality TV."

At the office, each went to their respective offices and Sonia noticed how quiet they were. Maybe relishing safe, familiar surroundings. At one, Raymond arrived, entering quietly, anticipating a heavy sickroom environment. Instead, Ito was working with Sonia on his schedule, ready to leave for the airport and New York. The interior sounds of phone conversations, energetic and bright voices, amazed him. Who were these women? Then he remembered not to underestimate Meredith. Like a porcelain figurine, but with a steel skeleton. He shook his head. Then he edged slowly into Meredith's workspace. She looked up with her biggest smile, her hair well-coiffed, wearing casual but professional slacks and a silk blouse, the elegant paisley scarf braided into her hair, strategically draped to cover the bandage over her swollen eye and cheek.

"Thank you," she said simply.

He blushed. "Just taking care of my girls," he answered. Ito pulled on his arm and handed him a page with typed notes.

"My airport cab is here so please take these notes. I talked to my friend at Quality. The company is putting a lot of marbles in this Roborabbit basket. It's their big Christmas product but they're waiting for the final truckload of bunny forms from Mexico to produce the final batch of toys to meet the already overburdened orders. The shipment is several days late now, but they expect it this Saturday and they have the whole crew coming in over the weekend to start the assembly. Right now, they only have about one-third of the toys ready to fulfill their orders."

Raymond took the page and thanked Ito, who grabbed the handle of his roll-on case, his jacket and briefcase and started for the door. "Have a great trip!" Raymond called.

"Call us in the morning and catch us up," Sonia reminded.

"Have fun!" Meredith yelled.

Sonia handed Raymond another page of notes she had from her conversation with the publicist from MEGAWATT Productions. He took them and Ito's page, went into the conference room and shut the door. For the next forty-five minutes he manipulated the case grid on the white board. New post-it notes in different colors, new lines drawn with the erasable marker but still as Bristow put it, "gaps."

☆☆☆

Raymond's outside invitees arrived through the back door of the conference room, curious about the purpose of the meeting. Sonia had set up a full coffee urn and cups on the sideboard, cookies in the center of the table. Meredith had slipped into the room early hoping to stay slightly less visible with her strange facial adornment. Cassie swayed into the room with her crutch and smiled brightly at the group.

She tabulated the participants: LAPD Deputy Chief Bernie Bristow and Raymond from Special Cases, two FBI branches— Jerrold from D.C. with LA's Norm Tallyure—and DEA. "What a distinguished assembly," she greeted as introductions were made. "We seldom see this many people—and certainly not law enforcement and never of this level—in our little editorial office. Legend tells us there might be territorial issues. Please not."

"This is unusual for the rest of us as well," murmured Jerrold, who had brought LA office's Tallyure to the meeting. They all looked around at each other, nonplussed when Reuben Rodriguez entered and introduced himself from the DEA.

Raymond spoke up immediately before idle chatter took over. "Rules first: everything here is OFF the record. We're here to gain facts and some connections in a very disjointed case about money laundering and drugs coming into the country. Maybe the death of a young man. There are a lot of moving parts and we have some of the links here today. Everyone at the table has some piece of the puzzle—including our members of the press, and it was easier and more discreet to meet here than elsewhere. Second: Nothing leaves this room about this discussion except in the context of investigation and law enforcement. Everyone on board with that? I want a verbal from each of you." They gave it. He then turned to the case grid now covering most of the large rolling whiteboard.

"Three cases—crimes, each on one panel. First, FBI case of paid invoices for nonexistent services or equipment. Various companies across the country involved, including Sterling Music here in LA. Astute headquarters accountant/whistleblower and a rumor of drug payments from those bogus invoices. Second, a prominent movie director abducted and left in the desert to die because he reported seeing drugs being transported in a studio truck from New Mexico movie location to LA. And finally, the overdose death of a teenager on the location of the same movie in New Mexico, but possible connections to both previous cases.

"It's complex. So, we set up the flow charts and grids. Some of you may have information to add as we move along." Raymond began to explain the connections, illustrating with a laser pointer on the boards. "Sterling Music, and four other 'entertainment' companies in four different areas—noted on your sheet—paid invoices for goods or services that were found to be nonexistent. All companies were subsidiaries of MNS, Inc., supposedly a Swiss company but run from U.S. headquarters in New Jersey. The U.S. Financial Officer from the company headquarters noticed the discrepancies, alerted top management. She was killed a few days later in a hit and run accident. Her assistant, our whistleblower, collected all the documents he could and called the FBI. With his help, and a few others who've been willing to do some undercover sleuthing, we've managed to locate all the fake companies. Most are in the West Texas area near the Mexican border, and all consist simply of a post office box address...."

"We traced the payments, the checks," Jerrold interjected, "and managed to identify about three of them flowing into Mexican banks. We're working to get idents on the names on the accounts. So far, we're at a dead end until we can locate them and connect them to drug shipments here. We have the rumor that came from the accounting supervisor that she heard the company was paying for drug imports from Mexico. And we have private memos between Sterling Music's financial officer and one or more MEGAWATT headquarters' top management about 'ghost payments' being tracked. We haven't made that final connection yet."

Raymond stepped back to the white board. "Case number two. The abduction of Dustin Reed who was left in the Arizona desert apparently to die. He was driving back from several months filming near Albuquerque to Los Angeles when he was overtaken and kidnapped. Just before he left, he was at the ranch adjacent to the production headquarters, checking shipments of equipment in the production company truck and found a case of what he believed to be drugs. He called one of the producers and reported it. The truck arrived at the company's warehouse, but no drugs were found. Fortunately, Reed was found and saved. He went home from the hospital with guards two days ago, after another aborted attempt on his life. He's back here in LA at an undisclosed location."

"What Raymond hasn't mentioned," Meredith spoke up softly, a rare moment of self-deprecation, "was that much of both of these cases were reported by our team in our columns. Shortly before Dusty Reed's abduction, Raymond was shot by an intruder at home, our home, by an intruder who has never yet been identified. We aren't sure who was supposed to be the target."

Comments arose, but Raymond went on, "Case number three, the death of movie star Sonora Hutchinson's son during filming of *Sunset West*. Found in his backpack later was a toy stuffed rabbit, heroin as its innards. The rabbit was a duplicate of one found at Quality Fun game company here in Culver City a week or so before, only empty and limp, with just heroin granules, but no other stuffing—yet. Quality is producing a high-tech toy soon to be marketed. It's supposed to be filled with a recording device so you can record messages for whoever you'd like to gift the rabbit to. Parent to kid, girlfriend to boyfriend. You get the idea. Quality seems genuinely unaware of how the heroin granules could have gotten into the product and we investigated that. That rabbit was the only one we found on the premises with heroin traces. No other evidence of drugs on the property.

"But…," he added, "Meredith picked up a tattered bandana—very much like the one worn by the two bunnies—from the warehouse floor of the ranch associated with the movie production in New Mexico during her and Cassie's visit yesterday. Another rabbit connection between New Mexico and the toy company in Culver City."

"The board looks pretty scarred up, though. Stitch it together for us, Raymond?" Bristow's voice sounded impatient but intense.

"There are some…elements that have common bonds. MNS Inc., the Swiss company—holding company—parent to MEGAWATT America, parent to Sterling Music, and five other 'entertainment companies' where bogus invoices were located. Sterling is the parent company of Quality Fun computer games where the heroin-infected bunny came from. MEGAWATT produces movies and TV shows, including *Sunset West*, filming in the New Mexico desert."

Cassie spoke up, "Albert K. Solver is one of the principals in MNS Inc., and MEGAWATT America."

"He is also a principal in MEGAWATT Productions, the major funder and production group of *Sunset West, Donaldsons in the Desert* TV series and three other movies that have filmed in New Mexico, headquartered at the ranch and villa in the last three years," Meredith added. "And he's the owner of the ranch and villa, where Carlton Hutchinson died." She noticed the frowns and thoughtful stares of everyone around the table.

"Hate to see the other guy," muttered Bristow, aside to Meredith. She self-consciously laid a palm against her wrapped cheek and eye.

"Long story and you don't want to see him."

Raymond took a sip of coffee and started in again. "Then there's the rabbits themselves. We first found heroin powder in a limp bunny toy one of our media members here was given from a friend who works at Quality. The unstuffed forms are the ones they use for their new toy product. We tested and tested other rabbit toys and forms, but found no other evidence of drugs, as I already said. Then, a fully loaded bunny—same materials, same outfit, obviously same manufacturer—came from the infamous Villa and set of *Sunset West*. It was in the backpack belonging to Carlton Hutchinson, the young man who died of an overdose. We don't know where it came from yet. His mother, Sonora Hutchinson, found it in his satchel when she packed up to leave the location for home in LA. Meredith noticed it when she was visiting with Sonora, who had no idea where the boy got it and how it landed in his backpack. Meredith subsequently picked up another bunny artifact at the ranch."

"So, a connection between drugs and the movie location, not sure what yet." Meredith added.

"Tell me again where you got this information about young Hutchinson's rabbit and the backpack? Why didn't the authorities know about this?" asked FBI Chief Tallyure. Meredith reiterated the story and added, "the pack was in Dusty Reed's car. He, Sonora and Carlton went out to dinner and then Dusty tossed the backpack into the trunk. Carlton didn't realize it and forgot about it when Dusty dropped him off. No one else knew it was there. The adults went off and later Carlton overdosed while they were gone." Tallyure grunted his understanding.

"We still only hypothesize it came from the ranch where the boys would hang out on many days," Raymond clarified. "The bandana Meredith found yesterday may have some connection, but there's still a definite gap in the chain."

"Second phase of this maze," he continued, "the drugs allegedly in the studio truck and the abduction of Dustin Reed after he reported their discovery to the producers. We believe the two situations are related, but...."

"Who did he tell? What producers?" asked Jerrold.

"His good friend Renn Burton, superstar and his mentor. Dusty stunt-doubled for Renn for years, began directing the action sections of his movies and Renn put him into *Sunset West*. Dusty swears Renn would have had nothing to do with his abduction and Renn insists he passed the information along to the major day-to-day producer on the film, Steve Bankleman. Bankleman says he found no one at the New Mexico location who knew anything about drugs on the truck and by the time it arrived back at the studio in LA, nothing was there," Raymond shrugged. "So far as we know, only an hourly worker may have noticed Dusty in the truck, but no one is admitting to it."

"DEA has had its eye on the film companies shooting in the Flecha Dorada area, in the whole southern New Mexico area, for some time," came the deep but sedate voice of Reuben Rodriguez. He sat upright from his languid slump in the farthest chair from the table center. "We've had someone embedded in the organization for 18 months after a studio truck driver told his cousin, who worked for the DEA, that he'd seen a case of what looked like bags of heroin in one of the equipment trucks returning to LA from a movie location near Albuquerque. By the time we heard about it, the truck was unloaded and in the studio lot. An undercover agent found nothing to indicate drugs. But it was an alert. There've been reports—rumors—of other kinds of on-site drug activity on some of the locations. We know there are two permanent drivers/truck hands who work directly for the production company. It's their job to oversee and approve every shipment in and out, sometimes drive the vehicles.

"We've looked closely at Renn Burton for the abduction. But feel pretty clear that he was just an unwitting conduit. We're keeping an eye on him for his own security mostly. He's been thrust into the web only by association. But the hijacking of a traveler, Reed, wasn't random. It's opened up a gate we've been trying to pry open for quite a while. And remember that the production company—companies—are more responsible for the operations like equipment movement, and so on, than the studio per se. CenturySonic Studios is probably clean."

"It sounds like everyone has been 'looking into' the abduction of Dusty Reed," Meredith said assertively, brushing away her scarf, which had drooped toward her mouth. "FBI, DEA, LA Police, probably the Arizona Sheriff's Department. Has anyone come up with any ideas of who actually pulled him from his car? Where they came from or went?" Heads were subtly shaken around the table.

"He's 'home' in an undisclosed location with round the clock security," Bristow said quietly. The table settled down before Raymond continued.

"Our press colleagues here had an adventurous day of investigating on their own yesterday. We have some new data thanks to their...efforts." He passed out copies of the check-in logs from the Villa.

"These show the arrivals and departures of visitors to the Villa," Cassie explained. "We haven't dissected them yet, haven't seen any obvious patterns. But take a look."

Raymond circulated copies of the photos from the minicamera and the wall schedule from the ranch, as well as a copy of the production company schedule of equipment transport by truck from the movie location to LA. "The photos show what appear to be delivery schedules of some product out of Mexico to the ranch."

Cassie explained that they seemed to indicate "what trucks were due in from what sources in Mexico, apparently checked off if they had arrived, and how the deliveries were then sent on to Los Angeles-based firms including Quality Fun Games."

"Looking at this calendar, it seems like a delivery came in the day before the studio truck left with equipment back to LA—and the day before Dusty went missing." Raymond reported. "Then notice that deliveries were made the day or night before every studio truck over the past ninety days left for LA. Quality Fun expects a delivery of rabbits from Mexico this Saturday. They're poised to start producing the bulk of their techno-bunnies as quickly as the bunny components arrive."

"How'd you get these?" asked the FBI head.

"Blood, sweat and tears, literally," said Meredith, adjusting her cover-up scarf. "And by the way, I personally heard a statement that 'they,' the apparent group behind the shipments, expected trucks arriving at the ranch on Thursday for a Friday transport."

"*Los Juguetes 'Jolly'* is the name of the toy company in Mexico, headquartered in Mexico City with a production facility in Juarez, just over the border from El Paso," Reuben commented matter of factly. "They make a variety of different toys and toy components that are trucked into the U.S. through El Paso and a couple of other border crossing towns nearby."

Jerrold excused himself and moved quickly into Meredith's empty office to make a murmured phone call, returning a few minutes later.

"So, we still have what Barnie refers to as yawning gaps to plug or connect but I hope you can see how these various cases seem to relate and work off of each other. Figuring out how is the challenge. Why you are all here." Raymond appeared to be wearing down.

Meredith quickly spoke up again. "We know that the head ranch and Villa operator is a man called Caleb. Don't know the last name, but he was on hand to check me out when I arrived for the set visit, and the gentleman who supervised our visit to the ranch yesterday. The Villa house manager called him 'El Jefe' or the general." She stood up, tore off a new sheet from the large pad and pinned it to a side wall with push pins. "What do we need to know to close these loops?"

Jerrold stepped up and grabbed a marker. On the sheet, he wrote,

- Connect Mexican bank(s) to toy company - tough
- Connect toy company to ranch shipments - obvious
- Connect ranch shipments to drugs?
- Connect ranch shipments to studio or production company - easy
- Connect rabbit in LA to rabbit in backpack to ranch - obvious - how?

Meredith added to the chart:

- Who/what killed Carlton?
- Who abducted Dusty?

"Let's not forget these two," she reminded.

Raymond looked around and then said, "Media friends, could you give us the room for a while. I don't think you should—or want to—be privy to the rest of this. I think you've done enough. Let me rephrase that, 'contributed' certainly your share!"

"Tom Beltrom promised us a first exclusive on developments," Cassie said, resolute in every word. Raymond looked around at the group and finally Bristow nodded his head. Meredith and Cassie excused themselves and left the room.

"Oof," grunted Jerrold. "Tougher than I would have thought. Wouldn't want to meet them in a dark alley under the wrong circumstances."

"You'd never know what hit you," said Raymond.

CHAPTER 51
WEST LOS ANGELES
WEDNESDAY

"A lot less turf protecting than I would have imagined," smirked Cassie as the two women sat in Meredith's office.

"Raymond worked hard to make sure that happened," sighed Meredith. "Is it still only Wednesday? God, I'm tired. How about you?" Cassie slumped back into the side chair, leaning her head back dramatically.

"I hope Bob's flight is on time. He should be here in about 30 minutes. And hopefully by then the boys in the other room will be done and we can go home. I can't wait to crawl into my sweats and fall into bed. Or something close to that." Meredith laughed.

"I could probably sleep for days. But I have an ophthalmologist appointment tomorrow to make sure no damage was done to the eye itself. Gads! And we have to cover the new TV season intros that start next week." Cassie moaned, then called Sonia to join them. Over the next half-hour the three charted all of the interview sessions, screenings, luncheons and parties involved in welcoming the new TV season among the various networks and various studios involved in the Fall offerings.

Meredith slotted column subjects over a two-week period. Cassie scoped out the TV shots they would have to tape. Sonia would take the walk-around events, Cassie and Meredith alternating with the quieter luncheons and interviews except those they felt Sonia could handle. Three big evening parties loomed. Two network and one joint network/production studio.

"We'll have to do our best to be infirm yet still competent...."

"And glamorous," chimed in Sonia. "Sequined wheelchair and eye patch?"

"Not a bad idea," commented Cassie. Meredith shuddered. "And the Emmys. Let's think about that. We have to arrange tickets, decide who wants to go."

"And the thing we don't seem to talk about—your month away on book tour. We need to plan that out soon because it involves TV, columns and features," Meredith said with firm purpose. "We can't just hope we can fill in for you without a lot of advance planning and work."

Cassie looked guiltily at the two other women. "I know. After we both get some sleep, let's sit down and work it out. Ok?"

"Sleep sounds good." And as Meredith nodded her agreement, Bob Ainsworth blew into the office, crashing the door open. "Three thousand miles and two stop-overs. You're a sight for sore eyes." He rushed over to Cassie sitting placidly at Meredith's desk and hugged her. "Who did this?"

Cassie laughed. "You wouldn't want to know. Just a sprain and some bruises, and I'm already healing." She could see Bob gnashing his teeth. "And the experts are on it, Bob."

"I've got the cab waiting. Let's go get your car and go home. I need to talk and touch you to make sure you're still real...oh, hi Meredith."

"It's been a long couple of days," said the younger woman. "For everyone. Go home and let's all get some sleep!"

"Come on, Toots...."

"Oh, by the way," Cassie added as they collected her belongings, "we have police protection again for a while." Bob rolled his eyes, sighed and ushered her out the door.

Soon after, the conference room opened and Raymond came out, followed by Reuben, talking conspiratorially. The rest of the gathering had scattered hurriedly through the back door. Raymond stopped at Meredith's desk and looked at her intently.

"You doing okay?" he asked. She nodded. "Okay if Sonia drives you home? I'll be there in an hour or so." She nodded again and he quickly followed Reuben out the door.

As he drove toward his own office his phone rang. Jerrold.

"Saddle up partner," joked the big agent. "Pick you up tomorrow at 0600. New Mexico here we come. Word just came down that the truck left the toy company in Mexico an hour ago, headed for LA through Flecha Dorada if they stay true to course."

"We flying, driving?"

"Helicopter to location near the infamous ranch. Wear your field duds, your temporary badge, bring a vest, your weapon and anything else you need to feel safe. Reuben's people and the locals will be at the party, too."

"Okay," said Raymond, his heart beating with a mixture of excitement and trepidation. It had been a long time since he'd engaged in field work. None to any serious degree since Vietnam. He'd been pretty good at it then.

CHAPTER 52
BRENTWOOD
THURSDAY MORNING

Meredith hardly noticed Raymond leaving the townhouse at six a.m. Still pushing away exhaustion, she rose to her alarm at eight, later than usual, and made her way to the kitchen. Coffee. Paco fed. And a bagel smeared with cream cheese in front of her, she sat down at her desk in the den and called Russ Talbot in New York. He came on the line enthusiastically with his deep, executive-perfect voice.

"Hello Meredith. How are you? You know that Ito is here."

"How's he doing and what is he doing? He was both excited and terrified. A big adventure for him."

"He's fine. He's working with our finance department learning our new system that will come online soon. He's a smart guy. Almost ahead of his trainers. Are you in New York or have an ETA yet?"

"No, Russ. I can't come to New York right now, and let me explain. Allan told me you wanted to talk with me but this week I had one of those episodes you call 'kerfuffles.' She heard no response at the other end.

"I expected at least a groan or a sigh," she offered meekly.

"Would it help?" Russ asked, but she could hear a note of humor.

"No, but traveling is not on the agenda for a couple of weeks. First, I had a little run-in with folks who didn't like news. There are stitches. Then, well, it's intro week for the TV networks new season and it's hard to miss that. If I could leave today and be back Monday, fine, but I can't. I have medical appointments I don't dare miss."

"Gunshots or fists, strangulation?"

"No, just…well, when I see you, I'll explain. I can do show and tell. So can Cassie." At that, she heard the groan. Then silence.

"So, you win. I'll come out to the coast. Next week, though. What's your best day?"

Meredith thought about it and answered, "How about Thursday." She figured time with Russ, however long, would work with the calendar they had set up, and it would give her a week to heal some and maybe lose a little bruising. "Shall I make you a reservation? What hotel?"

"I'll take care of it from here, Meredith. I like the Marina Del Rey Hotel. Not so bustling and arrogant as the west side places. I'll let you know my plans but save me time on Thursday. It's important."

"Should I prepare anything? Tell or bring Cassie?"

"None of the above," he said.

"Am I in trouble?"

"Meredith," he scolded her. "Of course not but try to avoid kerfuffles between now and next Thursday."

Meredith hung up and went to get ready for work. She'd cancelled Sonia's pick-up offer, choosing to drive her own car. She reasoned that, injured, she had driven 90 minutes to the Albuquerque airport in the dark, and home from LAX in normal night-time LA traffic. She could maneuver around her small circle of destinations in Brentwood or West LA in the daylight.

She looked at herself in the bathroom mirror and grimaced. The swelling around her eye was beginning to diminish slightly, the stitches not so frightful looking, but the bruising on her temple and cheek still vividly purple. She thought about the day and aside from a check-up to the ophthalmologist in the afternoon, she planned to stay in the office all day. She decided to use the eye patch provided by the ER and forego the fashion camouflage. Make-up would do enough.

Resigned to her situation, Meredith left for work, determined to go natural—simple eyepatch and light makeup. But as she approached the intersection a block from the office, she noticed the tailor shop in a row of innocuous retail store fronts. She knew the shop and the tailor, Edna Ossif. Edna could make a ball gown from a gunny sack, a soldier uniform from a discarded pair of pajamas. Meredith impulsively swung her car through a fast turn into a parking spot two doors down and hastened into the tiny cluttered shop.

"Oh my gawd!" exclaimed Edna. "Who did that to you?"

"It doesn't matter," sighed Meredith. "Can you help me look at least interesting?" Edna laughed, held up a finger telling her to wait a moment and disappeared through a musty curtain and was gone for a few minutes. When she returned, she held two large plastic bags stuffed with fabric. She cleared off a space on the small worktable and began laying out the contents of the bag. All eye patches or coverings in a variety of fashion fabrics, even sequined.

"You want to look interesting, if not down-right glamorous. You need a lot more makeup, though, hun." Meredith blushed and nodded. Then she began to pick through the eye garments assembled on the table.

"You know you aren't the first person to have this problem, hun," crowed Edna. "I'm always prepared for something this typical." In the end, Meredith chose four pieces, two subtle colors but well-fashioned to look professional, one "basic black" satin with beautifully executed tucks and folds and one multicolored pure glamor fun with sparkling beads. A compliment to any star-studded outfit. Each had a small hair adornment to go with the patch. She left feeling a little more confident and buoyed. Meredith being Meredith. Of course she could overcome this...insult to her vanity. "Just be yourself," she heard her mother telling her so often. As did Raymond.

But for the office and her eye exam that day, plain ER vanilla fashion was in keeping. It would be a mundane day.

"Cassie is taping today," Sonia reported as Meredith settled herself in her office. "She'll be in about 11."

"It should have been me on camera today, but...well, we all have some rearranging to do. One day of craziness and two weeks to clean it up."

"Ito called and just said he was having a fascinating time, learning a lot. He sounded exhilarated. But I'll be glad when he gets back. Double duty for me in the meantime. I've been setting up all of our schedules and interviews during the network onslaught." Meredith's back was to Sonia and when she turned around, she had donned the beaded eye patch.

"What d'you think?" she chuckled.

Sonia gasped. "Perfect!" she trilled.

Replacing the glittery patch with the simple ER version, Meredith looked at the calendar. "I have a column to get out. Can you bring me all the recent items sent in by the PR people? And I have notes from Florida about the concert brouhaha yesterday that sent a rocker to the ER. Anything else I should know? I have to get out there and get some one-on-one stuff. I'm getting my confidence back. And there's a police car following me just about everywhere. Again."

"A couple of things I've noticed about the TV season schedule you should be aware of, somethings to check out…," Sonia began. Meredith made notes in the logbook she kept next to her phone just for these times.

☆☆☆

Cassie wiped off the last of the broadcast make-up in the restroom, stuffed her belongings into her shoulder bag, grasped her crutch and hobbled toward the exit. Her agent Mort Agee seemed to appear out of the side shadows of the sound stage and came up to her with a look of concern and question on his tanned face.

"Good morning, Cassie," he greeted her. "What happened to your foot?"

"Just an itinerant sprain, nothing to be concerned about. What a surprise to see you here," she answered back. "What brings you out?"

The somewhat portly agent, in his black silk suit, his hair darkly glistening and slicked back, held out a thick manila envelope. "Your contract, my dear. Everything we all agreed upon. I need your signature, but you may want to read this over first."

"Give me a ride to my office so I don't have to cab it, and I'll look it over in the car." He helped her to his car, parked in a space not far from the studio door. She settled into the leather passenger seat and read through the document.

"Want to take it home and let Bob look at it?"

Cassie shook her head. "I trust you, Mort. Let's close this loop. Do you have a pen?" Her heart pounded and she felt giddy. The advance was large and impressive and the promise of another hit book—this time with all the power of a major publishing company pushing it—was breathtaking. Mort pulled a gold pen from his inner pocket and handed it to her.

The helicopter put down at a local sheriff's station about 10 miles from the ranch. Donning vests, guns, and goggles, Raymond and Jerrold headed off with a young, local deputy named Roger driving them. They pulled to the side of the road about nine miles later. "We go by foot, out and around from here," he told them, handing both a radio. "The team—a big combined group—is already standing by. The toy company truck arrived and pulled into the warehouse last night. About ten men working inside all night and today with the contents. We're waiting to see what happens next. The studio truck was already in place, backed up to the warehouse. We think they'll be loading the equipment vehicle from the toy truck." The trio took off into the desert and around the perimeter of the ranch.

Heat and grit confronted them on the hike, early September on the sand. They stopped when they reached a visual sighting of the fence, crouching low in place, waiting for instructions from the lead officer, a local FBI agent. With a burst of static, the voice spurted out, "Crates being loaded into the studio vehicle. Stand by...." Intense activity went forward from there.

Raymond closed his eyes for one second and hoped that the crates were filled with heroin bags. It would cause a great deal of embarrassment for a lot of agents if they weren't. Law enforcement vehicles and two SWAT trucks rumbled onto the ranch property, through the parking area, through the barbed wire fence and into the yard surrounding the warehouse. Shouting, weapons drawn and confusion ensued for a few seconds before gunfire was exchanged. Far enough away to watch and hear it, Raymond and Jerrold were not personally involved. But Raymond was breathing hard with the exhilaration that came with the frenetic action. He hadn't expected to relish it so much. Out of the corner of his eye, he noticed a brown truck far against the horizon rushing away from the scene.

"Give me the keys to your car," he commanded of the sheriff's deputy. Roger looked at him, surprised. "Quick. The truck's leaving and I know it's headed for the Villa. I'm going after it."

"I'm going with you," the deputy said.

Jerrold retorted, "Stay on the radio and wait for me and back-up before you two do anything. Hear?" The two men were rushing toward the desert, thumbs up with acknowledgment.

As they pulled away, Raymond used the satellite phone in the car to make a call. Roger heard a series of rapid commands in a level, uncompromising voice, ending with "stories later. Please take care of it." Roger was surprised that the voice never exuded anger, panic or fear. Just a command.

A short distance before the massive walls and gates for the Villa, the deputy slowed down and crept the vehicle forward. Raymond saw a squarely built older woman hunched against the outside wall, a terrified look on her face. But the gate was open.

"Park here," he told the driver, the car just outside the entrance. "We go on foot." He crouched low and crabbed over to the woman. "Fastida?" She nodded, her eyes saucer-like and clearly in shock. "Go hide—anywhere where no one can see you or find you. Thank you for opening the gate...."

"The reporter lady, she told me...,"

"I know," said Raymond. "She's wonderful. Now go."

"Four men inside, tearing apart the office...."

"Caleb?" Fastida nodded and Raymond grabbed her gently by the shoulder and pushed her toward an outcrop of bushes and trees. She skittled off in a frightened waddle.

"Four," said Deputy Roger. "We should wait for the others."

"No," insisted Raymond. "Everyone inside will be gone before they get here." Roger pulled his radio to his mouth and called Jerrold who reported he was a few minutes out.

Raymond slipped inside the wide opening, crept forward toward the portico, staying close to the wall, the deputy close on his heels. Once inside the foyer, the wide breezeway stretched all the way to the terrace. Only a series of columns shielded them from view. Guns drawn, they continued to crouch and move toward the office area on the right, near the open terrace. Their movement, however, caught the eye of an operative through the office's wide window and a gunshot popped, pinging against the pillar that buffered Raymond. He dropped toward the ground. Another shot followed and then a barrage. Damn, he thought to himself. Where's Jerrold?

"Hit!" yelled Roger, catching Raymond's attention. The young man hobbled to a deep side doorway as blood streamed down his leg from his thigh and bullets slammed into the wall around him. Raymond assumed the deputy was hidden well enough to avoid further fire, his gun was still out, and alert, ready for action. Suddenly the young man slumped against the door and slid to the floor. Raymond closed ranks, tightening his muscles and breathing slowly. Jerrold would arrive shortly and the firestorm would be over. He repeated the determined mantra. And waited. Minutes passed. He focused at ready. The barrage of shots began to taper off. He repeated the mantra.

Hard metal pressed against his skull, just behind his ear. He closed his eyes. No mistaking the feel of a gun barrel. "Caleb," he said softly.

"And yet I don't know you," mused the voice behind.

"No need. Just a police grunt." The response was a quiet chuckle. "Not a good day to visit the Villa."

"So it seems." Raymond knew it would be only a few seconds before the gun exploded in his ear. The crew in the Villa office were already evacuating to avoid being caught as the posse arrived. Without the luxury of heroic karate or martial arts maneuvers against his assailant—too many years, not enough practice, too compromised—his thoughts flashed to the promise he'd only recently made. "Don't get killed," Meredith had implored. And he promised.

"Sorry," he said out loud, so seriously Caleb laughed. Raymond heard the trigger click and felt the earthquake of explosion, saw red and yellow streaks and then nothing. Floating in blackness.

"Hey, hey, city boy, pull yourself together!" He felt someone kicking his shoe over and over, struggled to rise up on his elbows wondering if he was in Heaven or Hell, then realizing he was in New Mexico. FBI agent Margo Flaherty stood over him, wrapped in camo gear, a pistol dangling at her side. Against the bright wall of the Villa, she was backlit, and her red hair seemed to stream everywhere. Medusa? He wondered, squinting and shaking his head.

No. Margo.

"Jesus, Raymond. If you'd waited three minutes, you'd have had the whole of the local sheriff's department," she said. "Sonny boy over there wouldn't walk with a limp for the next few months and you wouldn't have had the scare of a lifetime. We have some training to do with this one," she snickered as Jerrold trotted over.

"No cowboys allowed," he said.

Raymond shook his head to clear the confusion. His hearing was only marginal, but he'd managed to catch the words from the two FBI agents. He was disgusted and suddenly tired. Standing up, he held on to the column he'd hidden behind, and brushed off his clothes. He drank deeply from a bottle of water handed to him. Slumped on the terra cotta tiles was the man named Caleb, an ugly head wound, no indication of continuing life and framed by a large puddle of red. Two agents were working with the Deputy Roger in the nearby doorway.

"He okay?" Raymond asked.

"Yeah, just injured—some time off and lots of sympathy."

"How about Fastida?"

"Who?" asked Margo.

"She's hiding in the trees outside. She opened the gate for us. Were there drugs? In the trucks?"

"Yes, there were," smiled Jerrold, stripping off his vest and taking a deep breath.

"A whole big truck from Juarez with cute little bunnies—stuffed full of heroin baggies—and a dozen guys pulling them out, tossing them into crates for the studio truck to take to LA, and the flaccid little rabbits going to Culver City to make innocent cute Christmas toys for kids. Wow, what a concept. You all figured well."

Agents were processing Caleb's men from the office.

Raymond asked to borrow the satellite phone carried by one of the sheriff's deputies. He made a quick call, said simply he was okay. Then hung up.

"What was that?" asked Margo.

"I had to call Meredith. I needed to talk to her, tell her I'm okay."

"Sure," said the agent, holstering her gun and walking off.

CHAPTER 55
WEST LOS ANGELES
THURSDAY AFTERNOON

Meredith stood up to walk down the block and bring back a cappuccino. Columns were completed and ready to send to New York, another drafted for the next day, the afternoon was at midpoint. As she passed the front desk, she picked up a ringing phone and was startled into shock and attention.

"I need your help. Don't ask questions," Raymond's voice commanded, quietly but without either opening or quarrel. "Don't talk—just call Fastida and tell her to get out of the Villa right now. She has about five minutes. But if there is a locked front gate or entrance, ask her to open it first—electronic or however. Just open the gate and get out. Stories to tell later." And he was gone.

Meredith started to interject but was left with only confusion and fear. She realized she was shaking, but also recognized the severity of Raymond's voice and apparent situation. She dropped the phone in the cradle and dug through her purse for her small notebook with contact numbers. And did as she was told.

Then she paced. Cassie and Sonia fumbled at their desks, grasping that the situation was dire and also very deeply classified. Tension sat like a heavy blanket. Finally, the phone jangled and Sonia picked it up. She handed it rapidly to Meredith who only said, "Okay. Good. Okay. Thank God."

Meredith sat down heavily in a visitor chair, her two colleagues quickly joining her in the front office. "He's okay. But he says the villa and ranch took a huge hit from a SWAT operation. All he said was 'It was a shit show. But it was successful.' I don't know what that means, but we're still off the record. He'll call later."

"Cappuccino anyone?" breathed Sonia.

Meredith sat quietly at her desk, rubbing her hand through her hair, loose and tumbling around her injured eye and face, breathing deeply but still on edge. She kept wondering when the other shoe would fall, knowing there was more to the story than seemed obvious, understanding that law enforcement "shit shows" rarely left everyone unscathed. She found attempts to work fruitless, and mostly thumbed through the current issue of *Time Magazine*.

"Meredith, Laurie Shoup needs to talk to you immediately," Sonia, barely back with sugared caffeine, broke into the tense reverie. "Urgent, she says and she's whispering." Laurie was the good friend and the publicist on *Sunset West*. She snatched up her phone.

Laurie's voice came on, truly a whisper. "Meredith, I'm calling from my car, don't want to be overheard. Something's going on down there at Flecha Dorada. I just got a call from the Albuquerque newspaper asking about a raid on El Rancho Descanso, the Villa and the ranch that's connected with it. They didn't know much except someone saw a huge bunch of law enforcement officers, some with FBI on their jackets, converging on the place. I tried to call the Villa but no one answered. I know you've been following stories from the movie there, so I wondered if you knew anything about it?"

"Me? No, but it sounds like I should be talking to someone at your office. Have you briefed the producers?"

"I wanted to see if you knew anything yet. The reporter in Albuquerque said he had nothing other than the eyewitness account, from the highway, of the infusion of feds on the ranch."

"Laurie, I'll see what I can find out in the next fifteen minutes, but I also want to talk with Steve Bankleman or at least get a comment from him or one of the other producers. This may have nothing to do with the movie. See if you can catch him. I'll call you and let you know if I find out anything else. No matter what, if Albuquerque already has a story going, you guys will have to issue a comment anyhow." Every nerve ending in her body was firing on full load as she hung up the phone. She yelled to Sonia and Cassie to come into her office quickly.

"Albuquerque just informed the studio of 'something' going down in Flecha Dorada. We need to jump on this, warp speed," She absently twisted her long hair into a knot at her neck as she barked out instructions. "Cassie, call Norm Tallyure, head of the LA FBI office, and remind him of his promise to give us first dibs on new information. If he's away or noncooperative, Call Tom Beltrom—your first exclusive promiser."

"I can at least get a statement even if they don't know anything." Cassie was out the door going to her own office.

"I'll pull today's column and get ready to rewrite," said Sonia rising quickly.

"And I'm calling Albuquerque. We know the folks at the paper. They carry our column and we've spent time with them when they were here," said Meredith, reaching for her Rolodex and her phone.

Exactly fifteen minutes later Meredith phoned Laurie Shoup who was waiting for the call. Meredith put the call on speaker so Cassie could take notes. "Here's what we know, Laurie.

According to LA FBI's Norman Tallyure, there was a law enforcement raid on Rancho Descanso—the Villa—but it started at a nearby ranch owned by the same person, Albert K. Solver. Several law enforcement agencies were involved including the FBI and local authorities. We know from other sources there were drugs involved. Eyewitnesses in Albuquerque reported seeing a truck from CenturySonic Studios on the premises. The ranch owner Solver was also a producer on the film *Sunset West* which just completed filming near the location of the raid. That's according to your own CenturySonic release. One eyewitness told us that there were shots fired at both locations but no information on arrests, victims or injuries yet." Meredith heard a deep sigh at the other end of the line. "Bankleman or any other producer have a comment?"

"Bankleman's only comment was, and I quote, 'We've just heard about this situation and we are investigating it now.' Not very helpful. He's busy chewing his nails and pacing. He's keen to find out about the details, but most likely more worried about his movie!"

"That's today's story," said Meredith. We need to talk tomorrow. We're just faxing the copy to New York!" As she hung up, she quickly turned to put the final quote from Bankleman into the text for the breaking story. She turned to Cassie and said, "You have to write this story as a side story and for the column update tomorrow. I'm too close to it. We'll work together on the final, and we have lots of usable background for the side feature." Cassie nodded, took her notes and went into her office, then hesitated, and asked, "Who was the eyewitness?"

"The lady whose sister serves great menudo!"

As Meredith settled deep into the cushions of the lounge chair by the pool of her best friend Gloria Masner Holmby Hills house, the sun's glow helped heal and soothe her face as well as her body and soul. Some would call this place a mansion, thought Meredith. To her it was just Gloria's house. The irony of friendship amused her with nothing else to rattle around in her mind that day. Gloria, former college roommate and long-time pal in the Los Angeles world, had married a highly respected theatrical agent, George Masner. Meredith had been maid of honor at their wedding.

"Told you older men were miraculous," Gloria kidded Meredith as they sipped gin and tonics and picked at tuna sandwiches. Meredith could only chuckle.

"No argument or complaints from me." Both Masner and Raymond had a dozen years on their younger partners. Meredith was spending the day at Gloria's to escape the stress of the last week and enjoy time not stitched with work, New Mexico and drugs. "I'll just be glad when this whole thing is over."

"Isn't it over now—with the raid and the arrests and all."

"Part of it for sure. Raymond is due back either tonight or tomorrow. Probably tomorrow. There's so much paperwork and interviews and what not in Albuquerque. But there's still the question of how young Carlton Hutchinson died."

"But is that your problem? Really?"

"Well, it will be someone's since there was no real answer determined and Sonora and everyone else around don't believe it was a suicidal overdose."

"But T.K. isn't involved in that investigation, is he?"

"No, but I am. I was one of the first on the scene, brought in to report on it. I never really finished the story."

"Ah yes, the 'story.' It's always about the story. How's Dusty, have you heard?"

"I talk with Sonora almost every day. He's doing great, back at work about half-time starting next week. The studio is keeping his name on the film and letting him have the final say on the editing."

"That's great."

"Well, Sonora wouldn't have it any other way and she is…kind of the queen bee and all…．"

"Being the super star at the studio," smiled Gloria. The two women sunk deeper into their lounges for a while until Gloria hesitantly spoke up.

"So, what's with Raymond? Status quo? Future?"

"No, not status quo. Definitely future. But we're both closed in at the townhouse. He'd like to get back to Malibu. Misses the beach. And I feel like I've outgrown the townhouse in so many ways. But it has been my cocoon of safety and sanity for a lot of years. Hard to give it up. But life seems very expanded now."

"No ring?"

Meredith laughed heartily. "No and none desired. I'm fine with the relationship as it is right now, good and solid with no demands." Gloria rolled her eyes. "The only thing we're contemplating right now is whether to move into the Malibu house. It's always been a great beach house—what it was always intended to be. But now with Will and Sophie living there and all the work demands, it seems just too small and not quite as accommodating as it could be."

"Remodel?"

"Somehow Raymond kind of feels about that place as I feel about the townhouse. But we don't know exactly how to fix that. Maybe too much going on to focus. Maybe we're reluctant to say goodbye to the past."

"You two have hunkered down for nearly three years. Almost hiding out. I think it's time to stop grieving for…well, the guy who died from your early Hollywood days, T.K.'s late wife Lily, Bettina Grant and her legacy—and her demands that keep you on the hamster wheel even from her grave."

"Well, change is coming, I can see that," smirked Meredith. "My boss from the syndicate, Russ Talbot, wanted me in New York this week but with the eye and bruises, and the breaking story and then the network's new season intros, I had to turn him down so he's coming here."

"Is everything okay?" Gloria sat up on alert.

Meredith shrugged. "I guess. He says so. Alan has talked with him and he also tells me everything is fine. But I can tell that things are about to change."

"For T.K. as well, I guess. He told George he's being recruited heavily by the FBI."

Jolted awake, Meredith sat up. "What? Recruited? That's news to me. I thought he was just on loan for a case he's working." Images quickly filled her mind—the break-in and gunfire in the townhouse, the raid and shoot out at the ranch, the red-headed bitch Margo, and more. Meredith sat up so abruptly she jostled her drink.

"Don't get mad yet. He may have dismissed the whole thing. It's been a while since he brought it up. He's a big boy—a veteran professional, not a green recruit. He knows what he's doing, Meredith. Remember, he's the older guy, the mature dude." Meredith closed her eyes and thought of the color blue. Someone told her it was the color of relaxation.

"George and I are talking about escaping the maddening crowd of Hollywood over Thanksgiving, going to Hawaii for a week. Why don't you two come with us? Great break!" Meredith flashed on palm trees, gentle trade winds, luxurious accommodations, maybe even a hot tub, spa, a quiet beach and no phones, celebrities or deadlines.

"I think it's the 'madding' crowd—Is there more gin?" she asked.

CHAPTER 57
FLECHA DORADA, NEW MEXICO
SATURDAY NIGHT

There's something about a spartan no-frills motel along a desert highway that offers a uniquely private kind of solace and sanctuary to the weary traveler. T.K. Raymond was that traveler. Saturday night he reflected on the special hominess of his plain vanilla room at the Wee Cactus Motel on the interstate just outside Flecha Dorada. Two small slivers of soap, a small vial of shampoo and mini-bar accessories that included a plastic ice bucket and ice bag with two plastic glasses.

After the raid, there had been two full days of interviews with the detainees from the ranch and the Villa and long discussions with other staff who were not involved in the raid but had information and perspective, including Fastida. Paperwork, reports written and sent to the LA bosses, follow-up meetings with the locals, his FBI colleagues. He could have driven to Albuquerque and flown home to LA later Saturday night, but chose to stay in the quiet of the simple motel and catch the helicopter ride home the next day.

After dinner with Jerrold and the local sheriff, Raymond picked up a six pack of beer, split it with Jerrold, and headed to his own room. He showered off a complex day, hoped the water would wash down the drain the memory of the gun against his head and the heavy heart it had caused. He settled against the pillows of the bed, ran a hand through his damp hair and called Meredith. As agreed, she called him back on a less expensive connection. Nestled into the sofa, wrapped in her oldest bathrobe and sipping chamomile tea, she felt a profound relief to hear what sounded like a healthy voice.

She had questions. He had some answers. Some he could not provide, though, because of the rules of investigation. She understood. He had disclosed his petrifying moment with Caleb. He didn't mention the name Caleb, nor the fact that Margo had saved his life. But he said, "It was such a clarifying moment."

"How so?" she prodded.

"I can't even articulate it yet. But a good night's sleep and some quiet time here in the therapeutic Wee Cactus Motel and I should be able to tamp down the cacophony in my brain." He explained the confusion between his anticipatory exhilaration of the raid on the ranch—the hunger for the action and friction in pursuit of righteousness, of "victory." "It was the thrill—the glory—of the hunt. Disgusting but satisfying." And the sublime sense of relief when he realized he had not been shot through the head and was actually alive and unharmed. "Maybe a part of the hunt metaphor," he said. "Winning the gamble. But there was so much more to the relief—visions of people and places and experiences I never thought of as special or important. Such irony." He thought silently for a moment. "I was shocked at how unprepared I was for what I'd be facing. Both physically and mentally."

Meredith listened and gave feedback in simple verbal nods and clucks. It seemed an important moment for Raymond. He asked her about her day and she laughed. "Too mundane to even talk about. As you know we released lots of info that was given to us—properly and legitimately—by Tom and Barnie and on and on. The doc said my eye is fine, a little traumatized and gave me some ointment. Nothing serious. The bruises are healing and I have an appointment to see the stitch doc next week. I got some great colorful haute couture eye patches...."

"I figured you'd find a way to merchandise that injury," snarked Raymond.

"Something occurred to me, Raymond. I'm puzzled." She interjected.

"Tell me," Raymond said, now on alert. Meredith's hunches, tied to her precise memory, usually bore fruit.

"Fastida told me that she was called to the Villa almost as quickly as Sonora found her son's body and cried for help. The producer Steve Bankleman called her, briefly met her and told her to keep everyone from the pool house except the sheriff's people. To talk to NO ONE about anything. Refer everything to the sheriff's office until the studio was on board. Dusty told me, later that morning, that Bankleman was at that moment on his way to New Mexico from LA. And, Bankleman, himself, mentioned he'd flown back immediately when he got word."

Raymond had no real context and needed to process the puzzle himself. "Let's not make any rash assumptions. The whole situation was a big blow to everyone and must have been a shock to all, including Fastida. We'll play it out when I get back."

Meredith demurred to her previous recounting of the heavy work schedule coming up with the introductions to the new TV season.

"Am I involved? Do I have to go?"

"Only if you want. Maybe one evening when...," she described one elegant network dinner party and presentation she thought he might enjoy.

"Another night, while you're busy, I'll take an evening with Will. Sophie's going to visit family for a couple of days. Will and

I haven't spent as much time together as I'd like. This is a good opportunity." Meredith understood fully. There were decisions they'd discussed recently but the moment seemed to have arrived when resolution seemed imminent.

The two talked like high school buddies for nearly an hour, Raymond relaxed into the thin, worn spread adorned with faded desert scenes over flimsy bedding, Meredith against the sofa in the comfort and familiarity of her living room. "I'm reluctant to say good night and hang up," he said. "We're due out of here early tomorrow morning and I should be home mid-day. Weather permitting. I'll call when we get in. I miss you. Someday they'll make a phone that lets people see each other when they talk."

"Raymond?" Meredith responded in a quieter, provocative tone. "Tell me what you're wearing."

CHAPTER 58
WEST LOS ANGELES
MONDAY

Monday morning the world seemed to normalize for the news office and families. The introduction to the new network TV season was beginning with a luncheon and series of interviews for Meredith and Cassie. This year they shared the work with Sonia who was becoming adept at simple stories and interviews. Ito had returned from New York aglow from the respect and attention he'd received from the media syndicate. Yet he promised to continue as the office's gourmet barista since no one else could brew coffee as savory as his. And he smiled in a way that suggested he knew something no one else did. That was just Ito.

Meredith's swollen eye and lid had receded to the point where a patch and some make-up almost brought back her usual porcelain face. She was relieved to be concentrating on the normal activity of the office and the news. Cassie used a brand-new cane instead of the clumsy crutch, compliments of Bob who found it in an antique shop on Melrose Avenue. Polished rosewood with a silver mermaid on the top. Her ankle improved daily. And Sonia was flush with light in her eyes from a pleasant weekend with Art and their two boys.

Raymond had come home on Sunday afternoon and by Monday morning was settled in, focused and ready to go back to work. He was heading to meetings with the LAPD brass for debriefing among other things. Jerrold had already left for D.C., Margo following independently.

Warrants and FBI raids had taken place in companies across the country, a total of twelve, one of them Sterling Music. A major drug network had been revealed. The perpetrator companies, subsidiaries of Swiss company MNS Inc., paid hundreds of thousands of dollars over several years to nonexistent vendors through bogus invoices. The money, collected through post office boxes and copy shop mailboxes, went into Mexican bank accounts from which drugs were purchased from cartels, smuggled into the U.S. mostly through Juarez/El Paso, TX, and San Luis/Sonora/Nogales, AZ. Other more covert MNS organizations then sold the drugs on the U.S. market at prices many times higher than they originally paid. The toy rabbits from Juarez came into the U.S., heroin packed inside the toy bunnies, separated from them in Flecha Dorada and delivered to LA through the movie company trucks. The deflated toys made an innocent run to the Culver City techno toy company that had no knowledge of the perilous route. But it was only one of many such networks, many yet to be uncovered. But it had far reaching impact on the movie industry. MEGAWATT Productions was highly respected, visible and well-integrated into various communities in New Mexico where their TV shows and movies were filmed. Albert Solver, "Bert," was a principal of MEGAWATT, also owned the ranch and Villa, and was a producer on many of their company's projects, including *Sunset West*. His projects were overseen and distributed by several major film companies which were not complicit in the web.

Bert was now in custody along with many of his colleagues and a number of operatives in Flecha Dorada. In Los Angeles, Sterling Music's future was uncertain, as were the futures of other companies across the country implicated by the various sting operations. But there were other similar networks laundering money, smuggling drugs through shadow enterprises.

From the outside, it seemed like a completed case, a closed story. Yet they all knew there was one seam waiting to be stitched closed. Young Carlton's death—how and why—and what the rabbit in his backpack had to do with it. The mystery plagued Meredith and troubled Raymond.

The puzzle occupied Meredith even as she attended the start-studded luncheons that week, sat through screenings and group interviews. She worked to push the questions aside as she conducted her own individual interviews and wrote columns and features from the activities. Cassie seemed hyper-energized. She mentioned that she and Bob were exploring houses to buy and threw herself happily into the extra work necessary to prepare for her upcoming month away from the office while on a press tour for her book.

Peaks and valleys, thought Meredith. Good days—weeks—months and some not so good. Everyone seemed more centered and focused.

Raymond returned from his Monday meetings smiling and settled. He seemed happy to be back at his usual work with the special status investigative office. Tuesday evening Meredith put on "good" jeans, T-shirt, a windbreaker and her funkiest eye patch and attended a screening of a returning series about a crew of young rag tag tour boat operators, a screening and reception held on the actual film yacht docked in Marina Del Rey. She joined up with her old boss and pal Fred Barton who took great pride in escorting a "beautiful woman dressed like a pirate!"

Raymond, meanwhile, took the evening with his son and headed to the Sea Shack for calamari and beer. The relationship between the two had been affectionate and as close as a limited active family can be, ever since Will moved through and out of puberty with his widowed father. Now he was an adult about to embark on his first big job, master's degree in engineering in hand and a girlfriend who Raymond assumed would be wife and even mother very soon. Will had a job offer from a prestigious firm in Seattle. It meant he and Sophie would be leaving Malibu by the end of the year when both graduated. Sophie had job offers as well, so their career paths were about to formalize, and Raymond knew he'd soon lose sight of them, or at least see them even less often than he did now.

Father and son shared the kind of strong and connected conversation they had on the rare occasions before when they did have time together without work, family, or just the world's interruptions. Raymond mused that his young son was now dealing with the same kinds of life dilemmas as his own: job, significant relationship, living spaces. They chuckled together at the irony. Then Raymond told Will about both near-death shooting experiences and the conflicting emotions that followed. "It's brought up a lot of stuff I seldom even think about."

"Like what?" asked the lean, angular-faced young man. Kind but intense eyes regarded his father through wire rimmed glasses, as he leaned his tall runner's body forward onto his elbows, a shock of dark brown hair falling over his forehead. Raymond tried to explain the thoughts that had wrapped around him.

Will put his head in his hands and groaned. "Can you please not let someone try to kill you in the future?" he said, half in jest but with a serious undertone. "I'd like to have more dinners like this. We'll be leaving right after Christmas," he explained. "We graduate earlier that month and will probably go to Seattle in late November or the first week in December to find a place to live. I'd like to anticipate visits up north or here in the south for a long time to come, no surprise announcements about a shooting or a deadly assault, please."

"I've enjoyed just having you close by for the past couple of years," Raymond said quietly. "In my best of worlds, I'd hoped to be in Malibu a lot more often with a lot more time spent with you...and Sophie of course. But, well...Meredith...."

Will laughed out loud, surprising even the diners nearby. "Dad. What a choice! Are you kidding! Even grandma says what a good influence she's been on you and your...joie de vivre! It's not an either—or—her or us. Not a competition.

"I only wish you would spend more time in Malibu before we leave. We're all busy, and it would be cramped, but at least we'd have some meals together and maybe run the beach. Maybe even really get to know Meredith." He looked at the detective with the wishful eyes of the five-year-old kid Raymond remembered. His heart melted.

A few hours later, the normally stolid detective sat on the patio of the townhouse, staring into the verdant hedges that surrounded the place. He sipped good scotch, the mellow sounds of a jazz album he liked stroking the evening air. Meredith burst in the front door, fresh from her event, energetic and full of chatter about the attendees, Fred's new lady friend and more. As she slipped out of her windbreaker and kicked off her sneakers, she noticed the sense of melancholy shrouding Raymond, who continued to regard the hedge undeterred. She walked over and put her arms around him from behind. "How was Will?"

"Great," he replied quickly. "He's a great kid. I'm lucky."

"Then why the sadness? The long face? You look like you've even been crying...but no! T.K. Raymond, stalwart detective, doesn't weep." She smiled quietly.

"I'm probably a little emotionally vulnerable these days. A gun pressed to your head probably does that. And gives you some strange dreams! But seriously," he spoke, regaining his normal demeanor, "I have a favor to ask." Meredith nodded and sat down next to him on the patio. "I'd really like for us to stay in Malibu for a few weeks. Will's leaving in December. I'd like the chance to spend more time with him. I don't want to be away from you…but we've been talking about maybe relocating to the beach, later, anyway. This would be a temporary run-through."

Meredith now stared into the bushes. "Give me a minute. I need to process this," she said. She went into the kitchen and poured herself a glass of wine, walked slowly, thoughtfully, back out to the patio. She sat down, kicked her feet up on a small ottoman and said with enthusiasm, "Sure."

Raymond parked in front of a large, modern glass and wood A-frame house on the hillside and made his way up a long flight of steps to the front door. Beau Hastings' Hollywood Hills home fit the celebrity well. Co-star of *Sunset West* and a major long-running TV western series, the well-worn face and craggy tough guy character was known to millions of Americans.

The detective visit was motivated by Meredith's inadvertent discovery of a straw western hat she'd found in her closet the day before. She'd "borrowed" it from Bitsy, the wardrober on *Sunset West*, during her set visit a few weeks before and forgotten to return it. As Meredith pulled it from the closet shelf, she recalled Bitsy's stories of the kids hanging out on the set and their summer hijinks, including Carlton.

"Raymond," she said, as they both dressed for work. "you should talk with Beau Hastings' son. He hung out with Carlton—and the kids from the ranch. He apparently saw drugs at the ranch, and his dad extracted him from the location and sent him home and even to some camp in Florida right after Carlton overdosed. Maybe there's some insight to be found. Maybe."

So that afternoon, an attractive woman in her forties opened the door to the actor's home. "Hi Detective Raymond. I'm Jen,

Beau's wife. But you know that. We shared a table at last year's all-charity ball." The detective smiled broadly and shook her hand.

"Of course."

"Beau and Trent are in the family room, waiting for you." She led him into a warm and comfortable room that obviously served as the central activity point for the family. A massive window spanned the entire room, showing off the Los Angeles basin—impressive even in the late summer smog. A third person was also waiting. "This is our attorney, Arnold Bessinger." The man stood up, slight of build, thin brown hair and insightful eyes behind heavy horn-rimmed glasses.

"Hey, Raymond." Both chuckled. They knew each other from various courtroom appearances.

"You really don't need an attorney here," said Raymond.

"Well, we want assurances that this conversation is off the record."

"It is," said Raymond. "You both know my significant other is a journalist, but we have a strict policy of discretion. We don't share stories unless they would normally be shared by the source itself."

Beau Hastings nodded. "My wife Jen is an agent with one of the big theatrical firms. We have the same agreement. We have to. But you know, from what I hear, you might put Meredith Ogden and her partner Cassie O'Connell on your payroll. My God, they are determined and smart. I've seen that firsthand."

"Now, there's a conflict of interest," murmured Raymond.

"Anyhow," Hastings continued, "this is my son Trent." He gently pushed a young teenager forward. The boy had the reddish hair of his mom, freckles and an awkward grin. His face was acne-speckled like most boys his age, and he looked terrified. Raymond thought one day he would be handsome. One day. He shook hands with the boy, and they all sat down.

"Trent, your dad tells me you just got home from Space Camp in Florida a couple of weeks ago. That must have been fascinating." Trent nodded.

"This is not an interrogation and I'm not here to pile any blame. I'm trying to find out what happened to Carlton— because it may help us better understand what happened to Dusty Reed." All "tsked-tsked" about the director's close call in the desert, and Raymond quickly went on.

"Trent, you and Carlton hung out together and spent some time with the boys from the ranch down the road from the Villa, Frankie Solver and his friends, is that right?" Trent nodded and murmured, "Yes."

"When you were at the ranch what did you guys do? What kept you all busy?"

"Sometimes we rode. Sometimes we just helped clean up the horses or hung around the corrals. Once in a while we'd play some cards in the warehouse."

"Do you know if Carlton took drugs?"

Trent shook his head. "No sir, I'm sure he didn't."

"I understand you might have seen some bags of drugs at the ranch?"

The teen was already picking at his cuticles and looking down at his hands. He answered in a soft squeak. "Yes sir, I think so. Just one plastic bag in the corner of the big room, caught on a splinter in the molding. But just one."

"What happened when you found it?"

"Carlton said, 'Wow looks like a bag of drugs. Like the ones on *Miami Vice.*'"

"Then what? What did Frankie do?"

"He was snide and uppity with us all, said if we wanted drugs, he could get them. Did we want to try it? He'd offered us marijuana a couple of times before."

"Don't ask," warned Bessinger, the attorney, protecting his young client from errant admissions.

"Not my interest," Raymond reiterated. "Did Carlton join you all the time for these visits?"

"Yeah, mostly. He had nothing else to do but wander the desert."

"What else did you see at the ranch? What else went on there?"

"Some ag stuff, you know, tractors and stuff. And the movie company also parked their trucks in the yard sometimes. I guess when they had to take equipment to the location or something."

"What kinds of trucks?"

"I just saw the big like haul-it-yourselves, big with closed-beds, like for equipment. Some of them actually had the MEGAWATT logo."

"Who else was there at the ranch besides you boys?"

"Usually the manager, but he was always busy in the office or out in the yards. A guy named Julio was there sometimes. He was young and kind of a bully. Liked to show how important he was, but I think he only came in Friday and the weekends. I don't exactly remember. He always tried to be a part of the gang. Guess he kind of identified with us...oh, and Caleb, the older guy from the Villa. He seemed to get everyone's attention when he showed up."

Raymond consulted his notes and put a pencil against his lips, thinking. "Were you ever there when trucks besides the studio trucks were around?"

"No sir!" snapped Trent. "Absolutely not allowed. Frankie said his dad did some importing of toys and other stuff from Mexico and didn't want any 'strangers' around because there were customs regulations. Once we didn't know a shipment—truckload—was coming in and as it came through the gate, the manager told us to leave." The boy stopped his dialogue and squinted as he worked to recall the episode. "Carlton asked what toys were in the truck? Frankie opened up a crate sitting in the room and tossed him a stuffed bunny. 'Here,' he told Carlton, take this. Perfect for a momma's boy.' They teased and bullied him something awful. Seemed like because his mom was a glamorous star. 'Even your mother might enjoy it,' Frankie said."

"And did Carlton take it?"

"Yes, because Caleb came in and chased us out. Carlton stuffed it into the backpack he always carried with him. We were all a little scared of Caleb." Trent's voice had become less firm, more hesitant.

"Trent? Did he keep the bunny? Do you know if he gave it to his mother?"

Trent looked out the windows and he cleared his throat. "Yes sir. He kept it. But...." He looked at his father. Beau nodded resolutely.

"His mom never saw it. Just before I left, the morning he...died...I ran into him at breakfast and he told me Frankie and Xander, Frankie's school buddy who was with him for the summer, had come to his room the day before. Carlton's mom was on the set. Frankie demanded the bunny back, but Carlton couldn't find his backpack. It was in Dusty's room. He'd completely forgotten about the rabbit. He didn't even remember where he put it. He told Frankie he'd find it and return it." Tears ran down the boy's face and he hiccupped.

"I was scared. Carlton was kind of messed up. Frankie told him his own father was furious he'd given the rabbit away. 'He'll kill me,' Frankie said. Worse, he said the old man, Caleb, would come to kill Carlton if he didn't return the rabbit. We thought he was exaggerating but then Carlton decided it wasn't a big deal and would just go away. His mom had bought tickets for him to leave for home—Europe—barely even two days later. I left that day I saw him…and only heard about his…overdose when I got home."

"Then," interjected Beau, "we all went to ground. We sent Trent to camp in Florida, Jen and our daughter went to stay with friends up north and I joined them as quickly as I could wrap up." Raymond looked at them all calmly.

"Everyone went to ground it seems," he said. He looked at Beau, "You knew about this?"

"Not all of it. I knew Trent had seen drugs and that Carlton was afraid of something. Trent never told us all of this," he looked at his son.

"This is all off the record for the media," Arnold spoke up with exaggerated force.

"Absolutely," assured the detective, "whatever gets released will be released by the department itself and you'll be privy to it first. They protect sources."

"Promise?" implored a chastened superstar Beau Hastings.

"No problem now. You may have read about the raid on the ranch and the discovery of a drug operation." Everyone nodded.

"So we don't have to worry about anyone coming to threaten Trent or worse, hurt him?" Jen spoke up from the doorway. "School's started and we've all been guarded and worried."

"We're all pretty certain the entire network has been tagged and the operation is terminated." Raymond handed his business card to everyone in the room. "If you remember anything else at all that could be helpful, or notice something that worries you, please call me."

Trent continued to sniff, tears coursing down his face. "I probably could have done something but the whole thing was so fricken' stupid! Who kills a kid over a stuffed rabbit?"

"The Mexican cartels," said Arnold.

CHAPTER 60
BRENTWOOD
WEDNESDAY

Meredith twisted around in front of the floor-to-ceiling mirror, checking out her dress. Attending glamorous but work-related events required a subtle touch. Not too glamorous but enough to capture the event's sparkle. A simple black dress, heart-shaped neck, lightly capped sleeves and artsy silver necklace and earrings.

Raymond came into the room adjusting his tie and whistled. "Nice," he said, standing behind her and towering over her as they both regarded their images in the mirror.

"Better be," she answered. "I have to live up to being on the arm of the handsomest guy in the room—and also, I have to match the eye patch. It's an elegant black satin one."

Raymond chuckled. "I think you'll miss that patch when your eye is well."

"It is a conversation starter," Meredith agreed.

Small preparations for the coming stay in Malibu were evident around the bedroom. An open suitcase in a corner, cosmetic bag partially filled. But the plan was not without negotiation. The final agreement required his attendance with Meredith at several evening press events, including the Emmy Awards, and a week's vacation over Thanksgiving with the Masners. Evening show biz affairs were his least favorite.

Meredith was often engaged in conversations with colleagues and friends, leaving Raymond to find ways to occupy his time. So, while Meredith now often attended these events with her friend Fred Barton or with Sonia, she preferred Raymond's company. She told him she felt "safe" and "watched over" with him but could never explain why. Now he was committed to two studio dinners and the Emmys.

A week in Hawaii over Thanksgiving, however, was happily agreed to. He welcomed the idea of a total break as life stepped into a new pattern and format. Whatever those ended up being.

The network evening was nonstop chatter and small talk, Meredith scurrying off for a quick conversation with one or another network executive, or a TV show celebrity. Raymond was amused at how she had quickly incorporated the eye patch and its never-the-same story into her casual conversation.

He considered circulating, himself, and talking with the familiar faces and names with whom he had become acquainted in his own role as cop to the stars. But then reconsidered. Instead, he made small talk with the wife of a producer sitting at their dinner table. She wasn't any happier to be there than he was, but they both concurred that the evening was part and parcel of life in the upper ethos of the entertainment industry.

At one such soiree several months earlier, as he picked up a drink from the bar, the woman standing next to him turned and said, "Well, hello." She seemed familiar but he couldn't place a name or event. She reminded him. "You arrested me a few years ago for assaulting my husband with a frying pan." He then recalled the incident. The husband was one of the film industry's celebrated directors. The wife beat him over the head with the hot pan still dripping with bacon grease and chased him down the driveway of their massive Hollywood house. Given the stature of the victim, T.K. Raymond was sent along to assess and manage the situation. Ultimately, charges were dropped. And never made news. "We're fine now. In therapy," the haute-garbed woman had assured the detective. He smiled, nodded and excused himself.

Now, at the new season's dinner, he thought it was time to find his date and be the occasional social partner he knew she appreciated. She was lightly engaged in a conversation with several colleagues as he stepped in next to her and pleasantly said, "Hello." A few familiar faces nodded at him, all from one or another TV series he, personally, seldom watched.

Meredith turned to Raymond and surprising him, said, "There you are. It's time to go. Nice to see all of you." She smiled and turned from the group. As she made her way to their table she noticed Hank Torbin across the room laughing with Renn and Angelina Burton, and an errant thought passed through her mind: Torbin, her disturbed belongings—both at the Villa the same day....Then Cassie's words about Angelina Burton replayed. The small woman, swathed in too much hair and chiffon, was like a well-trained puppy for her movie star husband—fetching his drinks, straightening his sleeve, her eyes scanning the room checking for important faces. A super fan.

"Early isn't it?" Raymond spoke up. "There're still announcements and stuff, aren't there?"

"Russ is coming in from New York tomorrow. It's a big meeting for me. I want to be ready. Besides, I've had enough," she answered quietly. "I've heard it all before. Let's go."

"No argument here," he muttered, scooping up her stole from the chair and placing it around her shoulders.

CHAPTER 61
MARINA DEL REY, CALIFORNIA
THURSDAY AFTERNOON

Russ Talbot was waiting for Meredith on the deck of the Marina Del Ray Hotel, the afternoon sky brilliant, the breeze just enough to ruffle his silver hair, and his usual confident professional smile on his well-aging face. Meredith held out her hand and he grasped it enthusiastically. "Thanks for coming out here," he said. "Felt like we should have some privacy for this discussion." His words didn't calm Meredith's nerves at all. The managing director of one of the world's largest media networks—also incidentally her boss—traveling from New York for this seemingly casual seaside meeting had clenched her teeth for days.

Russ guided her out to the bar deck to a table at its farthest edge. They sat, Meredith adjusting her eye patch and ordering an iced tea, Russ, a gin and tonic, staring at the paisley adornment on her face. "Sure you don't want something stronger?" She declined and explained she still had work to do before the day was over. He looked at her intently and asked, "Jesus, that must have been some kerfuffle, Meredith, to get you into an eye covering—stylish as it is."

Meredith blushed. "It was, Russ. It really was." She explained as briefly and undramatically as possible about the incident in New Mexico and how she and Cassie had escaped from the compound where they had been held. Russ just shook his head. He knew better than to proffer judgment on this woman. He'd come out on the losing side of it. They talked about the Hollywood Newsroom office, Cassie, Sonia, Ito. About the stories that were currently in the works. She expressed her adamancy about finding how young Carlton Hutchinson died. Russ hoped she wasn't being too noble.

"So, Meredith," he cleared his throat. "How do you think the 'package' is going?" He referred to the show business news operation she ran in West LA.

She took a deep breath and said, "Not to anyone's best, Russ. It's been three years since we set up the new offices and assignments. But the news ethos and the gossip world has changed. You probably know more specifics about that than I do. And, we've all heaved-to so hard and so well. But it feels…um…thin. This week the networks have brought in the bigger newspaper entertainment editors and I've had a chance to talk with many of them. Even they acknowledge that a daily gossip column has slipped to the back pages and pretty heavily edited to fit smaller spaces.

"Where do we go from here?" She shook her head. "I think every one of us at the office will give you a different suggestion."

"Where do you want to go, Meredith?" he asked, slouching into his chair and regarding her more closely. "You came to me after Bettina died and said being her replacement was your desire, that you'd do whatever was needed to live up to the position. Make no mistake, I know you have done that. You are well respected, your work is excellent. The editors who work with us and run the columns all support you."

Meredith shrugged. "Bettina Grant was one of a kind. Truly the 'Queen of Gossip.' Maybe she could reignite the print excitement about 'Hollywood.' But Gossip isn't gossip anymore. Hollywood isn't 'Hollywood' anymore. Everyone gets a dose of it on every TV station, network, magazine now—as 'news.' There are no more 'confidantes' to the stars.' The stars would rather confess their own sins publicly and get the attention. But more than that, I can't get my teeth into much in three paragraphs or less.

"Hollywood was once a small town with the Capitol Record's round music building, some TV and radio stations, Grauman's Chinese Theater, Paramount Studios and trendy show biz restaurants. It crept out to Burbank, NBC, Warner Brothers and to the west to 20th Century and on and on. Then it left geographical boundaries and became wherever films, music and news were being made. And where celebrities walked. And then it infiltrated every walk of life from high technology to medicine to fashion...well, you know the landscape now." She again shrugged and picked up her iced tea. "It went from Hollywood as a place to HOLLYWOOD as an ethos—all caps. It's an idea now that I don't know how to adjust the work to fit well, Russ."

"Nice discourse, Meredith, and you've hit the sweet spot in your analysis," he said, leaning on a golf analogy, golf being his sport of choice. "We agreed initially that the current set up was experimental. I'm here to lay out a scenario for you. I'd like to say, 'it's up to you,' but if this isn't the solution, we need to find one very quickly. You're really the managing head of your news office even though Cassie drew up the bones of the structure. You have the visibility and reputation and frankly what seems like the major interest in the operations."

"Bettina Grant's spirit rubbed off on me after a decade working with her."

Russ pulled a single sheet of white paper from his shirt pocket and smoothed it out on the table. He summarized it quickly. "You will be doing two pieces a week, one a longer opinion type piece to be included as part of our major columnists' package, like the political, sports and now the new technology pieces. Like your AIDS piece. You move from kind of a secondary level at the syndicate offerings to a top level. Kind of like moving from the red carpet 'B' list to the 'A' list. Your special features have shown us how well you fit into this role." Meredith's mind reeled grasping for clarity.

"Then," he continued, we'd like you to do one good movie or TV feature—like the weekly piece you usually do, in depth on a celebrity, industry executive, production or situation. You know the drill." She nodded, stunned.

"And the newest focus. UAM doesn't own stations, but we are moving into TV production and bought the *Morning Coffee Show*. Here in LA it will remain on its home station for now but becomes a little less local. You'll be appearing on one show a week—start to finish—not the little five-minute gigs you and Cassie have been putting together. You'll engage in commentary on whatever the day's subject is. Some of it will be entertainment-related, some not. That's the scenario."

"Cassie?" Meredith asked, trying to control her voice and hide her confusion.

"She'll produce two shows a week of the new *Morning Coffee Show*," Russ answered without affect. "And write her books. She'll eventually evolve into a celebrity writer. But you know that."

"Ito?"

"Going to New York to work in our headquarters."

Meredith nearly levitated from her chair. "What? When? How? He was wearing that silly little white coat and making tea and cooking for Bettina Grant only three years ago. I'm not saying he shouldn't excel, but...."

"With the MBA and a brilliant mind. We're getting his visa situation made permanent, and well, he'll tell you he's thrilled."

"I am too, for him, Russ. Just shocked. But Sonia. Oh lord, what will I tell her. What will she do?"

"I'm happy to pay her to do the weekly celebrity question and answer column. I know she's been compiling and writing those for a long time. We took Cassie's byline off them two years ago and added Sonia's, as you know. I'm also offering her a days' worth of work each week to help you. But you two will have to work that out. Maybe Cassie will have something additional for her on the show."

"How will you tell them or are you leaving that to me?"

"I have appointments with Ito and Cassie tomorrow."

Meredith sighed and nodded. "But the office. The files."

"Office will have to close. I suggest you work from your home space. Bettina did it for years. We'll reimburse phones, computers and other expenses like we always have." Meredith flashed on the small townhouse and then on the soon-to-be-cramped state of the beach house and winced. "The files are yours. They were left to you, and I imagine you will want to preserve them as best as you can. Someday they can all be put onto electronic storage. We're doing that with our own archives now.

"Moneywise," he went on, "You'll be doing better than you are now and it can only get better because your star will rise as an expert in the industry, not just about the celebrities and their bed mates. Think in terms of guest appearances and speeches. You should consider a topical book at some point."

"'Celebrities and their bed mates?' That's not fair, Russ," she snapped at him. He got it.

"Sorry. Learning to live with show biz as part of our news world has always been a bigger gulp than many of us old news horses were good at swallowing. Between you, and of course Bettina Grant, we were pushed and bullied into understanding and accepting it. A good thing especially in today's environment."

"Who else knows about this?" Meredith stammered, still trying to calm the confusion in her head and make sense of the situation.

"You, Ito—only parts of it—and the syndicate VP. While I'm here, I am taking advantage of talking with some of the editors who are staying over for the weekend. Like you, it's good to know what's on the mind of our subscribers. And I've asked for a Saturday morning meeting at your office, which you'll see when you get back there. So, we can happily and calmly all talk about it."

Meredith couldn't help but chuckle at the words, "happily and calmly." She sat silently looking out to the ocean. "I have to process this, Russ. Deep down, I see how this can be exactly what I'd like for myself. A chance to write serious and good stuff and use the years of working in this cacophony to put context to it. But the shock—it's a right angle turn at a high speed without notice." Russ only nodded his head and took a drink of his gin and tonic. They talked for a while about the syndicate, the news scene and their own situations. Meredith was surprised and a little taken aback by Russ's candor about life at the giant media organization.

"Something I should also mention," he said with unusual frankness. "Politics are always afoot in New York. You know that and remember how often Bettina used to crash into New York to resolve issues. Well, that hasn't changed, only worse. And our new overall boss, Walter Mayhew, is a player of people and position like we've never seen before. Things could change and probably will, often. So, I'd like everyone to sign and agree to the new regime as quickly as possible. Especially you. I'm only trying to secure your position and make it permanent."

"So, are we okay here, Russ?" He nodded again. Then she quietly negotiated another paid workday for Sonia.

"But you'll have to ask for help and guidance when you need it, work more closely with us," Russ said forcefully. "Stop sparring with the editors. It's a new world for you, Meredith. New for all of us. So, no kerfuffles, please. "

"Oh Russ," she pouted. "You know better than that."

CHAPTER 62
WEST LOS ANGELES
FRIDAY

Meredith was strung tightly when she took Sonia to breakfast on Friday after most of the network events and visiting editors and writers had returned to their home states. Sonia obviously knew something important was happening with news of a command performance the next day, Saturday, with Russ Talbot. Hesitant to surmise about not only the outcome or the conversations, but about her own career path.

The two long-time collaborators sat in a shiny blue booth at the nearby diner and talked the tough subject. Meredith was contrite as she explained the entire situation and Sonia took it in mostly looking down at her coffee cup. "I'm sorry it can't be better news for you. I did get you two days of work with me, if you want it. If this could work, we have hopes Cassie will find more for you with the new TV show."

"But does Cassie know about that yet?"

"By now," said Meredith glancing at her watch, "she will. She's meeting with Russ now."

Sonia was surprisingly calm and thoughtful. She took a few sips of her coffee and looked out the window. "You know," she finally spoke up, "some things that seem terrible aren't always." Meredith regarded her curiously. "I've been worrying a problem—opportunity—and wondering how to manage it. Divine providence. You know I've been dating Art for quite a while." Meredith nodded.

"We're planning to get married around Christmas."

"How wonderful. Why didn't you tell us more about him. We only met him at Alan's a couple of weeks ago."

"Well, there are a lot of decisions to be made and it won't be a knock-out Hollywood wedding, believe me. Art's not a public guy as you might have noticed at Alan's barbeque."

"I didn't get that. He was cordial and conversational. Nice guy."

"But he's not the public persona of either Raymond or Cassie's Bob. And he's not hardly interested in show biz except for what I like to watch on TV, and sports."

Meredith scowled and said, "So what? You two have decided it works and it's good. Who cares about the rest of it?"

"My Pollyanna boss," chuckled Sonia. "You all are intimidating. Bigger and more special than most everyone. Honestly."

Meredith cringed. "But not more special than you, Sonia. You're one of us." The younger woman shook her head.

"You say that, and I know you believe it because it's how you treat me. After all the years with Bettina—who was practically a Macy's parade balloon in how she just usurped the air—it's been both flattering and lovely to have you all take me on the path with you. But I'm still a San Fernando Valley single mom who lucked out getting a secretary position with a Hollywood icon." Her words stung Meredith. She cocked her head to one side and gazed at Sonia in question.

"Sonia, we were all just silly kids hungering after Hollywood's glow and like you, we all just lucked out in crashing into Bettina. How lucky we were to happen into each other. You have talent and are doing a great job, maybe even understand the entire scope of our field more than we, who go out and flit amongst the star bees, do. And, you're doing your own flitting these days." Silence overtook the table.

"So, where does that leave us with the work right now?"

Sonia looked up almost in surprise. "I'm so sorry. I got diverted. I guess it has been on my mind for a long time. But there are more decisions than when and where to get married for Art and me. His service business is in Canoga Park and we'll live there. My mom will be close by and the two boys will go to the same school in that area. Then, two weeks ago we were having dinner with two close friends of Art's—they own the *Valley Chronicle* newspaper in Tarzana. When they heard about our plans, they offered me a great position as the managing editor of the paper. Me! But it publishes twice weekly and is really part-time. I couldn't see giving up what I have here for that. I told them we would talk about it." She smiled at Meredith and took a drink of coffee.

Meredith processed the information and tried to clear the confusion pulsating through her brain. "So it could work?" Sonia shrugged.

"I could handle two days a week in a big time Hollywood news office. The rest of the time in my own local digs."

"And a nationally syndicated question/answer column with your byline?" Both women began to quietly laugh.

"Yeah."

Meredith sighed dramatically. "I couldn't do it without you. And, the synergy between your column and my stories will help us both. We'll figure out the details later, but now, tell me about the wedding. Of course, we want to put on a shower...."

"Fine, fine all of it. But I hope you'll be my maid of honor."

☆☆☆

Meredith checked "Sonia" off her mental list of concerns. But her mind was now on housing issues. Short term and long term. For the next 60 days she was figuring out how to fit into the small beach house—already filled with two active young people, now adding the fulsome life she and Raymond shared in the townhouse. Half the closet space with two other adults sharing them. No separate work space. And one garage for three cars with no on-street parking. I should have negotiated a better deal, she thought to herself, but then stopped the frenzy with, it's only temporary. And it's important to Raymond. Still, even when Will and Sophie leave, the Malibu house would still be small considering she'd be working full time in it, with Sonia eventually there two days a week. Then there was Paco the cat, undoubtedly facing serious adjustment issues with the top of the small, mostly inadequate refrigerator.

The subject had been tirelessly discussed with Raymond the night before. Notes were kept, detailing several solutions—none of them simple. But the serious discussion had come only after the celebratory conversation about Meredith's new work assignments. She had enthusiastically bounced into the townhouse after her meeting with Russ, announcing her upcoming role with the media syndicate. She had already put aside the sadness over the break-up of the current news-office team. "It's champagne time. Meredith Ogden finally gets to write important stuff, worthwhile material!"

Raymond had smiled as broadly as he ever did, hugged her and reminded her that "Meredith Ogden has always written worthwhile stuff—and written it well. Congratulations!"

Sipping champagne from a colorfully decorated promotional flute from a major movie, she asked him what decisions he'd made about his own future job. He gave his standard answer, "Still working it out."

"I'm still working out Carlton's death," she murmured. "Bankleman's conflicting arrival time after the discovery of the boy's death doesn't make sense, and it's been bugging me. There are other issues I'm puzzled about."

"I'm on that," Raymond said. "I've been looking into Steve Bankleman—and lots of other loose ends, but there're better things to talk about tonight." Later, after extensive after-dinner conversation about housing, he stood up and said, "Let's go to bed. We've hit the wall. Maybe we'll find inspiration overnight."

CHAPTER 63
MALIBU
SATURDAY

"How many clothes does one woman need?" asked Will.

"A lot," said Raymond. "Remember her wardrobe covers button-down meetings and interviews as well as fancy evening gowns to fashionable but practical travel clothes to…well, it goes on. Shoes to go with. She currently has a large—full—walk-in closet. And I have a full closet in the second bedroom that is fuller than usual thanks to a tuxedo and 'event' wardrobe of my own." The tall detective flinched just thinking about it.

Raymond and Will meandered through the Malibu house examining its layout and the life artifacts that filled it. Sophie was at the university library and Meredith was at the morning meeting of the news staff with Russ Talbot. "Two closets between the master bedroom and the bath," mumbled Raymond, shaking his head.

"You know the two most frightening words in the female vocabulary?" snickered Will. "Go with."

"Wait'll you see the eye patches. Although," he remembered, "her stitches came out yesterday and she's not required to wear one any longer. But I think she was enjoying the attention it brought her."

"I can't even guess what you two do in your recreational time," sighed Will.

"It may seem frivolous, but it's what she does for a living and it suits her well. And, she'll need a workspace."

"Doesn't she work out of an office?"

"Yes, but she's a writer and sometimes she comes home, shuts the door and works quietly without interruption." Will just nodded. "And sometimes I bring work home as well," said Raymond.

"Maybe we have to set up the living room like a study hall. Sophie and I are pretty much finished with our classes and projects, but we will have paperwork stuff to do. So, for now, how about a worktable the entire expanse of the living room wall with a space for each of us? Not pretty, but functional."

"We'll also need a second phone line for Meredith and me," Raymond added, gazing at the already littered living area. Books piled in corners, sweatshirts draped over chairs, an empty coke can hiding under the sofa. "She'll have to dress for the fancy gigs at the townhouse. She'll probably prefer it because the bathroom is a lot larger and more comfortable."

Finally, the two men migrated to the oceanfront deck, continuing their assessment of the arrangement. Late morning, Raymond broke from the planning to run the beach. He invited Will but the boy had other responsibilities and begged off. Raymond made a quick call to Meredith's car phone, relieved he caught her at the wheel heading to the post-meeting luncheon. He changed into shorts and a t-shirt and took off along the sand.

Sophie arrived a while later, struggling up the steps from the garage, slightly miffed but silent about having to jockey her car into an odd position to accommodate other vehicles in the space. She looked around the living room and suddenly felt embarrassed. The place was a mess...but she had other issues to handle, she rationalized. A willowy young woman, pleasant and lovely of face, born in Korea but educated from high school on in the U.S., Sophie was both strong willed and shy. Strong willed from her need to succeed without a lot of parental help and support once she landed in America. Shy by the nature of her Asian heritage. Living with distant relatives in Oregon, she had excelled in school but not necessarily in visibility among her classmates. She preferred to negotiate and barter information and grades one-on-one rather than stand out in class. She made one yearly family visit to a town about two hours from Seoul but spent most of her life as an American student. She met Will in a chemistry lab class during their junior year at the University of Oregon. He, too, was quieter and more introspective than most of her peers. Two years later they found a graduate program at Pepperdine University near Will's dad's Malibu home and were thrilled to be invited to live there. T.K. Raymond mostly spent his time with his lady friend Meredith at her townhouse. He was grateful to have them watching over the beach house.

Sophie had only met Meredith a few times, always in passing, never for an extended conversation. Honestly, thought Sophie, the woman intimidated her. She had a big, bold American presence, strikingly beautiful in a unique, nontypical way. And she didn't seem afraid of anything. Now Sophie, with her youthful, pristine face and shining black bobbed hair style, knew she would soon get to know both the tall detective father and his girlfriend very well. Life had maneuvered that nexus.

CHAPTER 64
MARINA DEL REY
SATURDAY

"I miss the elegant eye patch, Meredith," Russ Talbot noted as he paid the lunch tab at the hotel oceanside dining deck, "but your injury looks nearly healed and the swelling is gone. You look like the Meredith we all know." The Hollywood Newsroom group all laughed. Russ wasn't the first to lament Meredith's retired eye patch.

"But I only wore it for a couple of weeks," she mewed.

"But a stylishly rakish couple of weeks," said Ito.

"Where'd you learn a word like 'rakish'?" asked Cassie.

The media chief from New York had hosted the entire staff to lunch after their meeting to review and help put the new assignments into perspective. Even though he'd met with each independently, except for Sonia who'd worked out her plans with Meredith, he wanted everyone to feel comfortable, clear and without rancor about the changes coming. Lunch was to soften the lines of concern and the uncertainty with which each, no doubt, were grappling, no matter how certain he'd tried to make it seem. When he left, he knew there would be chatter and questions among them, and he wanted it to happen openly.

There was conversation and excitement, even sadness, that life for all would change. "But look at it like this, we all have promising new jobs—pretty much what we would ask for if it had been up to us," said Sonia. "And we still get to work together in some way."

"Except for Ito," moaned Cassie. "He'll be 3,000 miles away in New York."

"I'll send you coffee—and keep an eye on your expense accounts from there," he mused. He reported that Quality Fun game company was in dire straits with the bulk of their Roborabbit product delayed because of the raid on the trucks bringing the toys from Mexico. "What will they do?" asked Sonia.

"They've got two executives renting a truck in El Paso and bringing whatever remaining product the Juarez toy production facility has left over. They'll drive all night to try to get it back here so they can meet at least some of their orders." Everyone was quiet as they thought about the tragic result from the drug activities in which they'd all been involved. Sterling Music, Cassie reported, was in limbo, hoping several of the musicians might buy the company assets and keep it active.

The newsroom group hugged, quickly bid farewell and split off to their own Saturday pastimes. At the last minute, Meredith grabbed Cassie's arm. "This is fine with you?" she pushed.

"I had to process it hard," Cassie admitted. "But after all the maneuvering I did to step back into the Hollywood world, wooed, I guess, by memories of the glow, but the deadlines and constant pressure for news—some big but a lot of little—buried me. I'm glad to be back in the moment-to-moment production world—and only two days a week. And, we can still work together." Her colleague nodded, smiled and squeezed her arm.

Meredith watched as everyone went to their cars, feeling the stab of loss again. Only three years before they faced a similar precipice over job and future, as a result of Bettina's death. There was more safety and surety in this jump, and a boss they all knew who seemed, at least, to be pulling for them.

✩✩✩

By three, Meredith arrived at the Malibu house, hefting two bags of groceries requested by Raymond and, per his instructions, "just your PJs and toothbrush." Of course, she'd added a few more things. Raymond jogged up to the house by four after a long, strenuous run. His eyes were alive with energy and enthusiasm even though he was out of breath and wet with sweat.

"How'd it go?" he asked Meredith about her meeting and follow-on lunch with the whole news team. She beamed.

"I'd never have thought this whole change could work out well. Everyone is jazzed about their new assignments. Sonia— wow! Can you imagine? And Ito? He was wearing his cute little houseman's coat three years ago, serving Bettina coffee, making hors d'oeuvres for her guests and now he's a junior corporate financial coordinator for one of the biggest media companies in the country." She sighed.

"Cassie?" Raymond probed. "I'm not hearing a lot about her. How'd she take the change?"

"She's fine, actually relieved. Two early mornings a week will be a big adjustment, but they'll make it work. And, she'll be moving on soon. Her next book is being pushed big time and there's talk of a movie deal. You know she'll be in the middle of it." Raymond reached out and hugged Meredith.

"We're celebrating tonight. I'm heading to the shower now."

"Good," she grinned. "I brought my pajamas." They both chuckled at the subtle history of the phrase. Then remembered about the full house and thin walls.

CHAPTER 65
MALIBU
SATURDAY NIGHT

"Just to warn you," Raymond murmured quietly, "there's been some negotiation and the plan is altered a bit." Meredith scowled as she stepped in close to him. Woody, savory smoke arose from the deck as steaks crackled on the grill and he poked the sizzling meat with a fork, testing for doneness. Peppered corn ears seared in one corner "You'll approve, I think." She shook her head and went to retrieve the garlic bread from the kitchen. The move—even temporary—to Malibu was his plan, she reminded herself, and she had agreed to go along. But she knew that Paco the cat was going to take it poorly. Too much noise, small refrigerator top, and not enough of his own turf.

"Will and I have been talking, planning," said Raymond, once dinner was over and empty plates languished around the wooden picnic table. Sunset was just painting the sky over the Pacific with fiery reds, yellow and purples. "As you know, Meredith and I are planning to spend more time here at the beach house before you two," he nodded at Will and Sophie, "leave for Seattle. We've thought about this long and hard and today Will and I decided that the best way to do that is for us to spend Fridays, Saturdays and Sundays here, but continue our work and weekly schedules from the Brentwood townhouse." Meredith swallowed a sigh of relief.

Sophie's eyes sprung open in surprise. "Really?"

Will nodded. "This way everyone will have plenty of space for their own work and school and we can get packed."

Sophie sighed loudly. "And make it easier with the wedding plans and all." Her words were rushed and tumbled through her light Asian accent. Everyone stared at her. Will dropped his head and cringed.

"Wedding?" probed Raymond. "Yours?"

Will nodded. "Well. Yes. A new development since our dinner last week, dad. See, you're going to be a grandpa." Raymond grasped the table with both hands. Meredith could hardly process the idea—Raymond, vital, virile, wise and energetic—too young to be slammed into a "grandad" role. She mentally shushed herself. Sophie simply stared at her hands, clearly embarrassed and frightened.

Raymond took a quiet but deep breath and attempted to assume the wise elder role. "When is all of this happening?"

"Before we move to Seattle," Will explained in a chastened voice.

"The next 60 days," calculated Meredith. Both Will and Sophie murmured agreement.

"We thought the weekend before Thanksgiving because we'll be in Seattle the week after to find a place to live and…," the younger man elaborated.

"When, where and who will this wedding involve?" asked Meredith. She noticed Raymond looked like he'd swallowed a large dose of hot pepper juice.

"Well," Will began. Sophie seemed ready to scurry to the bedroom, close the door and hide. "Sophie's parents can't come to America until summer next year because of their jobs and finances. So, we'll have a more traditional wedding then." He cleared his throat. "But I want my child to be born into a legal, real family. I don't want people raising eyebrows because we aren't married."

"When's the baby due?" Meredith interjected.

"March," murmured Sophie. Will looked down at the table.

"So," Meredith continued in a measured voice. "You're basically two months along?" Sophie said a quiet "Yes."

Raymond looked at Will puzzled. "You didn't mention this last week. I guess I would have liked to have known about it before we started making plans about the beach house and all."

"He didn't know," Sophie said in a whisper. "I wanted to be sure and get through the first couple of months. Friends told me to do that."

"So, let's go back to the original question. When and where is this wedding taking place. Is it a done deal? And do you need help?" Both young people shrugged.

"We haven't made any plans yet. We just talked about it for the first time yesterday," Will responded, looking years younger and more insecure that he had a few nights before. The conversation came to a halt as each reached for a question or topic that could be asked gently.

"Congratulations," said Raymond. "An exciting part of your next step into the future. A little complicating, perhaps, but nonetheless exciting. Why don't we get the dishes done and the kitchen cleaned up and in the next day or so we can work out the details on how Will and Sophie would like us to participate."

Meredith was out of her chair and picking up plates as quickly as possible, followed by Sophie. Will sat waiting for his dad to move and finally said, "Well, it's not optimal but we'll make it all work." Raymond stood up, ruffled his son's hair and smiled, "We will." But he had never felt so old or "mature" in his life.

CHAPTER 66
MALIBU
SUNDAY

The smell of hot, rich coffee woke Meredith. She stirred reluctantly, enjoying the sound of the surf. It brought back the memory of her first night and morning with Raymond in the beach house. Then she realized she was actually there, in Malibu. Opening her eyes, she saw the "stalwart" detective sitting on the edge of the bed holding out a steaming mug for her.

"Did I have a psychedelic experience last night or did we get caught up in a tsunami of feral parenting?"

"Wear your highwater boots," Raymond sighed. "Sorry we left you to clean up with Sophie. Will seemed to need some quiet conversation and Sophie seemed ready to implode. I took him down the beach for a beer."

Meredith groaned then stretched her supple body and shook out her hair, resting back into the pillows. "Sophie finally calmed down a bit. She told me she has a good friend—a former classmate—living in Seattle who is helping her with the move. And her former adviser from Oregon now teaches in Seattle. Sophie and Will are staying with her family while they find a place to live. I feel a lot better about them having a landing place in Seattle in their current situation. Mostly, she's terribly shy even though I've always seen her as a tough, smart, energetic young college student like every other high-energy college kid in America. Her Asian demeanor was well hidden. She said we intimidate her—especially me. I'm 'on TV.'"

"Will kind of faded into his kid-self. He's overwhelmed and confused. I told him we'd help him 'organize' but he'd have to man-up, grow up and take responsibility for his future. I felt harsh, but...," Raymond said, handing her the coffee mug.

"Don't look at me for wisdom," she sighed. "I've had almost no contact with kids. Really. A couple of hours here or there at social events with friends' kids, but not much else. I never even baby sat. So...."

"Well, they're old enough to make these decisions for themselves. I might still see Will as a little boy, but he showed me a long time ago that he could do fine independently—with a little help—so he'll have to carry this load."

"I guess today is about making lists with them, figuring out timetables," yawned Meredith. "And whether we can actually take the vacation we've planned with the Masners over Thanksgiving." Raymond cringed.

"But first breakfast," he quickly changed the subject. "I'm doing omelets. Then you're going to run with me along the beach—no excuses. And then we can make lists. I hope by then they will have worked some of it out between themselves and we're just there to advise."

"Right. So, I'll get dressed while you play chef. Yell if you get in trouble."

"Ye of little faith," mused Raymond.

Omelets finished, dishes washed, some organization amid the cluttered house, and the young couple settled into the sofa to talk about their upcoming life plans. Meredith and Raymond pushed off from the sand in front and began a quiet trot down the beach toward Santa Monica. The view of his house gradually diminished as they passed the continuous row of upscale residences on a slight bluff one side of their path, a sunny day over the Pacific Ocean on the other side. After a while, winded and spent, Meredith called out, "Is there some unseen purpose in this journey?"

"Wait for it," Raymond called back. Unaccustomed to beach slogging, Meredith began to slow down and gulp for breath. "Almost there, let's cool it down," said the detective slowing to a walk. He reached for her hand then guided her across the sand toward a comely house, not too modern, not frivolously retro, languishing pleasantly on the embankment. A long wood-railed deck expanded across the beachside structure. And a grizzled older man was leaning on the rail.

"Come up the stairs, T.K.," he called out. The couple climbed up the tiled stairs.

"Irwin, this is Meredith. Meredith, meet my old friend Irwin Lemond," Raymond made the introductions.

"I've heard about you a lot," smiled the leprechaun of a man, slightly unruly grey hair, grey beard and flinty eyes. He wore a buttoned-up purple sweater with rumpled khaki trousers and no shoes. "My friend T.K. and I have been running together on this beach for...how many years T.K.?" Raymond shrugged. "Well, enough that I knew that kid of his when he was in grammar school. Come in, please."

Raymond cleared his throat and Meredith knew something important was about to emanate from it. "Yesterday when I was out jogging, Irwin was out walking. We got to talking as we have done for decades and I was telling him about the possible move to Malibu for us from Brentwood and how my little gem of a house has become too small and precious for the work and life that seems to have infiltrated my world."

"My wife passed on four years ago," the leprechaun explained. "I love it here, been here for over 30 years. But I'm old now. And my kids live a long ways away. My daughter and her husband are in Colorado and want me to come and live with them. They built me a little cabin next to a river. Can you imagine? Anyhow, I'd be nuts not to take them up. I get sick, my bones creak when I walk, the nights sometimes scare me, and it's time for me to be with someone other than myself—and him," he said pointing at Raymond. "He's been one constant for me but even he has other interests now." The old man grinned.

"Irwin made an interesting proposal yesterday. But how about we look at this wonderful house first," Raymond stepped in. Irwin walked them through the place, seeming to sprawl but actually so well designed its compactness was not obvious. "Garage across the front and a bedroom over it. Nice guest room with a small bath," graveled Irwin. "Master suite over the kitchen and laundry room," he explained as they climbed the terra cotta tiled steps. The view from the main bedroom was breathtaking.

"And look," Raymond expounded, "a large walk-in closet and separate shower!" Downstairs, however, was the clincher for Meredith, a large bedroom and bath that would make a great office with a lovely ocean view. And a small alcove. Instantly, her planner mind went to work and she could see room for Sonia either in the office or the alcove, or a dedicated office, as much as he needed, for Raymond in the alcove.

The whole house felt like a comfortably-fitting glove in cold weather. Some updates here or there, mostly cosmetic. Cracked tiles, some new ones in a couple of rooms, wood re-varnished in some areas, and updated appliances, but as Irwin put it, "the bones are great." He proudly gestured to the kitchen appliances. "New last year. The old ones broke down every few months, so I decided in honor of Ellie, the place deserved the best." Meredith carefully regarded the refrigerator, smiling at the extra-large fridge top, imagining how well Paco might enjoy both the space and the view.

The old man invited them to sit on the patio deck and have a beer. They talked about Irwin's years on the beach, his long history with Raymond and his family. "After Lilli died, Irwin's late wife Ellie often took Will for an evening or night or weekend when I was working. And, she fed us a lot of Sunday dinners."

"The boy still stops by to say hello," Irwin explained. "I'm not in any rush exactly—there's no problem selling this place but I'd rather it went to someone like you, T.K., who knows it and loves it. I think I'm offering a fair price. My kids want me to make the move the week or so before Christmas. Think it over. You have a lot to talk about. Don't feel pressured. Things have a way of working out."

CHAPTER 67
MALIBU
SUNDAY

Bidding Irwin goodbye with a promise to talk again in a few days, Meredith and Raymond walked toward the surf line and sat down on the sand. The afternoon sun was high and a small breeze meandered. "Irwin and Ellie kind of grew me up," Raymond said. "We have a long history. First Lilli died and Will and I were on our own here. Then four years ago Ellie passed after a very long illness. I should have been more available to him but well, life."

"It seems like 'growing up' never stops," said Meredith. "The bridge from one phase to the next always seems to come with a crisis or at least chaos. This weekend feels a lot like a full-out marathon of new adjustments. Years of self-focus, protection... whatever you want to call it...cocooned in my Hollywood bubble and the townhouse. First that was burst open with Bettina's death, but you came with it and our entwined life has been the new normal. Suddenly after the last week—new job—promotion really, dissolution of my work family, new although temporary living quarters, now two weddings before Christmas. Both in which I'm involved. I'm a little breathless. I've always felt like the young ingenue, especially around you. Now I feel older, like life just kicked me in the butt—said, 'here, take this!'"

Raymond chuckled. "You seem like a wide-eyed ingenue to me," he said, "and your butt is terrific. But then compared to you, Ms. Springtime, I am old, and today feel it for sure," he sighed. "Yes, this house needs a lot of serious 'grown up' thought. Irwin's offered me a great deal. If I buy it and you join me living there, it would suggest that we are into this relationship one step deeper. You have to think that one through seriously. I'm comfortable, but I haven't a lot to lose—except maybe you. I hope not. I have some nostalgia about the beach house but feel like it's time to move on. So you know, I'll be heading up the enlarged, more advanced high-profile unit— larger, more professional fields and located in Beverly Hills not far from the PD building. For Barnie Bristow. It's good." Meredith felt a deep release of tension. Less likelihood of shoot outs in the desert—or worse.

"I don't ask you to give up the townhouse. I know how important that's been to you, so you'll have to decide if you want to settle into a domestic situation with a lot more moving parts than you're used to."

"Well," she began. "I have been giving the townhouse a lot of thought. I bought it a long time ago soon after I started working for Bettina. It was paid for with insurance money from my late fiancé. He was so sure about our future he went ahead and made me the beneficiary when he started a new job— months before we ever talked about marriage. We'd been officially engaged two weeks when he died. I tried to pass the settlement over to his family, but they refused it, wanted me to have it." She still felt the lingering guilt pangs over the questions that troubled her at the time, her desire to marry—anyone. Raymond shrugged.

"You have to take that into consideration and make your own decision. I'm fine however it works. Selling Brentwood isn't necessary. Maybe you want to live in two places, much like I have this last couple of years. It's not a bad way to go, but gets complicated. Believe me, I also have a lot of other personal issues to sort out as well. Let's agree to decide, independently, how to go with Irwin's offer by October one. How's that?"

She agreed and added, "Your decision to stay with the local gendarmes instead of riding with the FBI gang means a lot." Raymond look at her puzzled. "Chances of getting killed seem a lot less likely," she explained. They both laid back into the sand and quietly absorbed the day's warmth and the comforting sound of the sea's dependable surge.

CHAPTER 68
MALIBU
SUNDAY

The tall detective finally sat up and shook the sand from his shirt, brushed the grains from his hair and took a deep breath. "So, I know you've had a lot of change, upheaval and decisions the last few days," he began, leaning toward Meredith. "Nobody could have anticipated last night's domestic drama. Sorry. Although, I do have a gift that was supposed be the only surprise of the weekend, but…well…maybe this will make today a better day. Here it is. Those pesky Feebs took Carlton's killer into custody Friday—aided, I might add, by Jerrold and Margo." Meredith bolted upright from her beach slump and stared at him.

"Tell me about it all."

"First, Beau Hastings' son, Trent, told me about Bert Solver's kid, Frankie, visiting Carlton and threatening him if he didn't return the stuffed rabbit to the ranch. You told me about Carlton's father ordering an independent toxicology report after the boy's remains were shipped home to Switzerland. That info must have come from Reuben, so I contacted him and he delivered the Swiss autopsy report. Small traces of chloroform were found in Carlton's system—no evidence of it at the scene— but suggests he was unconscious when the heroin was injected into his arm. Officially an 'unattended death' but you can forget suicide or self-administered overdose. By the way, I never actually saw Reuben through all of the exchanges."

"He does that," murmured Meredith.

"Friday, the feds in Pennsylvania picked up Frankie and his friend Xander." Raymond went on. "The kids said they were 'ordered' by Caleb to knock out Carlton with chloroform and then search his room and belongings in the pool suite for the rabbit. Caleb gave them the drug and showed them how to soak a rag with it and, well...." Meredith could easily picture the scene in Flecha Dorada as Raymond described it.

The desert slumbered silent and dark, only stars lighting the sands as the two teenagers snuck into the Villa compound through the back gates and waited for Carlton to show up at the cottage. They watched Dusty and Sonora drop him off and drive around to the main entrance of the Villa into another totally separate environment. Carlton was leaving the next morning for home in Europe, bags stuffed full, trash cans overflowing. Carlton plopped down into bed and with a happy sigh, knowing he'd be home soon. He read for a while and finally put aside his book, snapped off his bedside lamp, was soon sleeping soundly.

The teens easily slipped into the room, unnoticed. Carlton hadn't locked the door, expecting his mother to return. Frankie gently laid the chloroform rag over Carlton's nose and mouth, Xander also carefully held his shoulders down. The young victim swam out of his sleep, already somewhat diminished by the drug, to find two friends hovering over him, one holding him against the bed. He fought to respond, trying to sit up, push against the physical and ethereal force but couldn't find voice, couldn't seem to lift his heavy limbs, to fight off the blackness engulfing him. Frankie would later admit, with a sob, that his friend had "horrible fear and sadness, a sense of betrayal and confusion in his eyes just before he closed them."

Carlton was out. The two boys began to search the rooms. Opening drawers, digging through partially packed suitcases and duffle bags, scouring closet floors and corners, under the beds, in the bathroom cabinets. They told authorities they searched everywhere, including Sonora's room and belongings. She was with Dusty at the main house. Frustrated, the two quietly left the cottage, closing the door behind them.

"Frankie and Xander left the pool house but decided to nose around Sonora's personal car parked in the space next to it, still looking for the toy," Raymond continued his narrative. "A few minutes later they saw someone entering Carlton's room dressed in dark clothes with a knit cap pulled down over the head. They watched through the window and watched as the intruder plunged a needle into Carlton's arm, apparently not realizing the kids had stayed on the premises or were watching. Obviously, the mission was to silence the only innocent person aware of the drug bunny's connection to the ranch. Ironically, the boys realized they were involved in Carlton's death even though they didn't administer the killer drugs. When the murderer slipped out the cottage door, they snuck out the rear gate and went back to the ranch. By the time the sun came up they were on their way back to New Jersey. The fact that they, personally, didn't kill Carlton loosened their tongues a lot. Frankie rolled over immediately."

"So, who was the killer? Bankleman? Logical and convenient. He was on the premises."

"Yes, logical, but no. In fact, he was an inside source for the DEA. Reuben said they had someone watching—which may have been why he stuck so close to your activities when you first showed up there. Protection, mostly. But I saw a name on the guest log of the Villa, from Fastida, for the day and night of the murder. The name was familiar—and it will be to you. Looking at a photo lineup, the boys managed to identify the intruder they saw in the pool house by the facial features alone. The name on the log was A. Burton."

Meredith took a deep breath. "Oh my god—Angelina—Renn Burton's wife?" She shook her head and stammered, "Was Renn involved, too? That's hard to believe. Hank Dorbin as well?"

"Renn didn't send Hank to Phoenix just before the second attempt on Dusty's life—the one in the hospital. Remember Hank delivered Renn's flowers to Dusty. Hank, apparently, knew nothing of what was going on. He thought visiting with flowers was the right thing to do. Angelina, however, was in Phoenix but never visited Dusty. She phoned Sonora. She also showed up often at the various movie sites, sometimes doing a walk-on role, sometimes with Renn, but innocuously enough that no one particularly noticed or disputed her presence.

"The DEA had eyes on the production company through Bankleman for a long time. Don't be shocked, but Hank Torbin had suspected something going on with drugs but was afraid to talk to anyone about it. He didn't know who he could trust. Angelina flipped on the whole group trying to save herself and Renn. Too late and too little for the star. Solver, himself, turned state's evidence against everyone key to the drug operation in the production company. He's trying to work out a plea deal.

"But for Carlton's death, Frankie and Xander's account handed Angelina to the authorities. Boots-on-the-ground detective stuff filled in the blanks. The little lady hardly tried to cover her tracks. I guess she thought he was so far out of the center no one would ever suspect her, so she stayed at the Villa, signed in and we found Phoenix travel receipts as well, with a connection to the attempt there on Dusty's life. Oh, of course, Fastida confirmed that Angelina arrived on site the morning before the boy's death. Her suite was empty by the time the authorities went to interview her. Renn had been there, too, but several days earlier when the whole rabbit began to unfold. He'd left her to do the dirty work."

"You talked to Fastida?"

"Just following up. Not surprisingly, no one answered the phone at the Villa, so I called her sister at the restaurant. I found Fastida here in LA—taking care of Sonora—and Dusty."

Meredith smiled. "Good detective work and great for Fastida—I think. I hope."

"Both Burtons were arrested yesterday. Everyone's trying to deal right now—Solver, Burton, couple of others in the periphery…they're rolling over so fast it seems like an acrobatic circus act!"

Meredith's eyes brimmed with tears as she thought about murderers making a deal over the sad death of the innocent teenager. And remembered the tortured look in Sonora's eyes after the murder. She choked back her sadness and was silent for a few minutes.

"The studio told me Renn Burton was chewing his nails over Dusty being lost in the desert," she murmured. "I'll bet he was— only it was over what would happen if Dusty was found and lived! And Renn, Dusty's mentor and long-time friend! How Hollywood a story could you get?"

"Renn's star billing and screen time was diminishing as he got older and he started working behind the scenes, producing, directing. Then, he got himself into this film production drug network through Bert Solver a few years ago. Very lucrative, but risky. Renn's always loved risk. Once you're in, there's no getting out. Friends, protégés and all the rest are just collateral to drug cartels."

Meredith sighed, her sadness palpable. "Well, I'm relieved Carlton's murder is solved. The story is finally over and with it, the violence. Although, right now I still carry a lot guilt about the consequences from the columns I wrote—you getting shot, Dusty almost dying in the desert, even my suspicion about Hank…but thanks, this is a gift."

The two sat on the sand for a long while, silent, watching the breeze toss waves and clouds around. Raymond reached over and took her hand. "I'm also relieved we don't have to live seven days a week at the beach house right now," she spoke up quietly.

"Too many people, too much high anxiety," said Raymond, "even though it is my own kid caught up in it."

"And Paco would hate it."

"So, does that mean I'm off the hook for the Emmys? That was the deal, wasn't it?"

"Are you kidding? With a perfectly tailored Armani tux in the closet and it fits you so well?" They stood up, he took her hand and they trudged through the sand toward his house.

"Let's go plan a wedding," he sighed.

ACKNOWLEDGMENTS

Stories never write themselves. Even the most imaginative raconteur calls on the characters from past experiences, those who inform today's dialogue and those who look at it and wince. I'm lucky to have them all—and generous ones at that. I'm grateful to my story weavers again who took the ride with me along this fictional journey: Deborah Baker and Ruth Walden, Butch Wilson—conscience to Meredith; Jean Timmons, Judy Turley, and Cindy Gunn, Saturday morning writing cheerleaders: Sal Mingano, Jamie McOuat, and Tamara Moan; the super-keen eyes of Susan Wagner and Dana Barnum. And my ever-supportive, often amused husband Dixon Smith with his OCD attention to spacing. Mostly thanks to the characters in a dazzling journalistic world who were, in real life, more colorful than the best storyteller could conjure. And to the readers of The Last Legwoman: A Novel of Hollywood, Murder and Gossip! Your enthusiasm and support allowed Sunset West to happen.

ABOUT THE AUTHOR

Penny Pence Smith began writing professionally as a teenager for the local Indio, California, daily newspaper. Later, after college graduation, she covered the entertainment industry as a movie magazine editor, as assistant ("legwoman") for a well-known gossip columnist, feature correspondent and bureau manager for the *New York Times Special Features Syndicate*, and as correspondent for the *Hollywood Reporter*. With a Ph.D. in communication, she has taught journalism and communication at UNC Chapel Hill and Hawaii Pacific University. Her *Under a Maui Sun* and *Reflections of Kauai* were best-selling tourism books in Hawaii.

Check my Author Page on BookBub for news about future
Meredith Ogden adventures and other books:
pennystories.wixsite.com/penny-smith-books.